PRAISE FOR *BEWARE THE ABBOTT BOYS*

"Gripping... Hayden's persistence and emotional authenticity make her a likable and relatable lead."

—*School Library Journal*

PRAISE FOR *WE WERE WARNED*

"A twisty whodunit set against the backdrop of a town haunted by a deadly curse... Everyone's a suspect in this thrilling tale that armchair sleuths will enjoy untangling."

—*Kirkus Reviews*

"An **action-packed, edge-of-your-seat thriller**... A great pick for thriller fans who enjoy slasher horror movie vibes."

—*School Library Journal*

PRAISE FOR *THE SUMMER SHE WENT MISSING*

A BARNES & NOBLE BEST BOOK OF 2024

★ "Crackling and propulsive."

—*Publishers Weekly*, Starred Review

PRAISE FOR *THEY'RE WATCHING YOU*

"Dungeons, catacombs, and crypts, oh my: Readers will be glued to the edges of their seats."

—*Kirkus Reviews*

"Frightening crypts, deadly schemes, devastating betrayals, and pulse-pounding chases through dark tunnels abound in this twisty read."

—*Publishers Weekly*

PRAISE FOR *DEAD GIRLS CAN'T TELL SECRETS*

"A well-paced page-turner about uncovering the truth at any cost."

—*Kirkus Reviews*

"Sure to grip readers with a blend of mystery and romance… An endearing and engrossing read."

—*Booklist*

PRAISE FOR *LITTLE CREEPING THINGS*

"Gripping twists and turns add suspense to this genre-solid whodunit and keep readers guessing until the very last page."

—*Publishers Weekly*

"Everyone's a suspect, and no one is safe, in this twisty debut from a compelling new voice in YA, Chelsea Ichaso. Don't miss it!"

—Kit Frick, author of *See All the Stars*, *All Eyes on Us*, and *I Killed Zoe Spanos*

"A stunning debut in every sense of the word. From the chilling opening pages to the jaw-dropping final reveal, the pacing is relentless, the twists dizzying."

—Dana Mele, author of *People Like Us*

ALSO BY CHELSEA ICHASO

They're Watching You

Dead Girls Can't Tell Secrets

Little Creeping Things

The Summer She Went Missing

We Were Warned

BEWARE THE ABBOTT BOYS

CHELSEA ICHASO

Cover design by Corina Lupp/Sourcebooks
Cover images © Arkhipenko Olga/Shutterstock, Phongsak Meedaenphai/Shutterstock, Elina Li/Shutterstock
Internal design by Tara Jaggers/Sourcebooks
Internal images © allanswart/Getty Images

Published by Sourcebooks Fire, an imprint of Sourcebooks
1935 Brookdale RD, Naperville, IL 60563–2773
(630) 961-3900
sourcebooks.com

Cataloging-in-Publication Data is on file with the Library of Congress.

Printed and bound in the United States of America.
PAH 10 9 8 7 6 5 4 3 2 1

For Kaylie, Jude, and Camryn

"It is true, we shall be monsters, cut off from all the world; but on that account we shall be more attached to one another."

—*Frankenstein*
by Mary Shelley

RESIDENTS BELIEVE 16-YEAR-OLD GIRL'S TRAGIC DEATH WAS NO ACCIDENT

In light of new findings, the truth surrounding a fatal accident and a small-town hero may prove sinister.

October 28

Silver Creek, VT—Nearly sixty years after Peter J. Abbott inherited a property worth millions under suspicious circumstances, a new tragedy brings this haunted history to the surface.

Two weeks after sixteen-year-old Mariana Sanchez's death, investigators are still searching for answers. According to police, on October 13, Sanchez's car underwent routine engine work by the Abbotts' three teenage sons, all part-time employees of Abbott Auto Repair, the family-owned shop located on their property. When Sanchez attempted to drive home, the car caught fire, soon bursting into flames with the young girl trapped inside. Sanchez was rushed to Central Springs Hospital, where she was pronounced dead upon arrival.

Sixteen-year-old local football star, Adam Abbott, sustained extensive injuries during an apparent attempt to free Sanchez from the burning vehicle. Though unable to rescue Sanchez, Abbott was initially hailed as a hero for his efforts; however, when investigators announced earlier this week that the fire was caused by an exposed engine wire, authorities stated they had not yet ruled out foul play. As these new findings lead to speculations concerning possible negligence or even homicide, some Silver Creek residents share recollections of the Abbott family's checkered past.

One resident, seventy-three-year-old Velma Perkins, says she has lived in Silver Creek since Peter J. Abbott was alive and running the then-private auto shop himself. "The second Peter moved into that mansion," Perkins said, "he let the place go to hell. The plants grew so high, they covered everything, and then he started making this huge racket. Called it working on cars. But we all knew something else was going on up there, behind that gate."

Though authorities have not yet determined the manner of Sanchez's death, many in the community have reached their own conclusions. "Always knew something was off with those people," said Timothy Shaw, owner of The Silver Spoon diner. "The repair shop is popular because it's the only shop in town—that's it. I took my truck there one time, and let me tell you, it was the last time. Those boys need to stay inside their big house and leave the rest of us *good* people alone. They have no business working on our cars, and they certainly shouldn't be allowed in our school, interacting with our children."

"They never belonged," added Perkins. "Never. Whatever's wrong with them, it runs in the blood."

1

We learn from failure, not from success!

That's what Mrs. Lieu has written in red at the top of my English paper, above the C-plus. She's quoting some book, no doubt. She likes to weave literary quotations into even the most mundane conversation. One time, a couple of girls in the front row were talking about their homecoming dresses, and Mrs. Lieu interrupted to inform them, "All that glisters is not gold." We all spent the rest of the day trying to misuse *glisters* in a sentence.

I resist the urge to crumple up the paper and tell my teacher that actually, a C-plus isn't a *failing* grade. But I know what she means; it feels like failing. Especially since I worked hard on this assignment.

The room is in a state of grumbling dissent, and I look around to find everyone with their heads bent over their papers. I make eye contact with Henry Abbott across the room, who puts on a silly expression and pantomimes death by choking. My cheeks heat, and I pretend to collapse as though my grade has ended me too. Even Sage Wheeler, who's on the path to valedictorian, has folded her paper in half to hide her grade.

"You okay?" I ask, leaning closer to her desk.

"This is bull," she says, rolling her eyes. "I'll have my dad call her. I'm not going to lose a spot in the Ivies just because Mrs. Lieu can't read."

"Um..." I frown, not really sure what to say to that.

"I've never gotten a B in my life." Sage flicks a strand of short blond hair out of her eye and, as if to emphasize how *together* she has everything, examines her acrylic nails, painted an autumnal brick-orange shade that perfectly matches her tank top.

"Right." If we were at a bigger school in a bigger town, Sage and Henry would be in a separate class for the ultra-advanced. At Silver Creek High, they have to sit among us mere honors students and do separate assignments here and there.

Up front, Mrs. Lieu, either failing to read the room or thoroughly enjoying our collective anguish, flashes a broad smile. "Okay, everyone. I don't usually do this, but since you all struggled so much with your papers, I'm going to give you the chance to rewrite them."

"Yeah, you are," Sage mutters smugly under her breath while the rest of us cheer.

I glance over at Henry again, who runs a hand through his brown hair in a gesture of relief. He looks at me, glasses skewed and hair a mess. He's adorable, and still, I wish I could walk over there and straighten his glasses, smooth his hair. Maybe rough it up even more. At his smile, my heartbeat kicks up.

But Henry's just my friend. Always has been, as much as I sometimes wish he'd see me as something else.

A *snap* sounds, right in front of my face. I jerk back to find Sage reaching over. "Hello? Hayden, eww. Stop looking at that creep."

"You know he's my best friend," I say.

Sage looks momentarily hurt, and I regret the slip of tongue. Not that she's ever been my *best* friend; still, we were close. Her expression returns to disapproval. "Then why are you looking at him like he's an ice cream cone?"

"That's gross, Sage."

"Okay, whatever. The point is you could do so much better than a murderer. Even a really hot one."

"Thanks," I droll. "But he's not—"

"A murderer's *brother*, then, sorry." She lifts her hands, absolving herself of any misgivings.

My jaw clenches. *This* is the reason she and I aren't close anymore. Mariana Sanchez was her cousin, and despite the fact that the police ruled Mariana's death an accident last October, Sage and the rest of this town refuse to accept it. They're all convinced that the Abbott triplets were involved.

Class is almost over. Mrs. Lieu tugs on the collar of her blue and white pinstripe button-down as she explains the rewrite assignment. "You'll choose a *new* prompt from the list. You have two weeks."

This is met with groans. At the back of the room, Todd Ellison, quarterback of the football team, asks, "Can we make it three?" The sentiment is echoed by a couple of his teammates.

"If you have a problem with my *magnanimous* offer," Mrs. Lieu says, throwing in a vocab word as she wanders over to her desk, "we can call the whole thing off."

"Two weeks is great," Todd says, stuffing his paper into his backpack.

At her desk, Mrs. Lieu shakes her head and mutters to the ceiling, "'Lord, what fools these mortals be.'"

The bell rings, and after everyone packs up for lunch, Sage sidles up next to me on my way out. "Hayden, I didn't see your name on the list for the student council retreat. You're coming, right?"

I pull my long sand-colored hair over one shoulder and twirl it around a finger. "Oh, we might have auditions that weekend for *The Wizard of Oz*," I say, even though there's no way we'll pull together the numbers to put on an actual production. At our small school, I'm one of five members of the drama club. Whenever we attempt a performance, each of us plays at least two parts—sometimes we go triple or even quadruple duty.

Then there's student council. Sage and I joined together freshman year as something to do once a week at lunchtime. We never planned on moving up in the ranks the way Mariana did—she was a junior class secretary with sights on becoming student body president. When Mariana passed away, Sage decided it was her new mission to take her cousin's place as well as guilt me into joining her. *Mariana would've wanted us to do our part to help the school, Hayden.* But Sage never quite got the numbers to win the schoolwide presidential race over popular cheer captain Kennedy Russo and had to be content with senior class president.

I, on the other hand, ran unopposed for my position as school treasurer.

The annual retreat is the best part of being on student council. But things are still a little tense with Sage, so I've been on the fence about attending.

"You have to come," she says, linking her arm through mine. "Please, don't leave me alone with the Abbotts."

"The Abbotts?" I scan the hall, spotting Henry waiting for me at the lockers.

"Apparently, they're really interested in student government all of a sudden. It's so obvious they're just trying to pad their high school résumés after everything last year. And Mr. Fuller is the only club advisor stupid enough to fall for it."

"He's stupid for letting high school students...join a club?"

"Yeah," she says, like it's obvious. "For letting murderers join a club."

"Bye, Sage," I say, tugging my arm out of hers.

"*Alleged* murderers, then," she calls as I stride ahead of her. "You'll come though, right?"

"Maybe," I call back. If Henry's going on the retreat, that changes things.

I make my way through the crammed hallway to him. "I guess congratulations are in order." When he arches a brow, I add, "On your student government appointment. What, uh, is your title exactly? Vice Keeper of the Striped Polos?" Henry rarely veers from his uniform of jeans and a striped polo shirt, though he's changed up the top half today. "Nice sweatshirt, by the way." It's the navy-blue zip-up hoodie I gave all three triplets last Christmas when no one else—not even their parents—gave them a present. Embroidered on the back of each hoodie is a large white *A* for *Abbott*.

"It's my favorite, though I think this one might actually be Bram's," he says, tugging at the pouch pocket.

"I thought it smelled a little like rain and gloom."

"And my position is *Keeper* of the Striped Polos, Second-in-Command to No One."

"Atta boy." I knock my fist against his arm. "So this is for real? And you're going on the retreat?"

"Well, yeah. I thought you'd be going," he says, causing my insides to melt.

"I am," I say. "But you never actually said what the three of you would be doing on student council."

"Mr. Fuller said we could be senior class reps. I guess he had to fire a couple of them for misuse of power—a.k.a. stealing snacks from the teacher's lounge when they were supposed to be making copies."

"You and Bram could easily get back on the football team," I suggest. "I mean, they obviously need you. They haven't won a—"

"Not without Adam," he says, shutting the idea down.

I get it. Football has never truly been Henry or Bram's thing. They only played for the sake of their brother, Adam, who'd been the team's star wide receiver and hero of both the school and the town—at least until last year. The accident that killed Mariana left him physically incapable of playing again, as well as the town's number one murder suspect.

I guess student government is the only thing all three brothers can do together. And considering how their schoolmates have treated them since they returned to Silver Creek High last month, they need each other. Strength in numbers.

The brothers—fraternal triplets actually, who look nothing alike—have been working in their family's auto repair shop since they were old enough to hold tools. The shop is located at the base of their massive property, just down a winding dirt road from their nineteenth-century hilltop mansion. Back in the 1950s, the boys' great-grandfather Peter J. Abbott worked as a private auto mechanic for the reclusive elderly mansion owner. The wealthy man who'd first built the place had collected some of the earliest automobiles, including a Ford Model B that's still displayed in a special showroom in the house. Cars back then were luxury items that needed constant work, so the mansion had its own dedicated repair shop. The wealthy family's enthusiasm for cars continued to the next generation: the man who hired Peter. Over the years the old man came to consider Peter a son more than a hired hand, and when he passed away, he left the entire property and the shop to Peter.

The inheritance made waves in town, stirring up talk that the old man hadn't died of natural causes. The story goes that someone even came forth claiming to be the man's real son and demanding to see the will. But Peter's employer had been well into his eighties, and his lawyer had overseen the changes in the will himself. There wasn't any substance to the whispers—they'd likely come from the town's elites, the snobs with homes up in the hills near the mansion. The Abbotts, in their eyes, didn't deserve a place beside them.

Eventually the suspicions died down, and Peter Abbott thrived in his newfound life, living in the mansion with his family and training his son to be a mechanic. His son, the triplets' grandfather, saw the opportunity to expand and opened the repair shop to the public, singlehandedly turning it into the go-to auto shop for the residents of Silver Creek.

The triplets' father, Jonathan Abbott, never took to the auto business—he prefers spending money to earning it, jetting off to Bali or Marrakesh whenever he can. The boys, though, have no intentions of living off trust funds forever. They learned everything from their grandfather and took over as much of the business as they could after he passed away, working after school and on weekends to keep up with the town's auto repair needs.

One day after school, the brothers were working on Mariana's sedan. When they finished, Mariana said goodbye and started driving the car, which burst into flames before she'd even exited the property gate. The ambulance had to come all the way from Central Springs, the nearest hospital, and by the time it finally arrived, Mariana was dead. Adam, who'd attempted to pull her from the burning vehicle, sustained second- and third-degree burns to his hands, arms, and face.

Our town, having long awaited just such a scandal, began to speculate that the explosion was no accident. The car had been tampered with, they claimed. And Adam hadn't tried to *save* the girl—he'd been burned trying to keep her inside as the flames swallowed her whole.

It's nothing but ridiculous rumors. These people had been biding their time, waiting for some crack in the Abbott family's handsome and opulent exterior. Waiting so they could jump in and knock the family and their mansion to the ground.

But I've been the Abbott boys' neighbor my entire life. Okay, *neighbor* is a bit of a stretch. My house at the base of the hill is the closest one to their property. To get to their house, I have to trek twenty minutes along a dirt lane, past the fields of crops and the woods that span the Abbott property. We've been friends since we were kids, and when my mom passed away three years ago, the brothers took care of me. They left their lavish abode to come into my humble one, so Dad and I wouldn't be alone.

I know none of them could've hurt Mariana.

First of all, there was no motive. Mariana was Bram's girlfriend of a year, and the two were attached at the hip. He hasn't been the same since her death.

And as for Adam, why would he sacrifice his life and his football career to get rid of a kind soul like Mariana? It makes no sense.

"You want to work on our lit papers after school?" I ask Henry as I put away my books.

"Oh, um, sure," he says, reddening. "Though I might not redo it after all."

I narrow my eyes. "Show me your paper, Henry."

"What—why?" He isn't making eye contact.

"You didn't even get a bad grade, did you?" I should've known. That whole façade back in lit class was to make me feel better about my crappy grade.

"Well, I did get an A-minus," he says sheepishly, dragging the sole of his shoe over the linoleum.

"You're the worst, you know that?"

"You have mentioned this before, yes." He slings me a lopsided smile.

As for Henry, I know him best of all. He's the kindest and gentlest of souls. It just isn't possible.

We reach the cafeteria and join the line. When we get in the middle of debating which caf staple is most likely to give us *E. coli*, a commotion at a nearby table draws our attention.

A group of boys is gathered around the table, laughing. One of them picks up an apple from the ground, and the others call out, "Do it again!"

The boy tosses the apple into the center of the crowd, which parts enough for me to watch it nail someone in the head. The boys burst into laughter as the apple bounces off the table, hits the bench, and rolls along the floor. "What's wrong?" Todd Ellison jeers. "All-league receiver two years in a row, and now you can't even catch a piece of fruit? Guess that's karma for you."

His target, Adam Abbott, merely sits there, head lowered over his tray and navy-blue hoodie drawn, like he's trying to go unnoticed even as the boys continue to mock him. Beside me, Henry tenses.

Then he's out of the line, darting toward the fray.

I follow him, searching for whichever teacher is supposed to be on cafeteria duty and finding none. When I turn my eyes back to the scene, another football player, Neil Chen, snatches a plastic water bottle off the tray. Adam doesn't move as Neil winds up, bottle poised to nail him in the head. Henry and I are too far away, so I shout a warning at Adam. Only he ignores it.

I'm already flinching, bracing to watch the impact, when a dark lean figure swoops past the table and the other boys to grab Neil's wrist.

Bram. My tight chest lets out a breath. But Bram proceeds to twist Neil's arm until the boy screams, letting the bottle drop to the ground. My stomach mimics the wringing motion until Henry reaches the boys, coaxing his brother to let go.

The other football players stand there, wide-eyed. Todd Ellison starts in Bram's direction, but Henry steps out, cutting him off. Behind him, Adam slowly gets to his feet like a statue come to life.

"Let's just go," one of the boys says, nudging Todd.

Bram, wearing the same gifted hoodie, the crew neck of his

black T-shirt peeking through, glares icily at Neil. "Gotta release earlier, Chen. Aren't you like…fifth-string QB?"

"Sick freak," Neil mutters, gritting his teeth like he might risk another go at Bram. But the others hiss and tug at him, and when they turn for the cafeteria door, he reluctantly follows.

I feel the shift in the room. The way every student in this place has either moved closer to the door or scooted as far to the end of their benches as possible. I glance over to where pretty redhead and student council president, Kennedy Russo, sits with a rice bowl, watching with her mouth half-open. Her cheerleader friends are speaking in hushed tones and recording videos with their phones. One tugs on Kennedy's pink cashmere sweater, then leans over to whisper something in her ear. I don't need to get close to know that their thoughts—everyone's thoughts—echo Neil's words.

Sick freak.

They think the Abbott brothers are freaks. And their fear rises in the room, fast and hot as flames.

2

I slip past the boys to Adam. "Are you okay?" I ask, tugging back his sweatshirt hood to examine his head. Now that he no longer has to keep his blond hair short for football, it's grown out. I push it aside to find two large welts forming on his forehead. They're just above the thin and puckered flesh where his right eyebrow used to be, above the impaired eye and the scars running like tracks across the right side of his face. Hiding behind the hood and the hair, he's far from the clean-cut all-American boy and confident future prom king of last year.

Two bumps on Adam's head means we missed the first shot those jerks took at him. "Let me take you to the nurse for some ice." I attempt to pull him up by the hand, but he shrinks away, tugging his hood back up.

"I don't need the nurse."

"You could have a concussion," I protest as the bell rings, ending lunch.

"Who cares?" he says, standing. He pushes right between his brothers, soon lost in the crowd headed for the door.

"Why don't you stop him?" I ask Henry and Bram. "He could be—"

"Just, let him go, Hayden." Lightly, Henry touches my shoulder. "The last thing he wants is to be babied."

Unsatisfied, I glance at Bram, who looks like he wishes he'd kept twisting Neil's arm. I imagine the sound of the bone snapping and wince.

Before I can ask him to drag Adam into the nurse's office, Henry moves closer to his brother to mutter, "Can we have a word, please?"

"You can say whatever you want in front of her." Bram's gray-blue eyes meet mine, and my pulse accelerates. With his messy black hair, pale skin, and chiseled jaw, Bram's looks are nothing like the easy, disarming ones of his brother Henry.

Bram's dark beauty is something else. Something that causes my heart to seize in my chest for a moment whenever I see him. His charm and enigmatic allure have always had something of a choke hold on me. I used to think of him as nearly as close a friend as Henry, but now it's like I'm afraid to be alone with him. I see him, and feelings of attraction and guilt swarm in my stomach. I can't help but remember what happened the summer before last when we were alone together. Something I've never told Henry about, for fear of hurting him and ruining our friendship.

Henry casts a nervous look at me before nodding at Bram. "Fine then. What the hell was that? We don't exactly need proof that the whole town was right about some *violent* streak. Half the cafeteria was filming that whole show."

Bram shrugs. "Where were their cameras when Ellison and his crew were making a football target out of Adam's head?"

"You know that isn't the point. You'd already stopped it. You didn't need to—"

"He doesn't stand up for himself," Bram says, the words so pained they stab at my chest. "Adam, he just…sits there and takes it. But *I* couldn't."

Henry inhales slowly, and I'm torn between attempting to comfort him and heading out the door. For a moment, I wish I were anywhere but here. Though Bram insisted on making me a part of it, this space between the brothers is too taut with emotion. Too sacred. I've never felt more like an outsider.

"I know," Henry finally says. "If I'd gotten there first, I don't know what I would've done."

I try to picture it, Henry grabbing Neil by the arm. By the neck even. On the football field, Henry was always running. He was quick, so the coach put him at running back. I saw him knocked to the ground plenty, but I never saw him put a hand on another player. In fact, I've only seen him get physically violent once.

The tardy bell rings, and I start toward the door. I expect the boys to follow, only they don't. "Coming?" I ask.

"You go on ahead," Henry says. "We'll be along in a sec."

I force a smile and head out to my locker, somewhat relieved to be excused from their conversation.

In sixth period, my art elective, part of me is waiting to get called into the principal's office about the incident during lunch. Adam is supposed to be in this class, but he isn't here now. Which means he either got called to the office, or he actually listened to me and went to the school nurse. It has to be the former. First of all, Adam is a bit of a hothead who's never really listened to anyone. After his accident, he became even worse. He sank into himself and closed himself off to seemingly everyone, including his brothers.

Second of all, I know my schoolmates are trying to skew the facts. They want the Abbott brothers back in their mansion, isolated inside those walls the way they were last year. They probably went straight to Mr. Ortega's office with their videos.

Though it is odd that I didn't hear the principal's voice on the intercom. Maybe Adam decided to take the rest of the day off. I wouldn't blame him.

The idea eases my concerns. I let my guard down, let my mind fade into the world of the painting in front of me, when a harsh buzz sounds. Over and over. The fire alarm.

We look to the art teacher, Ms. Barrett, who apologizes for not having checked her bulletin that day. "It's probably a drill. Leave your things, and we'll head out the door and down the hall, single file."

Normally, we wouldn't complain about getting out of class. Except this is art, our easiest period of the day and the one in which half the class was napping. There's grumbling as everyone stuffs their phones in their pockets. I glance around for someone to walk with, remembering with a sinking feeling that, apart from Adam, I don't really have any friends in this class. But before I reach the door, Penelope Kaur, the best artist in the class, says midyawn, "I was just about to go into REM."

Sure, Penelope. She glances back at the precious painting she just slaved over, like she's about to abandon it to the flames.

The loud buzz continues as we march down the hall and exit through the back doors to the fields. The chatter is loud and easy, muffling Ms. Barrett's instructions. "Stay with your class! No wandering!" She starts counting us off, and as other classes swarm around us, the rest of the teachers do the same.

The alarm continues, and at my side, Penelope starts to moan and bob her head in time with the buzz. "Shouldn't they have turned that thing off by now?"

"Maybe it's a real fire," I say, new worries spiking about Adam, who could be in there somewhere, trapped.

But there's still no smoke to be seen, no flames. No smell, for that matter. Usually when there's a drill, Mr. Ortega will walk from class to class, taking down attendance numbers. Only I haven't seen him yet.

Penelope takes out her phone. "Whatever's going on, at least school is almost over. I just hope they let us back inside to get our stuff."

"They will," I assure her, knowing her thoughts are on that painting.

After another ten minutes, some of our classmates flop down into the grass, and Penelope and I follow suit. Two guys near us start making a TikTok about our plight, and I consider texting Adam, just to check on him.

When Penelope taps my arm, I look up to see Mr. Ortega striding through the back doors to speak with the teacher from the next class. He quickly makes his way to Ms. Barrett, but between the constant buzzing and the chatter, I can't make out a word.

The next class over starts to wander in herd formation back toward the building, and finally, Ms. Barrett nods and turns to us. "We have the all clear!" she shouts over the alarm.

"Great," I say, grabbing my ears as we near the doors. "It sounds like everything is totally resolved."

Behind me, some of the baseball players joke about taking their bats to the alarm. But before we reach the building, the buzzing stops.

"Oh, thank God," Penelope says. "My head was about to explode." We barely cross the classroom's threshold when another buzz sounds.

My body tenses, but it's only the final school bell, releasing us for the day.

I grab my things and head out the door to my locker, scanning the hall for Henry. Even though I have my license, the moment the boys turned sixteen, sophomore year, they started driving me to school and even home on days we didn't have extracurriculars.

They're probably waiting for me in the parking lot. I heft my backpack and head through the front doors. When I make it down the steps, spotting Henry and Adam talking beside the boys' shared black Mustang, a distant shriek tears through the air.

I continue toward the car, a joke on my tongue about the dramatics of the crows in Silver Creek, when I hear it again. Louder this time, the sound sends a chill down my spine.

Henry's wide eyes meet mine, and I know.

That wasn't a bird's call. That sound was a human scream.

ADAM

LAST OCTOBER

"Listen to my tale; when you have heard that, abandon or commiserate me, as you shall judge that I deserve. But hear me."

—*Frankenstein* by Mary Shelley

Adam scanned the list of outside reading novels, his eyes glazing over the titles. He hated to read and wasn't interested in anything apart from the sports section of the newspaper—though often enough, the school's online newspaper featured some flattering articles about his prowess on the football field. But all the books on this list sounded boring, and worse than that, Mr. Armstrong said they'd have to write a term paper on one of them.

They were to choose a book by the end of the week, only there was no bookstore in Silver Creek. He could try the school library, but they never kept more than one copy of any title. It would be cleared out by the time school was over. Adam considered online shopping, but the delivery drivers never bothered to try the gate at the edge of the Abbott property, which meant they never made it up the hill to the house. Packages were always left at the bottom of the dirt road and eventually stolen, or soaked and ruined by the automatic sprinklers. The brothers kept telling their father to fix the issue by getting a PO box in town. The man never listened.

Adam wandered over to the classroom bookshelf. Mr. Armstrong said that they could borrow a book from there if it was on the list.

"Hey, Adam." Tanya Rockwell gave a shy smile and sidled up next to him. Her eyes were on the books as she asked, "Are you excited about tonight's game?"

"Uh, sure. Nervous more than excited, I guess."

"You don't have anything to be nervous about." She patted him playfully on the arm. Tanya wasn't the only girl who kept doing *this*, trying to talk to him. He knew it was because homecoming was approaching; it happened every year around this time.

"Thanks. Well, I'd better get to it." He forced a smile and gestured to the bookshelf, effectively dismissing Tanya, whose face fell before she wandered off.

It was slim pickings on the shelf. Adam recognized one of the books on the list, a battered copy of Mary Shelley's *Frankenstein*, and his mind went to the old movie clips he'd seen of the monster with bolts protruding from its neck. The slow walk and the green skin—or maybe it had been in black and white. Adam hadn't watched the entire movie. He had no interest in reading the book either and scanned the shelves again for something slimmer.

But nearly everything had been claimed by Mr. Armstrong's morning class of juniors. The *smart* kids.

Adam glanced over to where Bram sat, looking completely unbothered as usual as he watched something on his phone. The reading list was folded up at the corner of his desk.

Bram was much smarter than Adam, but he only ever did the bare minimum in school. That was why they were both in this class. Today, though, even the bare minimum required finding a book. Adam ambled to his brother's desk. "So what are you going to pick?"

"I've already got a book."

"What is it?"

"None of your business," Bram answered grimly.

Adam smirked. "You're embarrassed. Is it *Twilight*?" He pretended to double-check the list.

"Something like that." Bram's eyes remained on his phone, and Adam realized he was watching the video of their last preseason game. So his brother wasn't as calm and collected as he appeared. Their first game of the season was tonight, and though he hid it well, Bram was obviously jittery.

"You'll do great tonight." Adam slapped his brother on the back, harder than necessary, before returning to his seat.

In the parking lot, Mariana Sanchez was leaning against the boys' Mustang. Adam's heart skipped at the sight.

But he soon spotted Bram in the driver's seat, and his heart sank again. The two were chatting through the open window, waiting for the others to arrive. Adam had forgotten they were giving Mariana a lift, so she could wait at the house while the brothers finished working on her car.

"Hi, Adam," Mariana said sweetly. Even dressed as she was in a modest pair of jeans and a turquoise sweater, Adam had trouble keeping his eyes off her.

"I'm driving," Adam said without returning the salutation. He opened the door and stood there, waiting. Finally, Bram lifted his hands off the wheel and got out of the car, exchanging a look with Mariana that said *I have no idea what this is about*.

That was the truth, Adam thought. Bram had no idea that Adam didn't want to sit in a car with Mariana. He had no clue that Adam would rather walk all the way home than share the back seat with that girl.

But Mariana knew. She was the one who had a reason to be sorry.

Fortunately, Adam had a plan. One that would fix everything.

"This thing only seats four," Adam grumbled. "And we already promised Hayden a ride."

"We can squeeze," Bram said, sliding into the back. Mariana followed, pressing in so close, she was practically on his lap. "Problem solved," he added. In the rearview window, Adam caught the vibrant blush on Mariana's cheeks.

"Not exactly legal," Adam said, though that wasn't what bothered him.

"It's a five-minute drive," Bram said.

When Henry and Hayden arrived, Henry took the passenger seat. Hayden squeezed in the back with the lovebirds, and Adam started the ignition. Even as he exited the school parking lot, he couldn't help but glance again at Bram and Mariana in the rearview mirror. Their fingers were interlocked, and Mariana giggled at something Bram whispered in her ear.

It all made Adam's stomach curl.

They wove through the residential streets and onto the open country road, soon reaching Hayden's house, a modest single-story with faded gray wood siding and white trim. Hayden hadn't even shut the car door behind her when Adam started to pull away.

"Wait!" Henry shouted. He glared at Adam, who braked. "Hayden's grabbing a book for me."

"Fine," Adam murmured, his skin itching to escape the car. "Why does she have your book?"

"It's not *my* book," he said as Hayden raced back down the steps. "She said she had an extra copy." Hayden reached the passenger side, thrusting a pristine copy of *Frankenstein* through the open window.

"Thanks," Henry said.

"No problem. I'll see you tonight at the—"

Adam stepped on the gas then, pulling away from the house before she finished the sentence.

"What the hell, Adam?" Henry snapped. "That was so rude."

Adam peeked in the rearview mirror, catching Bram's disapproving eye before he spotted Hayden standing by the side of the road, her diminishing figure as still as a scarecrow.

"I've got homework to do before the game," Adam barked. "And in case you forgot, we have to finish Mariana's car. So I don't have all day."

"We all have homework and football. Doesn't mean you can treat people that way." Henry huffed and started flipping through the pages of the novel.

"We're reading the same book," Adam said, trying to lighten the mood he'd single-handedly wrecked.

"Really?"

"Yeah, so now you can write my paper for me."

Henry whacked him in the arm with the book.

"Hey!" Adam laughed. "You're going to make me crash."

"So many hazards on this road," Bram chimed in from the back. "You could swerve straight into a cornfield, or even plow onto a pillowy soft bed of wildflowers."

Mariana giggled again. "Or into a man made out of straw."

At the sound of her voice, Adam darkened. "Whatever. Something happens to this car, it'll be one more we have to fix today for free." He felt the tension flood the space, as if it had wafted through the open windows, becoming trapped inside with them. He didn't dare look into the rearview mirror this time.

They reached the gate at the end of the property, on which hung a sign for *Abbott Auto Repair*. Henry hopped out to open the gate. Once he'd settled back inside, the car wound up the paved road of their property, veering left at the fork in the direction of the car repair shop.

Tucked away behind the hill, it wasn't the most optimal location for a business. Despite the sign, out-of-towners often drove right past the massive gate. Fortunately, locals knew the place, as they'd been coming for years for tune-ups, oil changes, and even major repairs.

When Mariana had driven her car up to the shop two days ago with a lit *CHECK ENGINE* light, Bram tried to convince his brothers to take on the job for free. Of course, Henry had readily agreed, and Adam was about to, thinking that perhaps it might be the right time to enact his plan. But then he noticed that Mariana herself wasn't at the shop. "Where is she?" he'd asked.

"In the Mustang," Bram had said. "I'm giving her a ride to the library." After school, Mariana worked at Silver Creek Town Library. It was one of the reasons all the old people knew and loved her.

Adam had a change of heart then. "I'm not going to work for free."

"She's my girlfriend," Bram had pressed.

"Well then, *you* handle it," Adam had responded. "I can take Mariana to the library, and you can check the car."

They both knew that Bram was the worst of the three of them at diagnosing an engine problem. "I'll take all your chores for the month," Bram had mumbled broodily, an offer Adam had accepted.

Now, Adam parked the Mustang and took out the key to the shop's lock. Instead of following him and Henry to the garage door, Bram tugged on his backpack. "I'll be right back," he said. "Just going to walk Mariana up to the house." It was a ten-minute walk back up the road, taking the right fork that winded up to the Abbott mansion. Bram would certainly not be "right back."

"Wonderful," Adam muttered under his breath as he watched Bram sling an arm around Mariana's delicate waist.

Adam's heart clenched, but he couldn't look away this time. The grass around him swayed and shivered, and when a bee buzzed too close to his ear, he swatted at it. It settled onto a wildflower, the buzzing sound drifting away.

But Adam kept hearing something. Something like the wind whispering through the tall blades of grass. It spoke to him of that thought, that plan.

The whispers said it had to be today.

3

What was that?" I ask, not really wanting to know.

"Maybe we should just go," Adam says, slipping into the driver's seat.

"But Bram isn't even here," I protest.

The screams continue. A few yards away in the lot, a girl begins to drift toward them. A group of freshmen boys gathered on the front steps get up and skirt the building, also following the wretched, bone-chilling shrieks.

"Oh my god," I breathe, my chest tightening at a horrible realization. Bram is always the first one out to the car. He and Adam have a long-standing competition for the driver's seat. Bram always wins since he rarely stops to gather books at the end of the day. But he isn't in the parking lot now. I start to run.

My mind is spinning a million miles per hour. Behind me, Henry is shouting something. I hear my name but nothing else over the sound of my heartbeat and my shoes pounding the asphalt.

I round the building, expecting to see a crowd on the grass or the basketball courts. Maybe even a cheerleading stunt gone wrong. But the sounds are coming from farther away, in the woods beyond the school grounds. There's no fence separating the campus from the woods, and a few students leave the fields to duck through the trees, seeking out the source of the commotion. I follow them.

By the time I spot where everyone is gathering, the screams have turned to sobs. I can't see through the onlookers to make out who is crying, or why.

Penelope is at the edge of the crowd, and when she turns away from the scene, her tear-filled eyes lock onto mine. She hurries toward me, and even though we barely speak outside of art class, she throws her arms around me. My heart plummets. Bram wasn't in the lot, and now Penelope is hugging me like I just lost a friend. *Because it's him.*

But then she cries, "It's Kennedy." My mind stalls for an instant until she inhales a deep, quaking breath to add, "I think she's *dead*."

I'm hit with an acute sense of disorientation, a fog rolling into my brain. "What?" I finally ask. Kennedy Russo can't be dead. I saw her in the cafeteria an hour ago. But I regain enough wherewithal to ask, "Did someone call 911?"

I feel Penelope's chin bump my shoulder as she nods. "You know the ambulance will take forever though."

"What about the school nurse?" I ask.

"Someone already went to get her," Penelope says, sniffling.

Slowly, I manage to pull away from her. My hair rustles as someone barrels past us, and I glance up to see a figure in a black T-shirt shove into the crowd. *Bram.* Right behind him is the school nurse. She makes it through, gasping audibly, then orders everyone to back away.

They obey, the wall they formed cracking and breaking apart, allowing me to glimpse what's behind it.

My feet refuse to step closer, but I see anyway. Red hair spilling over the pine needles, pink cashmere sweater splayed open and matted with dirt.

The tears start to come now, mottling the scene. I feel an arm wrap around my shoulders, a strong grip turning me away from the crowd, away from the nurse, who's growing more and more frantic as she works on the unmoving body.

The boy's touch is cold. I look up into his face, expecting to find Henry. Instead, it's Bram holding me. "We should go," he says, walking me out of the woods.

"We should?" I ask, so grateful he's alive that I don't try to slip free of his grasp. Instead, I lean into him more.

"The cops are already on their way over. I can't be here."

My head pulls back. "But you didn't do anything wrong."

"No, I know that." He glances over my shoulder, back at the woods and the crying students. "It's just..."

"And you went and got the nurse," I manage to get out.

"Because no one else was doing anything. They were just staring."

"Bram, what happened?" I ask, not sure I'm ready to find out.

"I don't know." His gray eyes are wide as he shakes his head. "I didn't look closely. It could've been an accident. Maybe she fell and hit her head or something? But...there was a lot of blood."

"What were you doing back here?" I ask.

He releases me now, putting his hands in his pockets and clearing his throat. "I was slow getting back after the drill, that's all."

He looks genuinely hurt by my questions. Without thinking, I reach out to touch his bare arm. But his attention isn't on my eyes anymore; it's on something behind me.

I crane my neck to see Henry standing on the path behind the school. My hand drops from Bram's arm, and I rush to him.

"What's going on?" he asks, peering into the woods.

"It's Kennedy. She's—the nurse is working on her."

"Kennedy?" Henry's skin pales. "What happened? Do you think she's okay?"

"Not really," Bram says, making his way to us.

"Well, did someone call her dad?" Kennedy's father, Dr. Arnold Russo, is a general surgeon out at Central Springs Hospital, but he also has a practice here in town.

"Yeah, I think so," Bram says, motioning us along. "But we need to get out of here." He scans the grounds. "Where's Adam?"

"Still in the car, I assume," Henry says, craning his neck to glance back at the woods.

We head around the building, reaching the front just as Dr. Russo's Mercedes screeches into the lot. He gets out, slamming the door and dropping his keys in the rush.

He looks around, but the keys seem to have disappeared beneath his car.

Bram walks over, bending down to retrieve them. He offers them to the man, adding solemnly, "They're working on her, behind the school."

Dr. Russo's head jerks back. His expression morphs to pure disgust as he tears the keys from Bram's hand and, without a word, pushes past him in the direction of the school.

4

The next morning, a knock at the door wakes me.

"Come in," I call out groggily, checking my phone on the nightstand: 10:37 a.m.

Last night, we learned that emergency personnel had pronounced Kennedy Russo dead at the scene. She was never even taken to the hospital. All after-school activities were canceled. School for today was canceled.

On the drive home yesterday, Bram kept saying he couldn't be locked away again, the way he had been after Mariana's death, when he and his brothers were forced to stay home from school to do independent study. For months they'd had to avoid going into town until the rumors subsided. They'd just come back to school, and now their world was collapsing all over again.

After the news last night, I'd tried calling Bram. But he didn't answer my calls or reply to my texts. Next I tried Henry, to no avail. Then I attempted to sleep, unsuccessfully for the most part. The last time I checked my phone, it was well after three in the morning.

Now, Dad walks in, looking red-eyed, and I can tell he had a rough night too. "You okay, hon?"

"Yeah." It wasn't like I was close with Kennedy. We ran in different circles. But growing up in Silver Creek means that no one is truly a stranger. Kennedy and I used to be friends in elementary school, before our personalities were fully developed and before she became…well, too popular for me.

"I just kept thinking about Betty and Arnold all night." He lowers onto the bed, and I let him hug me the way Kennedy's parents will never hold their daughter again. When he releases me, I can tell by his hesitation that it's going to be bad news. "The police are asking to interview you, Hayden."

"Me?" I get a sudden hot streak of guilt at what little I spied through the trees, through the crowd. "Why?"

"All they would tell me over the phone was that they're interviewing everyone who was there in the woods after school. Someone must've mentioned you. Sounds like it's routine."

"Routine when someone is murdered," I say.

"Routine when the police have questions," Dad corrects. "But I asked if I should be there, and the woman on the phone said it wasn't necessary. You'll be in and out in ten minutes."

"Okay," I say slowly, nodding. "Where? Central Springs?" Silver Creek doesn't have its own police station. The town's law enforcement is managed by the Vermont State Police, whose nearest location is a tiny office in Central Springs. We took a tour of it once, back in second grade, where this big officer with a kind smile inspired us all to want to be cops one day and to never do crime. I don't remember his name, but right now, I secretly hope he's the guy to interview me.

"No, the interviews are at the school. I took the morning off, so I can drive you."

"Thanks." Dad is a manager at the one bank in town. Before Mom got sick, he aspired to set out on his own and become an independent financial advisor. But after losing her and her modest yet steady preschool teacher salary, he decided the job security outweighed the dream. His hours and income are stable, for the most part. We aren't Abbott-level rich, but we're doing fine.

I sit for another moment, staring at the square on my quilted comforter that's stained red from a nail polish spill years ago. Mom and I were snuggled up here, watching a movie on her laptop. She was painting my nails bright red, and when she reached out to pause the movie, the polish dripped off the brush onto the comforter. The tiny drop sat in a bubble for a moment before bleeding out into a splotch. Mom said she'd try to get it out, but we both knew it was a lost cause. It only spread at her efforts.

Now, I look at the stain and can't help seeing Kennedy's blood spilling onto the forest floor. "Well, I should probably hop in the shower."

"Okay," Dad says, looking distracted for a moment as he fiddles with the corner of a throw pillow. "Hon, I know you're close with the Abbott boys. Uh"—he clears his throat, and I don't like where this is going—"you know I've never paid any mind to the rumors about them. But you will be careful, won't you?"

It feels like a gut punch. But before I can respond, he hugs me again, sniffling as he whispers into my hair, "You're the only thing I've got left, you know that."

My throat swells, and I force out a muffled "Yeah" past the retorts still lingering on my tongue. When he leaves the room, I get out of bed and search for something appropriate to wear to a police interview. I land on jeans and a white short-sleeve button-up shirt. Only instead of heading to the shower, I pick up my phone and call Henry. When he doesn't answer, I'm antsy enough to do something I know I'll regret; I open Instagram.

Sure enough, the first thing that pops up on my feed is a post from Kennedy's best friend, Lydia Costas. It's Kennedy's cheer photo from last year, along with a simple caption:

I will never be me again without you. Miss you so much, Ken.

My eyes sting, thinking not only of Kennedy but of Lydia. The pair had run for student council together this year, winning president and vice president. They'd been best friends since the third grade. My mind goes to Henry. Just the thought of losing him—of never being able to talk to him again—steals the air from my lungs.

I scroll down to the comments, where, true to form, my schoolmates are already speculating that one of the Abbott brothers must be responsible. It's full of baseless accusations, mostly from football players.

TELLISON: this has the looney bros written all over it

THEREALDEALNEIL: first that freak tries to break my arm, then when I show him up, he goes after poor kennedy

Nausea rises in my stomach. *You're a true saint, Neil.* I scroll further, finding, to no surprise whatsoever, that Sage has chimed in.

SAGEWHEELER: Ortega never should've let those monsters back in the school after what they did to my cousin

THEREALDEALNEIL: everyone was better off with them locked away in their castle on a hill

TELLISON: my grandparents were right about those weirdos

But after the back and forth, everyone echoing the exact same unfounded sentiment, there's a comment that stops me in my tracks. A strangely *specific* comment.

SPIKEATTACK77: I saw one of them walking off into the woods with Kennedy, yesterday during the fire drill.

TELLISON: seriously? I knew it

SAGEWHEELER: @spikeattack77 you have to tell the cops

SPIKEATTACK77: I did

SAGEWHEELER: which one was it?

SPIKEATTACK77: not sure but his hoodie had an A on it

I huff under my breath and click on *spikeattack77*'s profile, just so I can call this jerk out the next time I see him. The hoodie is the kind of detail anyone could easily make up. There's no proof.

I soon discover that the account belongs to Kacey Ross, a volleyball player—not a dude named Spike—and someone I'd always thought of as a nice person. Guess I misjudged her; she's just like every other hateful gossip in town. I close the app without reading another word and head to the shower.

Once I enter the school, I immediately see why the police chose it as their interrogation center. They've rounded up more students than would fit in the cardboard box–sized station over in Central Springs. Roughly ten kids sit slumped on the hallway floor outside the office, backs against the wall, awaiting their turn.

There's no sign of the Abbotts, but I spot Sage near the front of the line. Avoiding eye contact, I take a seat at the back.

My hands are fidgety, so I pull out my phone to play a game.

Only I have no attention span for it and lose in the first few seconds. Not knowing if the boys have already gone through this is making me anxious. I keep checking my text messages, though I would've heard the ding if Henry or Bram had texted me back. After twenty minutes or so, I text Dad to tell him about the wait and that he might as well head to work.

At some point I hear my name and start to get to my feet, thinking it must be my turn with the cops. Only when I look up, it's Sage standing over me, apparently having finished her interview. I keep my lips pressed flat, my eyes disinterested. I refuse to talk to someone who's been spouting off inflammatory rumors that could wreck the lives of real human beings. Human beings I care for deeply.

"You need to wake up, Hayden," she spits with enough venom that I flinch. "Your *friends* are murderers. And if you're not careful, you could be next."

She spins on her heels, and I'm too stunned to speak until she's way down the hall. My heart is thumping so loudly that I barely hear the man calling the next person in line—me—into the office.

I get up, still seething. When the man says hello and offers his hand, I merely grunt. "I'm Detective Chase," he tries again, looking more amused than offended. He's about fifty, with wrinkles around his green eyes and salt-and-pepper hair, and my only thought is that he's in good shape for an old guy. Immediately, I note his title: not *Officer*—and he's definitely not the friendly man who gave our second-grade tour—but *Detective*. "And this is my colleague, Detective Wilson." He gestures to a woman in her thirties, hair slicked back in a low bun. They're both wearing suits, and since they've taken over the principal's office, they direct me to the chair that usually seats kids who've either done something very good or very bad.

Why do I feel like the latter?

"Sorry, I'm Hayden," I say, settling into the chair. "Phillips."

"Ah," Detective Chase says, sharing a look I can't read with his colleague, "yes, Hayden. How are you this morning?"

"I mean," I say, my cheeks heating, "okay, I guess. My dad said you needed to speak to me because I was there yesterday, right? In the woods. Except by the time I arrived, there was already a crowd, so I couldn't really see anything."

Detective Chase clears his throat. "We're more interested in the events *leading up* to the discovery of Kennedy Russo's body."

At the word *body*, my mind threatens to unravel again. "Of course."

"Did you happen to see Kennedy earlier that afternoon? Maybe during the fire drill?"

I shake my head. "I was with my class. The last time I saw Kennedy"—*alive*, I keep to myself—"was at lunch."

"And how did she seem?" Detective Chase asks, taking the principal's seat behind the desk.

"Seem?" I shrug. "She seemed fine." I think of the fight in the cafeteria and how she watched it intently. But the detective isn't asking about the Abbott boys, and I'd like to keep it that way. "She was with some of the other cheerleaders. Maybe you should talk to them."

"Oh, we're in the process of doing just that," Detective Wilson assures me. Unlike Chase, she remains standing, leaning a palm on the notepad splayed open near the edge of the desk. "Only so far, none of them have been able to tell us exactly what Miss Russo was doing in the woods."

"Well, I don't—I mean, I didn't really talk to Kennedy much. Not since we were chemistry partners last year. Our teacher assigned the pairs."

"I see," Wilson says, jotting down notes in her pad. She then skirts the desk to approach my chair, carrying a Polaroid camera. "Would you mind if I take a look at your hands, Miss Phillips?"

She extends her own hand in demonstration, but I hesitate. "Are you sure this is routine?"

"Of course," she says, though it doesn't keep me from feeling like I'm a suspect.

"Is this—was Kennedy...?" Did Kennedy fight off her attacker? Are they looking for scratches? Blood or skin beneath my fingernails?

"There's evidence of foul play," Wilson says, "if that's what you're asking."

My fists are still clenched in my lap. I know I have nothing to hide. Still, I ask, "Well, can you tell me why you need to see my hands?"

"Like this," she says, ignoring my question and indicating that I hold both hands palm up.

I hold them both out, and she snaps a photo. When she gestures for me to turn my hands over, I do, and she snaps a second photo.

Before I can ask another question, Wilson says, "So you weren't friends with Kennedy. We heard you do have some good friends at the school, though. The Abbott triplets?"

My heart shoots up into my throat. "Yes," I force over the lump. "Why are you asking about them?" But I know exactly why she's asking. My fists curl in my lap as I ready myself to defend the Abbotts.

"Were any of them particularly friendly with Miss Russo?" Wilson asks, ignoring my question.

"No," I say more sharply than intended. "If anything, they stay far away from the Russo family."

The detectives exchange another look, surprise in this one, and I know I've said too much. "Why is that?" Chase asks. "Wasn't it Dr. Arnold Russo who handled Adam Abbott's surgery last year?"

I wring my hands now, wishing for a way out of here. "Yes, he was." Dr. Russo also organized a group of parents in petitioning the school board to have the Abbott boys expelled. It made no sense, since the boys were never charged with anything. But rather than add to the spectacle by fighting those parents, Mr. and Mrs. Abbott had the boys finish out the year through independent study.

"I didn't mean they stay away from the Russo family," I attempt to clarify. "I just meant that after everything last year, they're trying to keep...healthcare visits and bills to a minimum." I cringe at the terrible but necessary lie and then wonder if I can go down for perjury based on this *casual* interview.

"Mmhmm," Wilson says, tone unconvinced. "So there was no friendship—no relationship of any kind between any of the Abbott brothers and Miss Russo?"

"No—er, not that I'm aware of, at least."

"Miss Phillips, are you familiar with a blue sweatshirt that each of the Abbott brothers owned?"

I nod, my skin starting to prickle. This is about that rumor I read on Instagram. Kacey said she'd gone to the cops already. "I had them made for the triplets. They were Christmas presents." But it seems pretty obvious the detectives already know this.

"And did you see if any of the brothers were wearing the sweatshirt yesterday?"

I clench my teeth, not wanting to answer. "Yes, but you have to know something about the kids at this school—"

"Just, stick to answering the question, Miss Phillips," Chase says. "Did you see any of the brothers wearing the blue sweatshirt with the letter *A* on the back yesterday?"

"They were *all* wearing it," I say, throwing up a hand. "But it doesn't mean anything."

"Miss Phillips, I'd like to show you something," Wilson says, turning a laptop around on the desk to face me. She hits a button, and a video starts to play.

I watch for a moment. The image is grainy, but I can still make out Kennedy's long red hair and pink sweater as she walks through the grass behind the school. Instead of following her classmates to the right—in the direction of the playing fields—Kennedy scans the area before darting off to the left. She disappears behind the corner of the building. There are only two destinations off-screen in that direction: One, the parking lot, had she continued along that path that lines the building. And two, the woods, a straight shot ahead.

The video doesn't end there, though. For a split second, Kennedy's hand darts back into the frame to motion someone forward. In the direction of the woods.

And then it happens. A figure in a dark blue sweatshirt—hood drawn to cover its owner's head, the white letter *A* like a beacon on the murky screen—follows right behind her.

My mouth goes dry.

Wilson reaches forward to end the security footage, and all I can do is sit in stunned silence.

BRAM

LAST OCTOBER

"Welcome to my house! Enter freely and of your own will!"

—*Dracula* by Bram Stoker

Bram Abbott's body temperature always ran cold. But by the time he and Mariana reached the house, his hand was so sweaty, he couldn't wait to release hers. He was parched too.

"Ugh," Mariana said, a smile on her lips even while complaining. "What happened to fall weather?"

"I'll grab some water." Bram gestured for his girlfriend to settle on the living room couch. Before turning to the kitchen, however, Bram hurried upstairs to his room to grab the paperback stuffed behind all the rest of the books on the shelf.

"Thanks," Mariana said when he handed her the icy glass. She pursed her lips expectantly, and he lowered his head to kiss her.

Mariana's trigonometry textbook was open on the cushion

beside her, spiral notebook on her lap. Her backpack with half its contents spilled out occupied the only other cushion. She was a lovely little mess—that was what he'd endearingly called her the first time he saw her bedroom. Mariana was beautiful and never obsessed over the details. There was always a hair out of place, a button she'd missed. Maybe her bedroom was a disaster, but she'd baked three pies for the book club that met in the library on Wednesday nights. Bram admired that about her.

He settled in the chair next to the couch, sliding the novel from the crook of his arm.

"You're not going back to the shop?" Mariana asked, leaning forward to rest her water glass on the coffee table.

"They can handle it for a few minutes."

"Why are you all the way over there?" she asked, giggling as she reached her foot out to nudge his leg.

"Hm, I wonder." He arched a brow coyly.

"I can move all of this if you—"

"It's fine," he said. "I won't be here long anyway." A moment ago, Bram hadn't bothered asking her to move her things. Now he realized why, feeling a dash of relief mixed with a creeping sense of guilt. Being close to Mariana hadn't felt quite right in weeks. There was something he needed to take care of, something he had to do before things could go back to normal. Only he'd been too weak thus far.

He wondered if Mariana sensed it too—this chasm he had created between them—as she shrugged and turned back to her notebook.

Bram opened *Dracula*. He'd chosen the novel, of course, because he shared a name with its author. Bram Abbott's full name was Abraham, after the one in the Bible, only his mother never liked shortening it to Abe. So she'd settled on Bram. This had drawn the obvious comparison to Mr. Stoker over the years, mostly by old people asking if he'd been named after the author. And more recently, asking if he'd read the novel. Once, when he'd visited Mariana at the library, the elderly employee who took over her shift had actually thrust this worn copy at Bram. "Keep it," he'd said. "Read it, then tell me what you think."

The man's insistence had needled Bram, and up until now he'd intentionally avoided reading the book.

Maybe that was why Bram had kept quiet when his brothers asked about his book selection for the assignment. They would've laughed.

At least now he could say he'd read it the next time some old man made a joke. If he could get through all these pages.

Before long, though, Bram found himself immersed in the tale of Jonathan Harker, an accountant who'd been sent to work for a shady figure in a Transylvanian castle, where only terrible things could possibly happen.

At some point, Bram heard Mariana moving, and he mumbled that there were snacks in the pantry and sodas in the refrigerator. It wasn't until his phone buzzed in his pocket that Bram looked up from the book.

Frustration mounted in his chest as he reached for the phone.

It was probably Adam, whining about how Bram couldn't expect him and Henry to work on his girlfriend's car for free without him.

The message hadn't come from Adam, though.

Bram's neck heated as he closed the text conversation. He looked over at the couch, hoping Mariana was too preoccupied with her homework to notice.

Only she wasn't there. Bram listened for the sound of her footsteps but heard nothing. Her belongings were still sprawled out. Maybe she'd gone to the bathroom.

But when he went to check, Mariana wasn't there either.

5

"You know the brothers well," Detective Wilson prods, resting an elbow on the desk. "We're hoping you can tell us which one this is."

"I—" I blink, as if it will erase whatever I just saw on the footage. "I don't know," I answer honestly. The brothers' features are so distinct, and when they were little, they had different body types. But sometime after puberty, they all ended up with a similar lean, muscled build. That's why they all make decent football players, despite the fact that only Adam has a deep love for the game. Bram is the tallest by a couple of inches, Adam slightly more broad-shouldered. But while these differences may be clear when the boys stand next to one another, I have no idea here.

"The teachers took attendance at the drill," I say, like the most helpful little witness to have ever sat in this chair.

"Yes, we've spoken with their teachers." Wilson offers a condescending smile. Obviously, the detectives already thought of that.

"Did they tell you if one of the brothers was missing?" I press anyway.

"I'm afraid that's confidential at this point," Wilson says.

I can't read her expression. Either she knows which brother is in the footage—the one who was unaccounted for—and she's trying to use me for corroboration, or something else is going on. Maybe this footage was recorded after roll was taken. Or maybe more than one brother went missing during attendance. "But," Wilson adds, "we did hear from a couple of students that the person in the security camera footage might be Bram. Apparently, he was the first student on the scene where Kennedy was found."

"The first on the scene?" Bram's words ricochet back to me: *I was slow getting back after the drill.*

I try to swallow despite my arid throat. Then it hits me. "Bram wasn't wearing his sweatshirt in the afternoon," I practically bark. "I saw him, when he brought back the nurse."

The figure in the surveillance footage couldn't have been Bram. My body heaves with relief. Whoever told the cops they saw Bram with Kennedy was lying.

I'm not sure what I was expecting. Maybe I thought the detectives would nod and cross Bram's name off their notepad with a dramatic flick of the wrist. Instead, they exchange another look, this one even more smug and victorious than the last.

My stomach sinks. *I'm an idiot.* Just because Bram didn't have his hoodie on after Kennedy's body was found doesn't mean he wasn't the boy in the footage. I haven't vindicated him; I've merely given the cops a concrete piece of evidence to search for. They could track down that sweatshirt, test it for Kennedy's blood, and have themselves a smoking gun.

Or worse, maybe they already found a blood-covered sweatshirt out in those woods. They could be trying to establish which brother is missing a hoodie.

After a few more questions, which I answer in a fuzzy haze of shame, the detectives let me go, with instructions to call them if I think of anything helpful.

"Like I said before"—Wilson leans in close, even though Chase is the only other person in the room—"everything is confidential, so you can't tell anyone this. But all *three* Abbott brothers were missing from class when this footage was recorded. And the brothers aren't talking about where they were. They lawyered up immediately." She twists her lips. "I find that a little suspicious, don't you?"

I force a headshake. "It's only because people in this town say things about—"

"Oh," she cuts in, "and, again, just between us, there's already more evidence stacked against them." She tips her head like she's offering sympathy, only I know she's gloating.

I leave the office, my mind plagued with questions. Which Abbott brother would be talking to Kennedy Russo? And if it was Bram, like someone told the cops, should I warn him about his sweatshirt? Or should I let things play out?

And then the most crucial question of all: Could Bram have actually done this?

There's only one answer blaring through my head as I exit the school. *No.* Absolutely not.

But if he didn't do it, does it mean Adam or Henry did?

Dad offered to come back and pick me up after my interview, but I decide not to call him. I could use the lengthy walk home to clear my head.

Once I'm off the main street, where the school, the library, and the post office reside, I turn onto the road that snakes through the crop fields and country homes. It's lined with maple trees, their leaves the bright oranges and reds of fall. A white picket fence runs on either side, wild sunflowers woven through the slats. Little finches perch atop it until I come along, causing them to flutter off. I pass the white steepled church off to my left and continue on to where the trees grow thicker.

I shake off the detectives' implications about Bram, attempting to consider his brothers instead. Only I can't entertain the thought of Henry having anything to do with yesterday's events either. Even allowing it to cross my mind feels like a betrayal.

But Adam? He's changed so much since his accident. He's not the carefree boy or the up-for-anything friend I used to know. The real trouble I'm having is connecting the dots. Adam didn't talk to Kennedy Russo, and yesterday, he really didn't seem up for talking to anyone.

And then he wasn't in class. The thought sends a slight shiver through me. I assumed he'd gone to the nurse's office. This should still be the logical conclusion, considering he didn't head home. I saw him with Henry by the Mustang after school.

According to the detectives, though, Adam didn't give the nurse's office as his alibi—an alibi which would've easily been corroborated. Instead, Adam refused to talk about where he'd been during that time.

At the sound of an engine, I press closer to the fence, burying my feet in the weeds. A cloud of dust rises, and as it settles, a truck slows beside me. Henry leans over to call my name through the window.

I'm slightly taken aback seeing him in the driver's seat of his vintage Ford truck instead of the passenger side of the Mustang. His brothers drive him everywhere, so it's easy to forget he has his own mode of transportation.

"What are you doing?" he asks. His brown hair is combed for once, and he's wearing a light blue polo.

I point up the road. "Going home."

"Want to get lunch in town instead?"

"Town?" I bite my lower lip, my stomach starting to ache. He obviously doesn't know what everyone at school is saying—what the cops are saying about him and his brothers. "Maybe we should stick to your place."

His expression darkens as he glances down at the center console. "You were at the school. It's not true, what everyone's saying."

"I know that, Henry." I step closer to the truck, kicking up dirt. "I just think it might be best to lie low for a while until—"

"I'm not doing that again," he snaps, his glasses sliding down the bridge of his nose. He takes a deep breath, but his knuckles turn white over the steering wheel. "Look, Adam may be fine with hiding away, but I want to finish out the school year like everyone else. No more homeschooling. No more acting like everyone is right about us."

"Okay," I say softly, walking around to the passenger door and reaching for the handle. I heft myself inside the cab and strap on my seat belt. "Where were you just now?" I ask as he hits the gas.

Pulling into a dirt driveway, Henry turns the truck around. "I was with my dad and my brothers in Central Springs. Seeing the family lawyer, Mr. Swanson."

"Oh." I guess the detectives weren't lying about that.

"Bram had his interview with the cops this morning, and he could tell right away it was a witch hunt. He refused to say another word without a lawyer."

"That's wise," I say. "They went after you guys pretty hard during my interview."

"Really?" Henry asks, looking like a scared boy with his sea-green eyes wide. "Can't say I'm surprised," he mutters, focusing on the road again. "Not with everyone at this school convinced we had something to do with Mariana's death last year. And now this."

"And"—I lick my lips, almost too nervous to get the words out—"with the security camera footage of Kennedy and…you know."

He's silent for a long stretch before he finally shakes his head. "That's not what it looks like."

"What is it then, Henry? If you can explain it away, why don't you?"

"I can't," he mutters. "It's not up to me."

So my gut was right. It's not Henry on the footage. But he *is* covering for one of his brothers. "Look, I know you want to stay loyal to Bram and Adam, but this is your life."

"It's not like that," he says, a quiver running through his voice.

"Do you think they'll arrest you?"

Another headshake. "Our lawyer says they won't arrest anyone until they figure out who's on the video. And even then, he's ready to fight tooth and nail. The footage isn't clear, and without our faces, it's impossible to prove it's even one of us."

"Oh," I say, settling back in my seat. "That's good. I just don't understand why you can't tell *me* what you were really doing."

"Because I can't," Henry says, eyes still on the road. "Please, Hayden. Can you just trust me?"

Can I trust him? I always have in the past. But I really don't like this secrecy.

It's not the first time the brothers have kept something from me over the years. Not the only time they've made me feel like an outsider. They're triplets, close even before birth; naturally, they have secrets. When we were in second grade, they came up with a language all their own, and they refused to teach me how to speak it. I once got so frustrated, I stormed out of the mansion and down the road. Bram eventually chased me down and taught me how to say one word. It wasn't much, but he swore I could use it to get under Adam's skin the next time he did something annoying. And of course, it worked, and I felt like a part of the group.

Is this the same? Am I simply jealous they won't include me?

"Hayden," Henry says, his voice rough as he lifts a hand off the steering wheel to adjust his glasses, "I think the only way to prove that none of us were involved in Kennedy's murder is to prove that someone else was. And with Adam's current state of mind, and Bram essentially locked up, I *need* you." He turns to meet my gaze, his eyes pleading. "Will you help me figure this out?"

I don't answer at first, even though the words tug at my heart. "Why is Bram locked up?" I finally ask, avoiding his question.

"Not literally," Henry says. "But our parents won't let him out of the house because of what everyone's saying about him. That he was in the woods with Kennedy when she died."

"Poor Bram." Yesterday, he seemed as desperate as Henry not to be shut away again.

"You and I know he didn't do this," Henry says. "But the cops won't look anywhere else, not when they have Bram, the guy whose girlfriend *died* in a freak car explosion last year. Not when he happened to be the one to find Kennedy's body."

Henry's right about that. The obvious answer is right in front of the detectives. They won't go above and beyond to try and disprove it. "What does your dad—or your lawyer, for that matter—think about you going out in public?"

We've reached the downtown strip, and Henry pulls into a parking spot in front of the town diner, The Silver Spoon. "I don't care what they think," he grumbles as the door to the diner flings open.

Dan Wheeler, Sage's father, ducks out, a plastic takeout bag in hand. He squints at us through the windshield, then scowls. Lifting his chin, he strides off down the street to his car.

Indignation burns like a hot coal in my chest. I want to leap out of the car and shout at that man that Henry Abbott didn't do anything to his niece, Mariana. And he had nothing to do with what happened to Kennedy.

Instead, I turn to Henry. "Okay, I'll do it. I'll help you figure out who really killed Kennedy."

And for the look he offers in return, eyes glimmering with appreciation, and the way he throws his arm around me, burying his face in my hair—I would agree one thousand times over.

HENRY

LAST OCTOBER

"The world was to me a secret which I desired to divine. Curiosity, earnest research to learn the hidden laws of nature, gladness akin to rapture, as they were unfolded to me, are among the earliest sensations I can remember."

—*Frankenstein* by Mary Shelley

Didn't Bram say he'd be right back?" Adam huffed from beneath the hood of Mariana's car.

"Uh, yeah," Henry said absentmindedly, eyes on his phone screen. Hayden had texted him a question about their science homework. "Want me to ask him?"

"It's not like he'd be any help. But it is *his* girlfriend's car."

"That it is. I'll text him."

"No, it's—whatever. We don't need him."

"Okay," Henry said good-naturedly, his mind still half on asking Hayden if she needed a ride to tonight's game. "So we're all good then?"

"Oh yeah. We're just fantastic, covered in sweat and grease, while he's lounging around with his girlfriend."

"Then," Henry said, squinting at his brother through his frames, "we're *not* good?"

"No, we're not good, Henry!" Adam barked at the same time something in the engine popped and hissed, sending a gust of steam into his face.

He backed away, growling, and threw the wrench across the garage. It slammed against the far wall, knocking some tools off their pegs.

Henry rushed to retrieve the wrench, shoving his brother aside to contain the damage to the engine. "I thought the issue was the brakes," he muttered, twisting the radiator cap back on. The steam had fogged his lenses, which he removed and cleaned on his shirt.

"We still don't know what the problem is," Adam said, waving a hand. "Maybe we should tell Mariana she has to wait until Dad comes back. This is out of our depth."

"No, it's not." Maybe it was out of Adam's depth, but this car wasn't going to outsmart Henry. He hadn't really even tried to solve the issue yet. "And you really think Dad could do better than us?" Mr. Abbott took care of the books. He was, supposedly, away on business, trying to expand the auto shop into a chain. But the man hadn't stepped foot inside the garage in months. "You go up to the house," Henry said, putting his glasses back on. "Finish your homework. Do that pregame meditative mumbo jumbo you jocks love so much."

"I don't do that," Adam said defiantly. "And you're on the team too, you know."

"Yeah, I know." Henry had been on the football team since

freshman year, but he'd never really felt like one of them. Even on nights where he ended up with the highest yards per carry, he got the sense he'd only been placed on the field because of Adam. *You're Adam Abbott's brother? Oh, sure, we'll throw you a bone.* "I'll handle the car."

"Whatever," Adam said, clomping over to the door. He grabbed his backpack off the chair and, hefting it on, yanked on the straps like it might try to abscond from him.

"I think you meant to say *thank you*, and you are welcome." Henry pantomimed tipping an imaginary hat, which only made Adam stomp his feet louder.

Henry turned to face down his opponent, wondering how many additional problems his brother had caused in his impatience. Henry knew better than to get into it with Adam. And sure, Bram should've been back by now, but Henry didn't want to be the reason Bram was in a bad mood at the game tonight. If Bram's tendency was to get aggressive or hotheaded the way Adam did, anger improving his performance on the field, it might be worth interrupting his time with Mariana. But Bram always got broody and withdrawn.

Anyway, Henry didn't mind the solitude.

In fact, while he was the only person around, he thought he might even be able to work on his project, the thing that kept him awake for hours every night. The thing that had become a bit of an obsession. It was a secret, partly because he wanted it to be a surprise. And partly because he wasn't sure he would actually succeed.

Henry knew he should stay and work on the car like he'd

promised. The car needed fixing if Mariana was going to drive it out of there in a couple of hours. And though he was much faster than his brothers, he still needed time for his own homework before the game.

But it felt like he was being lured to the back of the shop, to the cardboard box where he'd hidden his experiment.

Lifting the box, Henry moved to the door, poking his head out to check that the coast was clear. Then, just to ensure that no one would stumble upon him, he ducked onto the dirt path that led to the garden shed. There he could tinker on his project in secret.

6

Lunch in town was predictably short. No sooner had Henry and I ordered when we noticed the middle-aged woman sitting at the bar, watching us.

"Got a problem?" I finally asked her like a six-year-old.

She shrugged. "Just wondering how he can sit there and enjoy a warm meal while Kennedy Russo's body is still going cold. Not even in the ground yet."

I press my lips flat, trying hard not to respond and failing. "You're saying that he shouldn't eat?"

"I'm saying he and his brothers should burn in hell for all the havoc they've wreaked." She wrapped her hands around herself like she needed protection. "Pure evil."

"Okay, well, thank you for that thorough report, ma'am," I said, blood simmering as the waitress placed a cold Coke in front of me. I picked it up and raised it to the woman. "You have yourself a nice day."

After that point, even the waitress started to look at us funny, apparently making the connection between the Abbott boy at my side and the recent murder. Suddenly unsure if we could trust the food, Henry paid for the Cokes, and we headed back to his house to make our own sandwiches.

"You were right," Henry says now, carrying both plates to where I'm seated at the kitchen nook. He places a turkey sandwich and a bag of potato chips in front of me, then removes a vase filled with withered flowers his mother must've collected from the garden weeks ago, setting it by the sink.

"Wish I hadn't been. You were brave to try anyway."

"Brave? Or stupid?"

"There is never one without the other," I say, trying to do a voice impersonation of a wizened, ancient sage before taking a bite of my sandwich.

"You should write a book of wise sayings," Henry jokes, but I can tell by the way he's pushing his chips around on the plate that his thoughts have already drifted elsewhere.

"What is it?" I put my sandwich down.

"How do we start?" he asks with a shrug. "This investigation, I mean. Should we talk to Kennedy's friends ourselves?"

"First of all—and I mean this in the nicest way—*you're* not talking to anyone. If we actually want these people to give us any information, you have to stay my silent, invisible partner."

Henry nibbles on a chip. His glasses have slid halfway down his nose, and at some point in his anxiousness, he must've stuck his fingers in his hair, undoing that neatly combed style. Even the collar of his polo shirt is upturned. Though I'm supposed to be thinking about how to help him and his brothers, my mind veers to how good he looks in this disheveled state. "You're right," he mutters. "Again."

"And it won't be the last time," I assure him with a smirk. "I think I want to start by talking to your brothers."

Henry's eyes widen in something like panic. "Why?"

I shrug, trying to calm him by keeping cool myself, though it's a complete act. If anything, Henry's fear has me wondering what the hell his brothers are hiding. "Because we're here, and they're here. And I think getting down their version of events—any part they're willing to tell—will help form a complete picture when I interview everyone else."

Henry takes a breath, considering this. When he meets my eyes, I cut him off and say, "Told you it wouldn't be the last time, didn't I?"

He kicks me under the table the way he used to when we were kids. I laugh and toss a chip at him.

"Well, good luck," he says. "I doubt they'll say much. I'll just… be in my room if you need me."

Before he lifts our plates off the table, I notice that he hasn't touched his chips.

Instead, he's arranged them on the crumb-sprinkled plate to form the letter *K*.

I take the stairs, noting the thick layer of dust coating the railing and the cobwebs strewn between the balustrades. The mansion has been in a slight state of disrepair since last year's accident. Mrs. Abbott used have a staff to help with the upkeep, but she fired them when she discovered someone was leaking photos of the family to the press. I haven't seen Mrs. Abbott around much lately—even less than I've seen her husband—and whenever I ask Henry, he says she's on another retreat to get away from the stress. I guess this new case isn't exactly going to help her self-renewal journey.

The staircase landing features a large arched window overlooking the gardens, and sunlight streams in, highlighting millions of dust motes. I reach the second floor and start down the long hall, passing portraits and wall sconces with unlit candles. The large black-framed mirror that always gives me a jump scare is not only filthy but curiously cracked. I try Adam's room first, but he's blasting heavy metal and apparently, doesn't hear my knock. You should never open someone's door uninvited, and I know from experience that Adam can be somewhat volatile. So I text him. Can we talk?

I wait outside the door, watching the screen. But the message goes unread.

Tentatively, I reach for the doorknob, just to peek. But I hear a deep voice and wrench my hand back. "Hey there."

I turn to find Bram behind me, leaning against the archway to the opposite wing. He takes a step forward, lifting his arms like he might embrace me. Instinctively, I back up.

He stops in his tracks, face falling.

"Sorry," I say, my breath shallow, "you startled me."

When he looks up again, his eyes are cold. "It's all bullshit, Hayden, what these idiots are saying. I didn't do anything to Kennedy. You know that."

I quickly nod, like I do know that. Only I don't, not really. Because I didn't see Bram during the drill, or even afterward.

"A girl is dead," he says. "Naturally, they're all going to blame *me*. The guy whose girlfriend died last year."

He has a point there. "That's exactly what I tried to tell the cops," I say.

Bram reaches up to rub the back of his neck. "Doubt it will do any good, but thanks. For vouching for me."

At the gratitude in his voice, I feel a stab of guilt that I didn't do more. That I didn't force those detectives to listen to what I had to say.

"That's what friends do." I say it like that's what we are, like it's all we've ever been. Like there isn't always this tension between us, ever since the day I made that horrible mistake with him. "But Bram, they have a video of one of you with Kennedy." I don't want to ask it aloud, but he's gone silent. "You're not the person in the video?"

"No," he says sharply. "I'm not the person in the video."

I put up my hands in a gesture of surrender, reminding him I'm not the bad guy here. We need to change the conversation.

"You want to watch a movie?" I ask, because when it's only Bram and me hanging out, that's what we do.

When I'm with Henry, we go for walks, maybe stopping by the library or hitting the diner, where whoever can finish an entire cup of stale coffee first wins a slice of pie, paid for by the loser. If Henry and I watch a movie together, we're talking over it the whole time, debating its merits, cracking jokes. It's not quiet like it is with Bram, where it's enough to just be in each other's presence.

As for Adam, I doubt he's ever sat through an entire movie in his life. Up until last year, he could never keep still. When we hung out, it always consisted of passing a ball of some sort on the mansion's lawn. He'd talk about which girl he liked at the moment; I'd stealthily avoid having to reciprocate and talk about my crush. Sometimes we'd pull pranks together, like when we taped *Looking for a Prom Date* ads with Jimmy Ciccone's photo on them around school after he'd trashed Adam's football performance in the school's sports column. I was there to tone down Adam's more extreme ideas of retribution and keep him out of jail. It's heartbreaking seeing Adam as a quiet recluse now, because he'd always been loud and *out there*, whether for good or bad.

Bram is Adam's opposite in many ways: He'd rather keep to the shadows than be in the spotlight and speaks only when he really has something to say. Now he simply nods, gesturing for me to lead the way to the home theater.

I do, with guilt creeping up again. The truth is, I'm not here to relax on the leather reclining seats with Bram and sit in contented silence. I'm here to find out why he was the one who found Kennedy in those woods yesterday. "Bram," I say, taking a seat front and center, "you said you took a while getting back after the fire drill."

"Yeah," he says, picking up the remote.

"Except the cops say that you weren't on the attendance sheet for the drill."

His spine stiffens, but he continues navigating the screen browser. "That's because I lied."

I flinch, shock hitting me like a fist. Somehow, I hoped the teachers were wrong, that Bram would be able to prove they simply missed him and his brothers. It sounds stupid, now that I really think through it. "You lied to me?" I hate how my voice cracks, how hurt I sound.

"I'm sorry," he says, dropping the remote on the seat nearest him and turning to me. "I wish I hadn't. But it doesn't mean I lied about everything else."

It doesn't? He must see the dilemma he's handed me. I'm expected to trust him, to believe the words that come out of his mouth. But yesterday he lied about the fire drill.

What's to say he didn't lie about not being the person on the video surveillance footage? "Where were you, then?" I ask. The question sounds sharp, almost like righteous indignation. Maybe it'll force the truth out of him. This is his chance to rectify things between us.

Bram rubs at his face, deep in thought. He rests his chin on his palm, the other arm crossed over his stomach. "You remember that Henry and I were together in the cafeteria when you left."

I nod.

"Well, we went to find Adam. And when we did, he was in bad shape."

"You mean the bumps on his head?"

Bram gives a headshake. "I mean more than the physical stuff. He was in a bad space...mentally."

My heart wrenches. Adam, always the toughest guy on the football field, hurting like that. It makes sense though. His former *friends* not only turned on him but used the worst thing he'd ever experienced to humiliate him.

"I wanted to get him away from the school before he did something."

"*Did* something?" I ask.

Bram lifts a hand. "Don't forget this is Adam. He's been like a lobotomy patient ever since the accident, but somewhere in there is the guy who would've marched right into Neil and Todd's classes and dragged them out of there by their shirt collars."

Another fair point. In fourth grade, Adam punched a kid in the face for joking that Henry wore *girl glasses*. "Anyway," Bram continues, "I told Henry to take him home. He handles Adam better than I do. You know that."

And I do. I've seen the brotherly dynamics unfold countless times. Bram isn't patient like Henry, who is careful and tactful as a crisis negotiator. Despite how close Bram and Adam are when it comes to managing conflict, Bram's methods resemble using kerosene to douse a fire. "And where did you go when you were supposed to be in class?"

His eyes lower. "I can't tell you that, Hayden."

"Why the hell not?"

"Because I don't want to lie to you again."

My jaw clamps. "Henry and Adam never went home," I say. "They were there in the parking lot, waiting for me."

"Henry said it was easier to wait out the bell than to go home and come back later for you and me." Bram sighs. "It's complicated."

"Is it?" I ask. My frustration rises like a river and I'm a dam about to burst. "You really won't tell me what you did during all of sixth period? You claim that you weren't the person shown with Kennedy in that video, and yet, you were in the woods! You were the one who found her body!"

He flinches at this accusation. "I see those detectives are really keeping key details under wraps."

I shrug. "*They* told me. *You* didn't. Even though I was there with you yesterday. That's the real reason you didn't want to be at school when the cops showed up. Because you had no excuse whatsoever to be there in the woods with Kennedy's body."

"I just—it was a lot yesterday." He rubs at his face, and I notice a long scratch on the back of his hand. "I didn't think I had to go around telling everyone I was the first person to find her."

"What happened there?" I ask, pointing to the scratch. Was

that what the cops were looking for when they examined my hands? Maybe this is just another reason why they've set their sights on Bram.

He frowns, lowering his hand to look. Then he shrugs and tucks it down at his side, in between his body and the armrest. "Mom fired the gardener, so I was trimming that obnoxious magnolia out back. You know, the one that's always blocking the path. It's not life or death, Phil." He uses his old nickname for me, the shortened version of my surname that used to drive me crazy at the same time it made me feel like one of the boys. I've started to feel different about the name over the last couple of years—this term of endearment meant for only me.

But right now, there's no warm, comforting feeling about it, since his tone is patronizing and he isn't making eye contact.

"Bram, yesterday afternoon you weren't wearing your sweatshirt, and I sort of...told the cops."

He squints, not following. Before he can say anything, I blurt, "I thought I was helping you! The guy on the surveillance footage was wearing a sweatshirt like the one I gave you. So I thought it was proof that he couldn't be you." I dig my fingertips into both temples. "Only now, I think they're going to try to use that sweatshirt as evidence."

"I see," Bram says, the words measured. But his face is stormy, his quiet fury sending an unsettling spike of fear through me. "And *why* are you telling me this?"

"In case you have it and want to...I don't know, get rid of it."

His eyes lock on to mine. "Get rid of it. Because I killed Kennedy, and then"—he tilts his head—"what exactly? Used the sweatshirt to clean her blood off my hands?"

Yes, exactly that. Maybe that. "No, Bram—I don't know! The cops have ways of twisting everything. If they get ahold of that sweatshirt, they could use it against you."

He's silent a moment, this logic seemingly having dulled his rage. Taking up the remote again, he turns to the television. "I can't get rid of it."

"Why not?"

"Because I have no idea where it is," he says in a clipped tone. "Yesterday afternoon in the cafeteria with Henry, I took it off and set it down on a bench. With everything going on, I forgot it. And when I went back a few minutes later, it was gone."

My insides go cold. "Someone stole it?"

If this is true, whoever stole Bram's sweatshirt could be the person on the footage. Someone impersonating him, maybe even framing him.

Only there's a flaw in this reasoning. If someone were trying to make it look like Bram killed Kennedy, it would make more sense to plant the sweatshirt somewhere—make sure it would be found covered in Kennedy's blood, ready for traces of Bram's DNA to turn up when tested. So far, though, that sweatshirt is still missing, and things aren't adding up. I have no idea why neither Bram nor Henry will be forthcoming with me—aside from the obvious implications.

The bad ones.

When I check my phone, Adam has left my text message on *read*. A lot of help he'll be. And Bram made it sound like Adam couldn't even help me if he wanted to, since he was in the car with Henry the entire time. All signs point to Bram, who swears he wasn't the guy caught on camera with Kennedy.

And the thing is—despite his shaky story and the fact that he lied to me yesterday—I believe him now. I want to help prove to those detectives that he didn't do it.

I try to rack my brain for who might've hated Kennedy—or even Bram—enough to do this, but the problem is that no one hated Kennedy Russo.

And *everyone* hates the Abbott brothers.

7

After knocking on Adam's door and getting no response again, I walk home and spend my time scrolling social media like a true winner.

As soon as I click on one post about Kennedy, another half dozen related posts pop onto my feed.

Then I see a new post by Lydia Costas, time-stamped ten minutes ago, this one decidedly darker than the first.

The caption accompanies a photo of Lydia and Kennedy as grade school students with matching pigtails:

To the person who did this, I know who you are. And it's only a matter of time before the cops have enough evidence to pull you in. I hope you get everything you deserve

An electric buzz rushes through me, and my spine stiffens. Who is she talking about?

Apparently, the rest of Lydia's followers have the same question, because already, the post has forty-nine comments.

STACYDORMER: 👀

LYDIACOSTAS: my lips are sealed

SAGEWHEELER: who are you talking about?

TELLISON: put this psycho on blast, Lyds

THEREALDEALNEIL: @Lydiacostas yeah this freak doesn't deserve to stay anonymous

But Lydia hasn't replied to anyone apart from Stacy. I have to assume one more attempt to get her attention in the comments will go unnoticed and that her DMs are likely flooded.

Still, I have to find out what she knows. If she saw whoever was out in the woods with Kennedy—if it's the same person who stole Bram's hoodie—then she has to go to the cops with what she knows.

Maybe there's a less direct way to go about this. Lydia and I have never really been friends, but as of the election two weeks ago, she's on the student council with me. And in a school the size of ours, everyone knows everyone. We've been at the same parties, in the same classes over the years. Once we were partnered up for an English project, and we hit it off pretty well. She came over to my house a few times and even stayed late for pizza and a movie. As soon as the project was turned in, though, we went our separate ways again. She'd find it strange if I suddenly reached out to check on her.

I go to Lydia's profile and scroll past the Kennedy posts, past her cheerleading headshot, pausing on a post from last week of Lydia holding a black kitten. The post is a slideshow, so I swipe to the second photo of a whole litter nestled on a blanket. There's a caption:

Aren't they adorable? Message if interested

A plan forms, along with a little knot of guilt. The timing would be insensitive—bordering on callous—but it's the only play I've got. I click on her DMs and type Hey Lydia, do you still have any kittens for sale?

Then I head to the kitchen to figure out dinner. Dad should be home soon. It's not like I'm expected to cook every night, but he appreciates it. And I did have the whole day off. I root around in the cupboard for something easy to whip up. Mom used to make the most amazing lasagna from scratch. I can barely remember how it tasted, those rich flavors, the intoxicating scent of the kitchen as she cooked. I'm sure that, like my other memories of her, that dish will eventually fade into oblivion.

I'm dumping a box of rotini into boiling water when my phone dings. It's an Instagram notification. I open the app to find a reply from Lydia. You can come by tomorrow morning around 9

Another message pops up from her. 43 Farrow Lane

I start to wonder if I missed a message about school being cancelled again, and then I remember that tomorrow is Saturday. I'll be there

---

Lydia lives in a modest farmhouse off a narrow, unpaved road I was expecting something bigger and newer, probably because she was Kennedy's friend and the Russo home is second in size only to the Abbott mansion.

Dad let me borrow his car for the morning, which I park on the weed-lined road outside the property. I take the dirt path up to the house. Passing a warped porch swing, I reach for the doorbell. But Lydia opens the door before I can ring it. "It's broken," she says in a rough voice, like she cheered too hard on the field. *Except there was no cheer practice*, I remind myself, *no Friday night game*. It's more likely she's been crying. She pushes through a ripped screen door to join me, wearing a matching green sweatsuit. Her dark brown hair is tied up in a messy bun. "The kittens are in the barn anyway."

"Oh," I say, my gaze veering to the building with the weathered red paint, some twenty yards away.

In the sunlight, I notice that Lydia, queen of the perfect cat-eye flick, is bare faced, her eyes red and swollen, nose raw and angry. I already regret coming here under false pretenses. I nearly apologize and tell her I've changed my mind when she brushes past me, leading the way across the weeds. "You like chickens?" she asks.

"Like for eating?"

She shoots me a look over her shoulder, and I smile disarmingly. "Kidding. Who doesn't like chickens?"

"We've got brand-new chicks. Want to see 'em?"

Somehow, this is not at all what I was expecting. "Definitely."

She leads me inside the barn, and we pass the horse stables to where little peeping sounds emerge from a brooder set up on a folding table in the corner.

"Want to hold one?" she offers.

"Sure." It's not my first time holding a newborn chick. Even so, I feel nervous when Lydia places the delicate, fuzzy animal in my cupped hands. "It's so cute. Are these for sale too?" I ask, even though Dad would think I've lost my mind.

"Nah, we're keeping these little guys. What you're looking for is over this way." She tips her head to the adjacent corner. Then she gingerly scoops the chick from my hands and places him back in the brooder.

I amble over to the large playpen structure housing the kittens. The mother cat is there, sleeping as the two kittens romp and roam around. "Just two, then?"

"The rest were snatched right up." She gazes down on them admiringly. "Think I'll keep whichever one you don't pick."

"Right." It just so happens that I have a slight cat allergy, so I will not be leaving here with a kitten. I'll have to tell her that the kittens and I didn't connect or something.

"You grab the orange one," Lydia says. "I sort of named him Tangerine already, but you can change it, obviously. I'll carry this one," she says, grabbing the calico kitten, "and we can do a little meet and greet out in the grass."

"Sounds good," I say, leaning down to lift the skittish kitten. When I finally wrangle it, Lydia has the calico one cradled to her chest, and I follow her, trying desperately not to lose the little orange ball of energy. "I think Fireball might be a more apt name for this guy," I say as Lydia settles in a shady spot.

She smiles and strokes the back of the calico kitten's neck. "That's a good one. This is Cal, which I know isn't very original. I try not to get too attached. But I plan to change the name of whichever one stays with me"—her voice breaks, and she clears it—"to Kennedy."

My chest tightens. "I'm so sorry, Lydia."

"Thanks," she says, nestling her cheek against the kitten's fur.

"You know what…I shouldn't have come here today." I start to get up but lose my grasp on the orange kitten, who leaps free onto the grass. "Not with everything you're going through. I can come back—"

"It's fine." Lydia motions for me to sit back down. "This is all I've been doing since I got the news anyway. The kittens and chicks are my therapy." For a moment, we both sit and watch the orange cat—who's looking more and more like a Fireball—raise a tiny paw to bat a dandelion, which subsequently springs back to whack him in the eye.

The glimmer of a smile crosses Lydia's face. She releases Cal, who pads tentatively over the grass. He only makes it a few steps before Fireball tackles him, the two rolling along like one striped ball of fur.

"You and Kennedy were friends for a long time," I say.

"Since kindergarten." The wind whips through the grass, and Lydia wraps her arms around herself. "It's like losing a sister."

"Wow," I say, scooting a little so that my top half is in the shade, my crossed legs in the sun. "Did the cops confirm what actually"—I drop my voice—"*happened*?"

"Not yet, but there's a press conference tonight. It's not like she bludgeoned herself to death." Lydia's hand darts to her mouth. "Sorry, I wasn't supposed to say how she was killed."

"It's okay," I assure her, trying to hide my horror. "I was there by the woods when they found her, so I...well, I saw her."

Lydia's eyes go wide. "You did?"

I nod, and suddenly, I can't help it. I sneeze. Once, then twice. "Sorry, it's uh...the pollen this time of year." Okay, so it's a *big* cat allergy.

Lydia nods. "The sunflowers. That's what always does my mom in."

"Exactly." *Get back on track.* "I caught your post yesterday, when you said you knew who the killer was. Did you see something in the woods?"

She's silent for an excruciating moment, and I start to wonder if she's onto me. But then she sighs. "Maybe I was exaggerating when I said I *know* who they are," she admits, brushing cat hair off her sweatpants. "Technically, I have it narrowed down to three people."

My heart drops. "You think it was an Abbott brother."

"Duh."

This was a waste of time, a complete dead end. "Because of Mariana's accident," I say.

"No." Lydia looks up at me like I'm an idiot. "Wait, aren't you *friends* with them?" The word *friends* comes out as if she'd said *infected* or *contagious*.

"We're neighbors," I say to downplay things.

At this, her interest perks up. "Well, did you ever see Kennedy with one of them?"

"With an Abbott brother?" I shake my head. "Never. Why?"

Lydia's brown eyes narrow, and she leans in conspiratorially. "Because Kennedy was seeing one of the triplets. *Secretly*."

Something pricks up in my chest. An unwelcome feeling. "How do you know it was an Abbott?" This is exactly what the detectives had hinted at yesterday, and just like then, I refuse to fall for it.

"I followed her," Lydia says, yanking a dandelion from the earth. "Kennedy had been real quiet and secretive since around the time school started. Skittish too, you know? This one time, I came up behind her while she was at her locker, and she literally jumped and then got all pissed. She even slammed her locker door. I figured she was, like, into drugs or something. Hiding them in her locker. I was worried about her."

"Had you ever seen her do drugs before?" Fireball prances up to me in the grass, trying to get my attention as he skirts me, his tail swerving dangerously close to my nose. I sneeze again, a violent sound.

"No, never," Lydia says, graciously oblivious to my condition. "She told me about this patient of her dad's, this addict who stole some shit out of the medicine cabinet when no one was looking. Dr. Russo realized it when he went back into the room. The guy was gone, and so were the drugs. And Kennedy was so vocal about how messed up it was and how she never wanted to end up that way." Lydia tosses the now petalless flower into the grass. "But something had to account for her behavior. I wanted to save her before she could turn into some loser, like that addict. One night, we were doing homework, and she kept getting distracted with her texts. Well, when she got up to use the bathroom, I took her phone. It hadn't locked yet, so I pulled up her messages and saw that she'd made plans to meet someone that night. The contact didn't have a name, just a number I didn't recognize."

"So you think it was drugs then?" I ask, brushing the orange cat fur off my sleeve, only to find that it's practically glued on. I try plucking individual hairs, letting each one blow off into the field with the wind.

"I wasn't sure. She came back before I could read much or write down the number. And then, what do you know? She grabbed her books, claiming she needed to go home and get to bed early." Lydia shrugs, her lips a tight line. "That's when I followed her. Whoever this guy was, he'd turned my best friend into a stranger. Someone who lied to me."

"You followed her in your car?" I ask, struggling to picture Lydia tailing Kennedy on these two-lane roads unnoticed.

"At the beginning, I had to keep my headlights off." She waves a hand. "I know, it was dangerous. But it was the only way. Eventually, we ended up in your part of town—I remembered from when we worked on that English project. That was when Ken parked outside the Abbott property."

I lean forward to listen, my posture mimicking the windswept weeds.

"Ken got out and started to push open the gate. Only it was so loud, I heard it through my closed window. So she changed tactics and climbed the gate. That's how I knew whatever was going on had to be shady. She didn't want anyone spotting her." Lydia gives me a smug look, which falls, like she only just remembered that there's no reason to feel triumphant.

I try with everything in me not to sniffle or sneeze again, and interrupt her focus. "Did you follow her over the gate?"

"Yeah, but I was too slow. She didn't take the path up to the mansion. She veered off into the woods on their property, and I lost track of her. Then I got creeped out. Everyone says the Abbott brothers are like modern-day Blackbeards."

She's trying to reference the old fairy tale about the rich man who murdered his wives. "I think you mean *Blue Beards*," I correct, though the damage is done. I'm already imagining the triplets with eye patches and peg legs.

"Anyway..." Lydia says, shivering, "Now, I think everyone might've been right. I don't think it was drugs at all. I think she was seeing one of the Abbott boys, and then..." Her gaze veers off to the trees lining the far end of the property.

"Okay," I say, letting the word drag. "But why would Kennedy keep a boyfriend from you? Is it because you don't like the Abbotts?"

"No." She pauses, her head doing a little swish from one side to the other. "I mean, I don't like them *now*. But before this week, I didn't have a problem with them. I think Ken kept her relationship from me because everyone else hates the Abbotts. Especially her dad."

This isn't exactly news. I'm aware that Dr. Russo hasn't been the Abbott brothers' biggest fan since Mariana's accident. And the fact that he was Adam Abbott's doctor yet clearly sided against him made the rest of the town believe he knew more about the case—knew things that patient-doctor privilege didn't allow him to disclose. And though I hate to admit it, while the idea of Kennedy and an Abbott brother having a relationship out in the open seems ridiculous, a secret relationship makes perfect sense. She was gorgeous; they're gorgeous. If we're basing this on appearances alone, Kennedy and any one of the Abbott triplets would've made a perfect match.

And I never explicitly heard Kennedy speak ill of the brothers.

"Plus, I mean," Lydia continues, "if I'm honest, I have a little bit of a problem keeping my mouth shut about basically everything. So Ken was probably afraid of not only the entire school's judgment but also of what her dad might do, you know, if I spilled."

Kennedy had been afraid of Dr. Russo? Her own father? "You never figured out which brother Kennedy was meeting?" I clear my throat and add, "Allegedly."

Lydia shakes her head, eyes tearing up. "This was only a few weeks ago. I tried to dig up something, but like I said, she was so secretive. And now, I'll never..." A sob racks her body and the words crumple. "I'll never forgive myself for not saving her."

I freeze, unsure how to help. Spotting Cal rolling in the grass, I scoop him up and, holding my breath, place him in her lap.

Fireball, because he's just as mischievous as he is energetic, bounds into my lap like a little devil. I sneeze again.

Lydia is cuddling Cal to her chest, letting her tears drip onto his spotted fur.

I attempt to nudge Fireball off my lap, but he stays planted, looking up at me with devious amber eyes. "I'd hate to separate these two," I say, which is both the truth and the only excuse that will save me from taking a tiny bundle of allergens home. "Do you think your parents would let you keep both?"

Lydia sighs. "Honestly? After everything with Kennedy? Yeah."

"Then you should," I say, handing over Fireball, who digs his baby claws into my sweatshirt sleeve like he's holding on for dear life. "You need them more than I do."

"Thanks, Hayden. I forgot what a good person you were."

I get to my feet, wiping grass and fur off my clothes, that knot of guilt solidifying in my chest.

8

I still don't believe it. I need someone else to corroborate Lydia's account, and maybe even point out which Abbott brother Kennedy had gone to see.

I open Instagram again and DM another of Kennedy's close cheer friends, Desiree Watts.

> Hey, I'm really sorry about Kennedy. I'm hoping I can ask you some questions about what you think happened to her. I'm wondering if I should be concerned for my own safety. If you know something, can we talk?

As soon as I send it, I feel horrible; it's a betrayal.

But in the end, I'm doing it for the triplets. For Henry, who asked me to help clear their names. I close the app and pray that none of the Abbott brothers ever find out I sent that message.

The whole drive back from Lydia's house, I tried to think up some other reason Kennedy may've been on the Abbotts' property the night Lydia followed her. I refused to believe it was drugs, since I've never seen the Abbotts with so much as a cigarette. But nothing else came to mind.

Now, I try in vain to picture any of the brothers having dated Kennedy in secret. Bram has always seemed too torn up over Mariana to move on, and Henry...well, I don't think Henry was seeing Kennedy.

That leaves Adam, a boy who, since the accident, is merely a shell of his former outgoing-king-of-Silver-Creek-High self. A boy who practically has to be dragged to school by his brothers and, apart from that, never goes beyond the mansion walls.

Unless he actually *has* been going beyond the mansion walls.

Henry lets me inside, his brows furrowing when I tell him I need to talk to Adam.

"For the investigation," I explain.

"It's your funeral." He points me to the backyard, which is more like botanic gardens than a *yard*, complete with a pond, a hedge maze, a white gazebo, and probably five hundred flower varietals.

I find Adam sitting cross-legged on the small arched bridge that overlooks the lily pad–strewn water. His head rests on his folded arms.

"Hey," I say, to which his chin lifts almost imperceptibly.

"Henry isn't out here," he mumbles.

"I know that," I say, trying not to sound as hurt as I feel about the state of our friendship.

I've never been as close to Adam as I am to Henry or Bram; still, I've always considered him a friend. I guess that's changed over the past year. Adam pushed me away like he did everyone else who cared for him. "I came to see *you*. I tried yesterday too, but you ignored my text."

He grumbles an inaudible response. As I round the path to step onto the bridge, he slips the hood of his gray sweatshirt over his head.

"You know you don't have to do that." I near him cautiously, like a child trying not to spook a lizard. He remains seated, making no move to pull back the hood or to look at me. "What are you doing out here?"

"Thinking," he says.

"About Kennedy?"

He darts me a withering look and goes back to staring at the water.

But I can't back down. People are going to keep talking about the Abbotts' possible involvement in Kennedy's murder regardless of how antisocial Adam behaves. Hell, Lydia apparently shared her secret boyfriend theory with the detectives. Time isn't exactly on the brothers' side.

"Lydia Costas is talking to the detectives, Adam. She's claiming that Kennedy was seeing one of you."

He scoffs. "*Seeing* one of us?"

"As in dating one of you. In secret."

He chuckles, and then, before I know what's happening, he pushes back the hood and thrusts his face closer to mine, teeth bared. "Look at me, Hayden," he spits, causing me to flinch.

But I do what he asks, my eyes following the paths of scars over the right half of his face, shiny and pink. The missing eyebrow, his right eye in a constant squinted state, having sustained damage from the flames. It's only a moment before he lifts his hand to shield that eye from the sun.

But the hand—that's where the real damage lies. I know that's what bothers Adam more than his face. His right hand, half of the equation when it came to receiving passes on the football field. Now, with the grafted skin still in delicate condition and most of the feeling gone in his fingers, Adam can barely hold a pencil. In fact, the doctors encouraged him to try to switch everything to his left. He's obstinate, so he keeps trying to use the right. From what Henry has told me, though, these efforts always result in frustration and meltdowns.

"Adam." I scoot closer to him, but he inches away again.

"You think any girl would want to be with me now that I look like this?"

"You want my honest answer?"

"Not really," he says dismally, still shielding his eyes as he watches a bird pause on the railing before flitting down to the pond.

I pretend to evaluate him. "I think that yes, any girl would want to be with you. I think the main thing you lost in the accident was your confidence. But you'll get it back. You're just as handsome as before, only with a slightly more…rugged look. Which has been hot ever since the dawn of time." I cut him off before he can tell me to go to hell. "But you've been hiding under that hood."

"It's chilly out."

I sigh. "You really won't tell me about Kennedy?"

"I didn't have a secret relationship with Kennedy Russo. I'd be happy if I never had to hear the name Russo again. The last thing I'd do is spend time with that girl."

"Because of the school board campaign?" I guess it makes sense. Dr. Russo's word holds a lot of weight with the people in this town. When he implied the brothers were dangerous, most of the parents turned against the boys. Their children, the student population of Silver Springs High, soon followed.

"Something like that," he says, running his fingers gently over the delicate flesh of his right hand. "Let's just say that as sorry as I am that Kennedy died, I'm not sorry *that man* lost a daughter."

I'm taken aback by his words. By the scorn and utter hatred in them. It isn't like Adam at all. He's used to people gossiping about him and his brothers. "You don't mean that."

His face is still hard when he says, "No, I guess not."

"Adam, did something happen in that hospital room?" What made the doctor turn against him the way he did?

When he doesn't respond, I add, "You can talk to me, anytime. Or...kick a soccer ball with me." I know it's not soccer he longs to play, but it's all I can offer, considering his limitations.

He starts picking the white paint off the bridge beam in front of him, his lack of response a dismissal. Only I can't help but push things. "What about your brothers?"

"What about them?" he snaps.

"Was one of them seeing Kennedy?"

He laughs, a scornful sound. "They're your *best friends*. You say it all the time. But you're asking *me*?"

My heart twists. I didn't realize how careless I'd been in the past. How much it hurt Adam. "They're your brothers, though. You guys share everything."

"Not anymore. Not in a long time." He pulls the hood back up, and I know he's done talking.

I get up, watching him for another moment, trying to come up with something to say before leaving him there on the bridge.

On my way back through the gardens, my phone dings with an Instagram notification. It's a DM from Desiree Watts. My nerves hum as I open it, but the adrenaline buzz is short-lived.

I've got nothing to say

A black haze hovers at the edge of my periphery. Something like hopelessness threatening to push in. Desiree has a reputation as a bit of a cold-hearted bitch. But I thought after what happened to Kennedy, she might be in a more pliant, empathetic mood. Even my bluff about fearing for my own safety didn't tug on her heartstrings.

Everyone in school knows I'm friends with the Abbotts. Either Desiree is really as icy cold as her reputation, or she doesn't believe the brothers truly pose any danger.

When I push the French doors shut behind me, Henry wanders into the room. "How did it go?" he asks, wincing with one eye shut.

"About how you'd expect. I never realized how much Adam hates Dr. Russo."

Henry nods. "Guy's a huge jerk."

"Yeah, I know. Hey, is Bram home?"

"Where else would he be?" Henry's face falls. "We're pretty much confined here per our lawyer's advice."

Exactly what Henry and Bram feared. "Look, I hate to ask this," I say, lowering my voice and peering over Henry's shoulder at the doorway, "but you don't know if he was seeing Kennedy, do you? The last few weeks, since the start of the school year?"

Henry's eyes drop to his feet, and he starts to fiddle with the collar of his polo. "Like *dating* her?"

"Yeah."

"Not that I know of," he says with a headshake. "He's still destroyed over Mariana." His tone shifts to something like spite. "Why would you ask that?"

"Sorry, it—I knew there was nothing to it, but Lydia Costas

said that Kennedy was seeing somebody and that she saw Kennedy sneak onto your property a few weeks ago."

"Lydia said that?"

"I told her I had a hard time believing it. Adam denies being the guy, and we both know Bram isn't ready for a relationship. Which," I say with a silly head tilt as I look at him, "just leaves you."

For a moment that drags on for a seeming eternity, Henry simply stares back at me. Then his eyes avert mine, and he lets out an uncomfortable laugh. "Me and Kennedy Russo? I don't think so."

"Yeah, I didn't actually believe Lydia's theory. Though, it's strange, isn't it? That Kennedy snuck onto your property."

Henry shrugs. "It wouldn't be the first time a kid from school exacted some sort of revenge prank on us. Remember the paint?" A couple of weeks after Mariana's accident, someone snuck onto the property and spray-painted the word *Killers* over the auto shop's garage door. "Maybe Kennedy tried something but got scared off by the security cameras." Ever since Mariana's accident and all the rumors circulating about the triplets, Mr. Abbott had a brand-new state-of-the-art security system installed around the mansion.

"Except Lydia said Kennedy didn't take the path up to the house. She went into the woods." Almost like she was avoiding being spotted by the family and the cameras.

"None of us were secretly seeing Kennedy," Henry says, an impatient edge to his voice now.

"Well, this is what Lydia believes, and I think it's what she told the cops."

Henry huffs out a breath, jamming his hands into his pockets. "Great. Perfect. It's always the boyfriend, so if the cops believe one of us was the boyfriend..."

"Yeah."

"It's ridiculous." He starts to pace through the foyer. "We have to give them a different story. Did Lydia say anything else?"

"Not really. I tried to contact Desiree, just to see if she could disprove Lydia's theory. But she refused to talk."

Henry rubs at his temple, still pacing in front of me. He looks beyond distraught, and I want nothing more than to calm him.

"Hey," I say, reaching out to touch his arm. "It's going to be okay. They need proof to put someone away for murder. Lydia's speculations won't cut it."

"I know," he says, nodding in an almost maniacal way. "I know. I just wish she would've kept her mouth shut about these unfounded theories. I've got to call our lawyer, Hayden. You can get home okay, right?" He steps away, and my hand falls down to my side.

"Sure," I say, though he's nearly out of the room.

I don't like this. My chest is tight, and it feels like I can't take a full breath. For the first time since I've known Henry, I'm getting the feeling that he is lying to me.

Since two-thirds of the Abbott triplets dismissed me, I'm back at home, staring at the sparkling ocean on my laptop's home screen. Something about Adam's reaction to dating Kennedy isn't sitting right with me. Adam has been known to get heated, to have a temper. But the way he nearly gloated about Dr. Russo's grave misfortune was so cold it felt almost...*inhuman*.

Yes, Dr. Russo seems to be an unpleasant man who likely spurred a movement to get the Abbott boys expelled by the school board. But in the wake of Mariana's accident, most of the town behaved similarly toward the brothers. And besides, Adam never wanted to go back to school. What about Dr. Russo made him react so strongly out in the garden?

Too bad Adam doesn't seem like he'll ever willingly answer that question, and most of what I've learned about the school board effort has been through word of mouth. That's not exactly helpful right now.

At a dead end, I decide to go back and read the news stories about Mariana's case, hoping it will spark something. Hoping it will remind me what I know to be true: Mariana's death was accidental. Back in the mansion, the tension was completely normal, given the circumstances. The Abbott brothers were not killers then, and they aren't killers now.

Though I read some of these publications before, back when we were all living through this, it was always from a position of guarded detachment. When journalists began to come after the triplets, I only absorbed what I needed to keep track of the gossip at school. To be on the defense. Now, I need to see what my brain couldn't handle back then.

The bulk of the early articles feature the tragic accident of a sweet small-town girl. There are a few that focus on Adam, such as "Small-Town Hero Fights for Life as Tragic Car Explosion Leaves One Dead," and another, titled "High School Football Star Risks It All in Failed Attempt to Save Girl."

Then, about two weeks after those first articles were published, came the bad stories, the ones that mention how the explosion was caused by an exposed engine wire. I skim a few, refreshing my memory on the details. According to the articles, investigators concluded that the fire originated in the engine, likely a wire that sparked and ignited when Mariana started the car.

They could not, however, say exactly why Mariana failed to escape the vehicle in time. When the fire reached the fuel tank, the entire car exploded with her inside. Police weren't ruling out foul play. Considering the brothers had been working on the car just minutes before the explosion, the detective on the case had stated that at the very least, they could be facing manslaughter.

The detective added, "At this moment, we have no reason to believe that Adam Abbott's injuries were caused by anything other than an act of heroism."

I clench my teeth. By saying this, the detective fed directly into people's suspicions that Adam's actions *could've* been something other than heroic. I read on to where the Abbotts' now-retired dentist said, "The Abbott brothers always gave me a bad feeling. Just something about them."

Real crackerjack journalism. And it's only outdone by the next source, Dennis Riggs, the mechanic in Alton Woods, one town over from Silver Creek. "Unfortunately, this isn't the only time the Abbotts have made catastrophic mistakes due to carelessness and insufficient automobile education and training. It's just the first time the results were fatal. At my shop, every one of our employees is certified through the National Institute for Automotive Service Excellence." My jaw starts to ache now. Dennis Riggs has been trying to poach auto repair jobs from the Abbotts for the past decade. When this story broke, he was more than happy to talk to journalists and post slander online.

Sebastian Moore, Mariana's neighbor, then disagreed with Riggs, stating, "That family worked on countless cars for the members of Silver Creek. This was more than carelessness or lack of *education*; it was sabotage. It was murder."

My stomach tenses. Why didn't Mr. and Mrs. Abbott ever sue this article's author for libel? The article goes on to quote an anonymous source, who said, "Abbott Auto Repair has been bleeding money for years. It's no surprise the boys would cut corners. Probably learned it from their father. And now, a young girl is dead."

If this were a physical newspaper, I'd ball it up and throw it at the wall. The boys wouldn't cut corners. They're honest and hardworking. But this source's words catch me off guard for another reason. Before Mariana's death, the repair shop had been a highly successful operation. That accident and its subsequent rumors were the reason business began to tank. So why would anyone claim the shop has been bleeding money for years?

I click out of the article, making a mental note to ask Henry about it. Eventually, all online publications reach the same conclusion as the detectives—Mariana's death was a horrible, tragic accident. The engine along with the wiring had sustained far too much damage to find any conclusive evidence of foul play.

I move on to Instagram next, scrolling back to the point when things started to take a turn, typing *Adam Abbott* and *Mariana Sanchez* into the search bar. Posts flood my feed, most featuring strangers talking to the camera, rehashing the same baseless rumors; the incident was somewhat of a viral phenomenon, at least in Vermont.

This was a space I avoided a year ago. If the journalism was sketchy, social media was a million times worse. The horrible things anonymous strangers said about my closest friends had me up at night in tears, worried for them. But if something in here can help them now, I have to face it. I narrow down my search by adding *murder* into the bar.

An image pops up at the top of my results—one that turns my stomach.

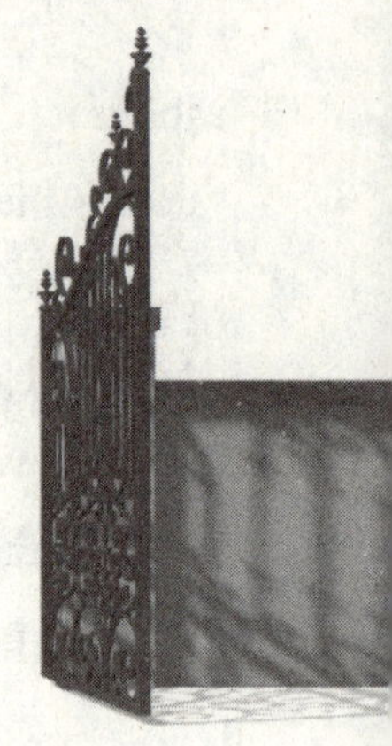

ADAM

LAST OCTOBER

"Why did I not die? More miserable than man ever was before, why did I not sink into forgetfulness and rest?... Of what materials was I made, that I could thus resist so many shocks, which, like the turning of the wheel, continually renewed the torture? But I was doomed to live."

—*Frankenstein* by Mary Shelley

When Adam awoke at Central Springs Hospital, he learned he'd already been there for three days. He was told that, during the hour-long ambulance ride, he'd gone in and out of consciousness. The burns had penetrated enough layers of skin to put him past the point of pain, so that when his gurney was rolled through the hospital doors, he wasn't crying or screaming. He only stared up at the ceiling as the medical team swept him into surgery, putting him into an induced coma.

Adam also learned that while he was under, having managed to stave off infection for two days, the team led by Dr. Arnold Russo deemed him ready for skin grafting. Apparently, his brothers had pushed back, wanting to wait for their parents to return from

Paris before continuing with surgery; however, Dr. Russo warned them that the risk of mortality increased with every hour they put it off. Healthy skin was taken from other parts of Adam's body and grafted onto the right side of his face and right hand—the areas that had been most affected by the explosion that occurred as Adam opened the door to the burning car and attempted to pull Mariana out.

At least, that's what everyone assumed those first couple of weeks.

But when Adam woke up, groggy and confused—the pain excruciating now—he had no memory of what had happened the day of the accident. And when his parents and brothers told him about Mariana, it was as though the flames had reached deep inside his chest to scorch his heart.

When his family left the room, Adam looked at his bandaged hand, imagining what lay beneath the gauze. All he knew was that it hurt like hell, but he hadn't wanted to bring up the pain in front of his parents. His face, including the right eye, was also bandaged, leaving him to wonder if he'd even see out of it again.

His mother had cried when she saw him, her beautiful, active son, bandaged and immobile.

Adam still debated pressing that red button beside the bed when Dr. Russo himself came in to check on him.

"I heard you were awake," the man said, sweeping into the room in a white lab coat like one of those cranes that settled on the banks of the creek.

Adam had been crying, the news of Mariana's death raw. His voice was still scratchy and rough, but he grated out, "Yes, sir."

"Good, good." The doctor stood at Adam's bedside and took his vitals. "Everything is looking good. No fever, which means there's likely no infection. How are you feeling?"

"Like hell," Adam said, sniffling. He wondered what his face looked like, but the doctor didn't touch the bandages.

"Pain level, from one to ten?"

"Twelve." Adam's parents weren't there, which meant he could finally answer truthfully.

The doctor gave him a tight-lipped smile. "I'll have the nurse up your morphine levels."

Adam thanked him, so grateful to have relief on the horizon. He expected the doctor to head out to find the nurse. Instead, the man sat down on the edge of his bed. "How are you feeling about… the accident?"

"The accident?" Adam didn't quite understand the question.

"About Mariana. Can you tell me what happened?"

"Oh." Adam's heart sank, and he feared he might cry again in front of this man. "I only just heard about her."

"The papers are saying you tried to save her. That you got your injuries by throwing yourself into the burning car to pull her out. That it exploded before you succeeded."

Adam didn't answer. He couldn't, since in his mind, the incident never existed.

Dr. Russo's eyes narrowed. "You don't want to tell me?"

"No, it's—it's not that I don't *want* to tell you. It's that I can't. I don't remember."

"Oh." Dr. Russo's face darkened. "I see."

Adam thought he recognized the look. Disappointment? Disbelief? Perhaps some combination of the two.

"Well, there are some detectives here to speak with you, if you're up to it."

Adam nodded, and the doctor rose and strode through the room. "Though I guess," the man added, pausing at the door, "if you can't *remember*, it will be rather difficult for you."

There was no mistaking the man's sardonic tone then. Dr. Russo thought Adam was lying about his memory.

Mysteriously, the nurse never received the message about the morphine.

For a while, Adam had many visitors. Friends from school flooded the reception area, taking turns, a few at a time. The entire team brought football-shaped balloons, repeating lines about how he needed to get better in time for next season. Adam saw the looks in their eyes, though. No one believed he could recover from such horrific injuries.

An entire team of doctors and nurses visited daily to change Adam's dressings. The process was excruciating and took over an hour. One afternoon, about two weeks into Adam's stay, Dr. Russo himself led the team primarily made up of interns. They removed the old dressing on Adam's hand. "This is healing up nicely," Dr. Russo said, squinting at the raw flesh.

Adam didn't think there was anything *nice* about the way his hand looked, and when the doctor poked at it with his sharp metal instrument, Adam couldn't feel a thing.

"Hmm," the doctor said. "It may simply take more time. Can you move your fingers?"

Adam could, just barely. Panic started to set in, a little insect in the pit of his stomach that started to spawn until it became dozens of skittering bugs. He was hyperventilating.

"Calm down, boy," the doctor snapped. "I've ordered a psychiatrist to come and speak with you about your memory issues. Seems like it couldn't come at a better time." He gave Adam another disdainful look and then removed the bandages from Adam's face himself. It was different than when the other doctors had performed the removal—lacking that careful, gentle touch. Adam thought it odd, since surgeons are known for having steady hands.

The pain built, and Adam started to feel woozy until a nurse, apparently unable to keep quiet, offered to take over.

"Fine," Dr. Russo said gruffly. "We'll need to take some pictures for educational purposes as well as for our records." He motioned for an intern with a digital camera to come closer.

The intern snapped a few photos of Adam's hand, then moved the lens up to his face, the light blinding to Adam's newly uncovered eye. When he blinked and squinted long enough, he felt dizzy, his focus and depth perception off.

But he could see.

This relief lasted only until Dr. Russo grabbed a small mirror from one of his interns and thrust it into Adam's good hand. "Thought you'd want to see how nicely this was coming along." The man sounded proud, and it sparked hope in Adam.

The feeling was immediately replaced by horror. A strangled sob emerged from Adam's throat. The mirror shook in his hand so violently that the nurse took it from him.

In all of his thoughts and imaginings, Adam had never pictured anything as grotesque as what had appeared in the mirror. The red-and-brown melted skin. White oozing patches scattered like geysers. His entire right eyebrow gone.

"I feel sick," Adam said, at which point an intern raced to grab an emesis basin.

The nurse helped him through it, placing a hand on his back as he emptied the meager contents of his stomach. Adam hadn't had much of an appetite since his accident. "It's still healing," the nurse said, moving her hand to the top of his good one, as if to settle the shaking.

The team began to replace the dressings on Adam's face, and Dr. Russo, looking even more disgusted than before, snatched the camera from the intern and removed himself from the room.

For another day or two, Adam's visitors continued, though less frequently than before. This was always the case with long hospital stays. At least people came. A few football teammates after practice, the girls who'd had huge crushes on Adam. They would cry, and Adam suspected it was because they knew he'd never look the same again.

But that day with Dr. Russo sparked a change. Adam perceived it, albeit gradually. Then one day, he realized that only his family and Hayden had been to see him for a long stretch of time. He wasn't sure what exactly had shifted—neither his brothers nor his parents wanted to talk much, claiming he should focus on healing. Not only were there physical injuries to overcome, but his mind needed to heal.

The psychiatrist had been in to "chat" with Adam a handful of times. This woman, Dr. Wen, hadn't seemed nearly as concerned about Adam's memory of the accident as Dr. Russo had been. She simply asked how he felt about his burns, how he felt about Mariana's passing. What worries he had regarding his future, and if he felt equipped to deal with them or hopeless.

Adam wasn't sure how to answer. Everything felt hopeless, like he was plunging into a black abyss.

And then he witnessed Bram trying to sneak his iPad out of the room. "Hey!" Adam called before his brother could slip it into the emptied bag of snacks and books their mother had packed. "What are you doing?"

"Nothing," Bram said, looking furious he'd been caught.

"I need that to watch movies. They've only got three channels on that damned thing, and they're all about fixing up houses." He gestured with his good hand at the mounted hospital room television.

"Okay, but..." Bram hesitated, still calm as ever but rubbing at the back of his neck. His tell.

"What's going on?"

"Don't go on social media, okay?"

Adam pressed his lips flat. "What is it?"

It wasn't that Adam hadn't thought about social media since the accident; it was that he couldn't bear to see the posts about Mariana. He'd been crying himself to sleep over her every night; he didn't need to cry all day too.

"Just..." Bram growled under his breath. "People are idiots."

Adam held out his hand. Whatever it was, he'd have to see it sooner or later. Thanks to Bram, that time would be now.

"It's not going to help you get better," Bram tried, but his gray eyes were resigned. "At least let me stay with you."

Adam consented. "Show me."

Bram did, bringing up the posts from their schoolmates debating whether Adam had actually killed Mariana or if the killer was her boyfriend, Bram. A normally shy sophomore was suddenly very vocal about how he'd always suspected the brothers were hiding a dark side. Adam found this especially hurtful, considering he'd saved that very kid from having his lunch stolen by Todd Ellison the previous year.

They'd turned on him. All of them. Every student, teammate—even some of his *teachers* who'd been singing Adam's praises only days before—were now calling him and his brothers the most abhorrent of names.

"I want to be alone," he told Bram in a clipped voice.

"No. Here, give me the—" Bram reached for the iPad, but Adam threw up his left shoulder, blocking his brother's actions. Bram let out a grunt but didn't force the issue. "You shouldn't do this to yourself."

But Adam wasn't listening. He continued the robotic game of scroll, click, read. "Should I be worried about this?" he eventually asked, his tone void of emotion.

"There's nothing to any of it," Bram said. "Supposedly, investigators are looking at Mariana's car. But if they found anything, they would've brought us in." Bram shrugged. "Dad says if the detectives come talk to you again, tell them you need your lawyer present."

Adam nodded, still sifting through the posts, most of which came from total strangers. He wondered how people he'd never met before could hold such passionate hatred toward him. Such immense love for Mariana—enough to make them wish death upon Adam.

For whatever reason, the more Adam read, the more he became numb. It was like burns. The way the lesser-degree burns caused agonizing pain while Adam's full-thickness burns had penetrated so deeply into the layers of skin, he barely felt a thing as he was rushed to the hospital.

Adam relinquished the iPad, the hazy feeling lingering, either from reading too much or from the morphine.

One month later, Adam still hadn't gone back online. That illicit draw hadn't niggled at him since the day with Bram in the hospital. But after a few days back at home, still bedridden with none of his usual activities to fill the day—no visitors and not even a phone call from anyone Adam had believed was his friend—he picked up his iPad to watch a movie and saw a little red circular notification in the top-right corner of the Instagram icon.

The temptation to click on it arose again. Like the glow of a fishing lure beneath the dark surface of the creek. Adam ignored whatever sharp hooks might be awaiting and opened social media again.

He soon came to a blurred photo with the little eye covering it—a graphic image warning. Without a thought, he clicked on the *Are you sure you want to proceed?* question to override the content warning. The image came into focus, and a sudden explosion of pain—visceral and real—came on. The numbness he'd felt while scrolling through the hateful comments and posts back in the hospital was gone, leaving the layers of him peeled back and exposed. Everything he never experienced in the hospital, Adam now felt in his room.

The image was Adam's own unbandaged face, the same red and pink burn wounds he saw when he looked in the mirror a month earlier. The post contained two photos of his face and another of his torched hand. The caption read:

Sixteen-year-old homicide suspect Adam Abbott's football days are over

It was a lie; Adam hadn't been named a suspect, nor had Mariana's death been ruled a homicide. Intellectually, Adam knew he should turn the iPad off and surrender it to his brother. Yet, Adam's emotions—rage, grief, humiliation—stirred within his core. He couldn't help it; he began to scroll through the comments.

SKIMOM33: disgusting

BRETTRAYMOND907: looks like the kid got what he deserved

LESTERTHEJESTER: isn't that the newest Marvel villain?

WHATKATYISWEARING: 😂😂😂

Rage started to boil in Adam's chest. His teeth clenched so ferociously that he started to feel lightheaded. These photos were taken in the hospital. The only way they could've made it on here was if they were leaked by a member of the medical staff. Could one of the interns have risked their own future to do this? Adam doubted it. He was willing to bet anything it was Dr. Russo, that smug, unfeeling bastard.

With the release of these photos, Adam wasn't simply being labeled a murderer anymore.

Now, he was a monster.

Adam almost closed the iPad when another comment caught his eye.

KENRICHARDSTHEBOXER: he can play football in prison

SAMILEETHEPOET: @kenrichardstheboxer no he can't. I read somewhere his hand doesn't work anymore

PENNYGREENE23: @samileethepoet why wasn't this kid

taken to a hospital with a dedicated burn unit? People are idiots

JAMESVANDERBEER: yeah, seems like something could've been done to keep him playing football. Why treat a major burn in Hicksville Creek? Any thoughts, @hendricksmd?

Suddenly, Adam's chest became tight. His vision started to go fuzzy.

SAMILEETHEPOET: @jamesvanderbeer who cares?? Anyone heard of poetic justice?

OLLIETHECATPERSON: I agree. Without his hand, hopefully he won't be able to murder anyone else. Maybe the doctor did it on purpose, as an act of mercy to humanity

JAMESVANDERBEER: just saying it's a crime for the football world. He was a great player

HENDRICKSMD: Hard to say from a photo, but burn centers with specialized teams exist for a reason. This reason

That was the last comment Adam read before his vision tunneled, then went black.

9

My heart is beating out of my chest. When Adam came home from the hospital, we'd heard that his hand was beyond repair. That Dr. Russo had done everything in his power to help Adam, and the best they could hope for was regaining more feeling in his fingers.

But among all the comments from Adam's haters, there are several football fanatics and medical professionals claiming that Dr. Russo failed his patient. And a handful of comments have tagged Adam; there's no way he hasn't seen this.

Maybe none of it's true. Maybe Dr. Russo gave Adam the very best treatment possible. But if Adam saw this post, he may have started to think otherwise. He may have grown resentful.

As I look at the photos and the label in the caption, *homicide suspect*, I remember how the doctor sided against the brothers after Mariana's accident.

Why would he have done that, going so far as to try and get them expelled? Was it really mob mentality—the town's collective fears—that caused the doctor to turn against his own patient? Or did Adam say something in those early days, maybe under sedation? Something that would cause Dr. Russo to not only spread the word that Adam had committed the crime but maybe even sabotage his healing?

I call Henry, who picks up on the second ring.

"Hey," he says, but it sounds like a question.

I grab a pen off the desk and search through the drawer for a scrap of paper, tearing a page from an old notebook. "Henry, did Adam ever mention his experience with Dr. Russo in the hospital? Or his treatment plans?"

There's a pause, and I can't blame him for being confused. "A little," he finally says, sounding tired. "The guy has a terrible bedside manner. Adam even asked to move hospitals. Said the guy had it out for him."

"And what did you think?" I ask, jotting down some notes.

"I thought Adam was going through a lot, and he was on a ton of meds. I'm sure you've noticed that he's not exactly an easy guy to get along with under normal circumstances. Bram and I figured he was overreacting. Plus, Russo said transferring him was too big a risk."

"What did your parents say?"

"I mean, they didn't have much choice," Henry says, voice taut now. "They had to make all the early decisions over the phone because they were in Paris. They basically put Bram and me in charge. And by the time they got here, Dr. Russo said further surgery was pointless. The burns on Adam's hand were too severe. Something about tissue and muscle damage. He told Adam there was nothing else he could do for him and to try physical therapy. Didn't even bother giving him a referral. Look, Hayden, I appreciate all you're doing. But like I said earlier, I've got to—"

"I know," I say quickly, staring down at the question I scribbled on my scrap paper and underlined three times. "I just keep thinking about the school board stuff and what made Dr. Russo turn on the three of you. You don't..." I hesitate, knowing that once this is out, I can't take it back. "You don't think maybe Adam said something... *incriminating*? Like while he was on all those meds. Or maybe during the surgery, Russo found—"

"No," Henry cuts in sharply. But a moment later, he sighs. "Sorry, I guess I'm angry at myself. Dr. Russo did turn out to be an arrogant jerk, didn't he? We should've listened to Adam."

"Don't beat yourself up, Henry," I say. "You and Bram were put in an impossible situation."

"Yeah," he says grimly. "Look, I still haven't gotten ahold of Mr. Swanson. Talk later?"

"Okay," I start to say, but he's already hung up.

Setting my phone and pen down, I take a deep, calming breath. My stomach starts to grumble. It's past two p.m. and I never paused my research to eat lunch.

I grab my phone and descend the stairs. In the kitchen, I find my dad rooting around in the pantry.

"Hey," I say, opting for something from the fridge.

"Hey, kiddo." He emerges with a box of crackers. "What are you up to?"

"Nothing much." I grab last night's leftovers as Dad settles down at the table. Once the rotini is in the microwave, I pour myself a glass of water and take a seat across from him. I'm still thinking about that question Henry answered all too quickly about the doctor. "Hey, Dad, remember back when those parents were trying to get signatures to keep the Abbott boys out of school?"

He nods, his mouth full.

"Dr. Russo supposedly spearheaded the whole thing. But what exactly did you hear? Did Dr. Russo ever make any actual accusations about Adam or his brothers?"

He swallows, shaking his head. "You know I didn't want anything to do with that school board agenda. I stayed far away."

"Yeah, I know," I say, my heart swelling. "You trust the boys."

"Well, that," he says, "and I know Arnold Russo has been bitter toward their family since long before Mariana was killed."

My heart jolts. "Bitter…how?"

He stops himself from stuffing another cracker into his mouth.

"Probably shouldn't be sharing this." He shuts one eye and tilts his head. "Then again, neither should've Russo's accountant. But a couple years back, Dr. Russo claimed Jonathan Abbott stole hundreds of thousands of dollars from him." At the look of shock on my face, my dad waves a hand. "The doctor invested in the auto shop. Apparently, Jonathan told him business was booming and that soon, there would be Abbott Auto Repair shops all over the country. Well, Russo, seeing dollar signs, jumped at the opportunity. Only the investment flopped, as they sometimes do."

The microwave beeps, but I ignore it. "I didn't know those two even spoke. I've never seen them in the same room together."

"Well, this may be the reason. If memory serves, the families were never close, but they weren't enemies. They grew up side by side, the sons of the two wealthiest families in town." Dad went to Silver Springs High around the same time as Dr. Russo and Mr. Abbott. "Your mother used to talk about the fancy parties Mrs. Russo would host up at her place. She was never invited, of course, but Mrs. Abbott always was."

"Up until this investment went sour?" I ask, reaching for my water glass.

Dad nods. "It sounded like Dr. Russo lost every penny he put into the shop. The accountant said Russo suspected the shop was actually in trouble and that Abbott never invested the money. That he'd stolen it to attempt to curb the damage and lied about everything."

I think of that article and the anonymous source who claimed the auto shop had been bleeding money for years. If Russo believed he'd been lied to, did he speak to the press, not as a doctor, but as a businessman who felt he'd been scammed? "So," I say, trying to connect the dots, "you think the whole school board thing was because of the money? Not because the doctor *actually* suspected one of the Abbott brothers?" Did Dr. Russo want revenge on the Abbotts in whatever way he could get it? Seeing the family name demolished, one of them locked up—was it all the same to him?

Dad clears his throat. "Look, Hayden, is there something you're worried about? Maybe you shouldn't be spending so much time over at the Abbott place. Not if you're...unsettled."

"I'm not unsettled," I say, though it's a lie. "Dad, did Dr. Russo ever try to take legal action?"

"That was part of the reason this accountant wanted my opinion." Dad shrugs. "But there was nothing illegal about the transaction. An investment's a risk. This one may've had more to do with dollar signs than good judgment. And I guess, if not for the accident, he still could've made a return on that investment, eventually."

"Do you think Russo told anyone else?" I ask, still thinking of that online article. "That Abbott Auto Repair had been in financial trouble?" I wonder if the boys know the extent of the shop's struggles. They've never mentioned anything to me.

"No idea, but I wouldn't put it past him."

So even if Russo wasn't that anonymous source, he wanted this story out there. He hated Jonathan Abbott, and he'd been biding his time, waiting for some way to ruin him. But as much as he'd been wronged, I don't see how he could extend his hatred to Mr. Abbott's children.

Then I remember the rest of that anonymous source's statement: *It's no surprise the boys would cut corners. Probably learned it from their father. And now, a young girl is dead.*

Another question needles its sharp point into my mind. Could Dr. Russo have believed that Adam knowingly endangered a life? If the anonymous source was the doctor, maybe, at least in *his* mind, there was more than revenge motivating him. And maybe, when the press failed to blow up the story the way he'd hoped, Dr. Russo decided to leak those medical photos and rumors about Adam as a murder suspect.

Would Mr. Abbott have asked his sons to take shortcuts in order to save money on jobs? For all the time I've spent in that house, the man remains an enigma. Sort of like Bram, in a way.

"Are you going to tell me what this is about?" Dad asks abruptly, causing me to lose my nerve. Besides, even if Mr. Abbott asked, the boys never would have complied. "Why are you asking about the doctor?" he presses. "Is this about Kennedy's murder? Do you need to speak to someone? Like"—his eyes veer to the table—"a professional?"

"No, Dad. I was just curious." Smiling, I get up to remove my food from the microwave. It's barely warm now. Still, I sit down and start to eat. When my dad says he's going to start watching "the game"—whatever that means—I set down my fork and grab my phone.

Navigating back to the social media post, I force myself to look at the photos again, at the raw flesh. I never personally witnessed Adam in this state. By the time he'd returned home and had his bandages removed, the wounds were much improved. I don't need the IV tube dangling in the corner of these photographs to tell me these photos aren't the same kind that Mrs. Abbott's home staff leaked. No, these were taken in the hospital, which means someone who worked there could have leaked them.

Regardless of whether it was Dr. Russo himself, it happened on his watch. He was the surgeon in charge of the case. Dr. Russo, who seems to hold a grudge against the Abbotts, stemming from what went down between him and Mr. Abbott. The doctor attempted to turn the press, the school board, and the entirety of Silver Creek against Adam Abbott. He's been accused online of making questionable medical decisions—ones that could keep Adam from ever playing football again.

And if Adam found out—which would've only required clicking on his social media notifications—what would he have done about it? I think back to Adam's icy comment this morning about the doctor and Kennedy. *I'm not sorry that man lost a daughter.*

Adam claims no one has wanted to date him since the accident. Maybe he lied. Maybe he knew Kennedy liked him, so he drew her in and lured her into the woods—a way to punish her father.

I banish the thought. Just because Adam made one cruel remark in his anger, doesn't mean he's capable of murder. I may not know Adam as well as I know Henry or Bram, but we grew up together.

The whole reason I agreed to help was because I trust all three of them.

So why am I having these doubts?

Henry will talk me through it. He'll know what to do. I need to see him, face-to-face. After hurrying through the rest of my lunch, I grab my phone and book it down the road to the Abbott mansion.

10

On the walk, I text Henry that I'm on my way. I stick to the shade, trying to work out exactly how to tell him about Adam without making it seem like I suspect him. It isn't until I ring the doorbell and Bram answers that I realize Henry never replied to my text.

"Oh," I say, "hi."

He rests a shoulder on the doorjamb, a coy grin on his lips. "Weren't you here earlier?"

"Yes," I admit. "I didn't see *you*, though. Were you spying on me or something?"

"Your visit put my little brother in bad spirits." Bram loves to call his brothers *younger*, simply because he was born first. And we're talking the oldest by seconds; they were all delivered via C-section, one right after another. "He slammed a door so hard my hair got a little messed up from the draft."

I cover my mouth with a hand in mock astonishment. "Whatever did you do?"

"Cried a little. Took a nap to recapture the bedhead look."

I roll my eyes. "Adam is always in bad spirits."

"Very true," Bram says, motioning me inside. "But I meant Henry."

I blink. "Henry's in a bad mood because of me?" That explains the tension on our phone call. I think back to our conversation here at the house about who Kennedy might've been dating. All I remember is that he seemed eager to speak to his lawyer, and he was somewhat dismissive of me. "Where is he?"

"Out." Bram furls a hand in the direction of the door.

Out? "I thought you weren't allowed to leave the house."

He lifts his dark brows mischievously. "We aren't."

It doesn't sound like Henry, going against his parents and the lawyers. "Well, where did he go?"

"He didn't tell me," Bram says matter-of-factly. But he softens, his cocky demeanor falling. "I wouldn't worry about him. He hates being holed up in here. He has ever since the whole thing with"—he shrugs—"you know."

"I would've gone with him," I say, hurt that Henry didn't invite me. He must've been really upset with me. Last year, when the boys were shut in after Mariana's death, Henry would often get restless.

He'd always invite me over to keep him company. To make his world seem a little bit bigger.

"I'm sure he just needed to clear his head," Bram says gently.

"I hope he stays out of sight. People are saying some messed-up things." My heart aches, thinking of the way Sage's father looked at Henry the other day.

"Well, he's used to it. He's the one who kept trying to go back to school last year, despite everything. And it sounds like if the detectives don't charge us with anything by Monday, we're going back this week."

"What?" I ask, failing to hide my shock. "I thought your lawyer—that Mr. Swanson guy—told you to stay home."

"Mr. Swanson didn't want us talking to anyone, letting something stupid slip." Bram gestures me along through the foyer, and I follow. "Now he's saying that hiding makes us look guilty. If we're not guilty and we're not being charged with anything, we need to carry on with our lives as usual."

"Wow."

"Yeah, and it's perfect timing, really. With the retreat coming up."

I balk. "There's no way you three are attending the retreat."

"Phil," Bram says, stepping close enough that I can smell the cedar and smoke of his cologne, the mint of his toothpaste. It brings me back to a day in his room over a year ago, when I felt almost intoxicated by that scent. Like he had some sort of magical power over me. "You're not listening. *Life as usual.* That means the student council retreat."

I cross my arms. "You guys are barely on student council."

"Take it up with Mr. Fuller," he says, smirking. "And don't act like you're not *thrilled* we're going with you."

My pulse hitches. I hate it when he reads me perfectly. "You're going to give Sage a heart attack." I tilt my head. "Which might be kind of funny, honestly. Not, like, a *literal* heart attack. But putting a healthy dose of fear in her."

"That's our girl." Bram knocks a fist lightly against my shoulder.

My cheeks heat. "I, uh, should probably get going. You'll tell Henry I came by?"

"Don't be so daft," Bram says, utilizing a vocab word from last week's honors list, even though he isn't even in honors. His hand is on my shoulder now. "Stay until Henry gets back. I've got another movie lined up."

His touch sends a thrill up to the base of my skull and down to my toes simultaneously. This is a bad idea. Very bad. For whatever reason, Bram has always had this effect on me. I know that Henry is the boy for me—I've known for a while now. And still, when Bram so much as looks at me a certain way, I feel this beguiling sense of danger.

I think about telling him I've got homework. I think about telling him I don't feel up for a movie. Instead, unwilling to douse that little spark, I let him nudge me ahead to the living room, his hand on my back now, radiating heat.

He sits me down on the couch. "Want coffee?"

"Are you having some?"

"Why not? You can tell me whatever it is that's got you all flustered. The coffee will help loosen your lips."

I can't help but notice his gaze on my mouth. "I think you've got coffee confused with liquor," I say, to which he quirks his own lips, amused. "And I am not all *flustered*," I add. But he's already ambling off, leaving me to sit here and regret my choices.

I *am* dying to hash out everything I learned about Dr. Russo with someone. Only Bram isn't the person I'd usually confide in about something serious, like my concerns about Adam.

With Henry, I feel like I can see straight through his lenses, his eyes, and his skull into his mind. It's like talking to myself.

But with Bram, things are never transparent. At least, not on my end. He always seems to know what I'm thinking, while *his* mind remains a locked box. He's always playing games, saying one thing but meaning another. For all I know, he could run straight to Adam and tell him everything.

I hear the machine brewing over in the kitchen and check my phone again. My text to Henry is still unread, and I'm antsy not knowing what I said to upset him earlier.

Bram's voice calls to me from the kitchen. "Cream and sugar?"

"Yes, please."

A moment later, he ambles back in, a mug in each hand. "Thanks," I say as he sits down beside me, slightly too close.

Again I get a flash of that day in his room.

I'd come over here to help Adam with his summer school assignment. For whatever reason—likely pride—he never allowed Henry to help with schoolwork, so I was his tutor. Only that day, Adam forgot about our session, and Bram was the only brother at home.

He invited me in, much like today, and I asked if I could see the painting he was working on. I expected an automatic *no*; he never showed anyone his paintings. It was part of the whole mystery that is Bram. In fact, hardly anyone even knows he paints. But if you look closely, there's often a trace of black or red beneath his fingernails.

Not that I look closely at Bram.

To my surprise, he hesitated, deliberating with his hands in the pockets of his black jeans and an endearing twist of the lips. "All right," he finally said. "But if you make fun of me, I'll tell everyone about that time you fed Igor cheese and he got sick all over Mom's rug."

"Hey! I never had a dog before."

"And we never did again, thanks to *you*." He grinned and bumped my shoulder with his.

Bram's paintings were stowed in his massive walk-in closet, the canvases covered in white sheets.

"Why don't you hang these up around the house?" I asked. "It's not like your family is short on wall space."

"Haven't felt like it." He shrugged, his rogue expression turning contemplative. "These paintings are about what's on the inside. I guess displaying them just seems…*wrong*."

"But isn't that what painting is? Showing others what you're thinking and feeling?"

"Maybe I don't want anyone to know what's in here," he said, tapping his temple.

I rolled my eyes. "Has Mariana seen it?"

Bram shook his head. "You're the first."

I was surprised. Mariana and Bram seemed so close. Their relationship was one of the reasons I failed to see the risk in stepping into the walk-in closet alone with Bram.

That may have been the first mistake I made that day.

He reached for the easel that faced the back of the closet. "I'll warn you, it's a work in progress. The beginning stages, really."

"Yeah, yeah, I know." I bounced on the balls of my feet, excitement building at seeing something no one else had laid eyes on.

"Please temper your expectations," Bram said, his brows drawing together.

"Just show me."

"Fine." He lifted the sheet between two fingers, like a magician revealing a birdcage. "Voila." He let the sheet fall to the floor. "I call it...well, nothing yet."

I looked upon the painting, stunned. I'd had no idea what to expect, but maybe I should have formed some visualization beforehand. Obviously, I wouldn't have pictured a landscape with colorful flowers or green hills. Nothing vibrant or cheerful, not from Bram.

But I never could've envisioned what perched on the easel before me. The blackness, texturized by the brush and palette knife, grays and dark blues blended to form an image, something like a face. The one bright streak of red. The abstractness, sharp lines meeting delicate curved ones, giving the macabre illusion of teeth sinking into soft flesh. The utter destruction represented on the canvas. The absence of life.

It was like I was viewing Death itself. It was visceral, grotesque, and shocking.

And yet, much like its creator, in a way, it was the most beautiful thing I'd ever seen. It drew me in, called me forward.

I must've been standing there in silent awe for far too long, because Bram picked up the sheet off the floor and started to cover the painting.

I rushed to the easel. "What are you doing?"

"You obviously hate it." He kept his back to me, still attempting to cover the painting.

"No, I-I..." I wanted to say I loved it, but that would've rung false. *Love* wouldn't have been the right word. How can you love something so ghastly? How can you love something that makes you feel like your very bones and innards are quaking in revulsion? And yet, the way I felt was far stronger than *admiration* or *like*. Maybe because it made me *feel* so strongly to begin with. It was as if the incarnation of death had made me feel more alive than I ever had.

Even now, recalling the details of that encounter, I can't come up with a word that describes how I felt about the painting.

"Hey," I said, reaching up for his shoulder and attempting to turn him around. "Hey, look at me."

He consented, his tall sturdy frame almost malleable beneath my fingers. Yet he refused to meet my eyes.

"I'm sorry I didn't say anything, but you're misunderstanding. I think it's amazing."

"You're just saying that because I got upset."

"No. *No*, I'm not." I tilted my head in front of his, trying to catch his gaze. My hands were up on both of his shoulders, and as he let his guard down, I let my hands slide down to his wrists.

And though I've hashed this scene out in my head often over the last year and a half, I think that was likely where I really went wrong.

Now, not wanting to repeat past mistakes, I scoot ever so slightly away from Bram under the guise of needing to cross my legs and get comfortable. "You're not worried about Henry?" I ask, because Henry seems like a safe conversation topic.

"I am not." Bram takes a sip of coffee. "Now, tell me what's on your mind."

"Is this Irish coffee?" I ask, taking a tentative sip.

"Come on, Phil. Talk to me. I know Henry had you acting as private investigator, and I'd like to be in the loop."

"I don't have anything just yet," I answer truthfully. "But I'm looking into how Mariana's death might be related to Kennedy's."

Bram's head pulls back. "As in the same person killed both girls?"

"Not exactly."

He leans forward, placing a hand so near my leg on the couch, it might as well be touching me. He looks me dead in the eyes. Whatever gift I thought I had for reading Henry's mind—Bram has it with me. He is seeing my thoughts in real time—about Adam, about Henry, about *him*.

All of my past mistakes come tumbling forward, like he's siphoning them out of me.

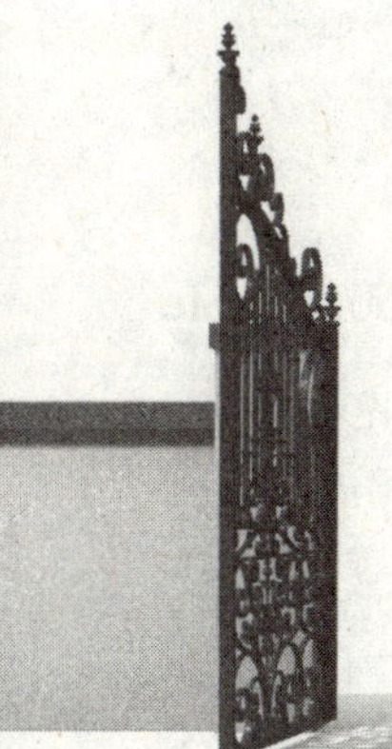

BRAM

LAST OCTOBER

"Souls and memories can do strange things during trance."

—*Dracula* by Bram Stoker

"Mariana?" Bram called again when he found the downstairs bathroom unoccupied.

It was very strange, the way she'd left her belongings there in the living room. And that she hadn't told him where she'd gone. Though maybe she was being considerate; he had been rather immersed in his novel.

Bram headed toward the back door to see if maybe she'd gone for a walk around the gardens when his phone buzzed in his back pocket again. And again, it wasn't Mariana.

It was *her*. The guilt returned in a wave, washing over him like sticky salt water. Leaving that filthy feeling behind. At least now he could reply without Mariana there in the room with him.

This has to end

He sent the text and stuffed his phone back in his pocket. He wanted to finally feel clean. He craved it. There was nothing he could do about the past, other than make sure it never happened again.

Another thought caused dread to rise in his chest: He had to tell Mariana. She needed to decide for herself if she would forgive Bram and give him another chance, or if she wanted to move on.

And he would never tell Mariana the other girl's name. He couldn't. It would create an even bigger mess out of this. And he wasn't sure how Mariana would take it.

One step in the right direction would be to actually fix her car. After calling her name out in the gardens and getting no response, Bram decided to head to the shop and help his brothers. Hopefully, Mariana had simply gone to check their progress, and he'd meet her there.

11

The sound of the front door wrenches me from Bram's trance. I stand up quickly, like I'm shaking a spider off my clothes. Fortunately, the foyer is one room over, so Henry can't see that it's actually his brother I've batted away.

"Hey!" I say brightly the moment he enters the room.

Henry glances up from where his gaze was planted on the floor, and his brows knit together. His eyes drift from me to Bram, to the mugs side by side on the table, and then back to me again. "Hayden. What are you doing here?"

"I texted you," I say somewhat defensively, even though I've come over unannounced a million times before.

"Oh." He frowns and tugs his phone from his pocket. "Sorry, it was on silent. I needed to think."

"That's okay. Do you have a minute to talk?"

"Of course," he says without meeting my eyes. He's still upset about earlier, which means he's really going to hate what I have to tell him now.

Bram stands, taking his mug. "I just remembered I've got a thing to do," he says, tipping his head in the direction of the staircase. "Later, Phil."

"Later." I keep my voice light, waiting until he's really gone to take a seat.

Henry slumps against the couch and removes his glasses to rub at an eye. He's starting to look sleep-deprived. "You and Bram had a little coffee date?"

I laugh, the sound forced. "Sort of. He was attempting to shake me down for information on the case."

He sits up straighter. "And did you ask him? About Kennedy?"

"Oh," I say, feeling stupid. "I didn't, sorry. I thought we'd agreed there was no way it could've been him. Did you talk to him?"

Henry's gaze shifts to the coffee table and then over to the staircase. "Maybe I shouldn't say."

"I can't exactly help you guys if you don't share anything."

He runs his fingers through his hair, then leans forward with his elbows on his knees. "I asked him, just to put it out of my mind, once and for all. At first he looked angry that I even suggested he might be over Mariana. But then he got this strange look on his face.

Almost guilty? And he admitted that he might've had feelings for someone he shouldn't have."

My body heats so fast, I look straight down into my mug. "So you think it was Kennedy?" I ask.

"No," Henry whispers, too quickly. "Of course not."

"Because if it was," I say, treading carefully, "it would look really bad for Bram."

Henry purses his lips in thought, one hand fiddling with his frames. "Are you sure Lydia already told the cops about Kennedy seeing someone?" he asks, desperation in his blue-green eyes. "Maybe it's not too late to change her mind."

"She said she already told them," I say. "I'm surprised the cops haven't asked about it."

Henry blows out a long puff of air. "Oh, they will. The good news is that at least now, we'll see it coming."

"Unfortunately, that wasn't what I came to talk to you about," I admit. "You know how I asked you about Adam and Dr. Russo earlier? Well, after my chat with Adam this morning, I couldn't get something out of my head." Henry's eyes go to my foot, which bounces in agitation. It takes all my concentration to still it. "He was so angry with Dr. Russo," I continue, "that he said he wasn't sorry the man lost a daughter."

Henry's eyes widen. "Adam said that?"

I nod. "I know, if I hadn't heard him myself, I probably wouldn't believe it either." I debate sharing what I learned about Dr. Russo's investment, the quarrel that may have driven him. But I decide against it, not wanting to pile onto Henry's list of problems. The last thing he needs to worry about is his parents' financial situation. "We both know that after the accident," I say, "Dr. Russo likely led that campaign against you guys with the school board. Only I don't think he stopped there."

"What do you mean?" Henry asks.

"I think he spread rumors that Adam had something to do with Mariana's death on social media, maybe even to the press." My hands are starting to shake, and coffee sloshes around in my mug. I lean forward to set it on the table and pull up the social media post on my phone, filling Henry in on my findings, including how Dr. Russo may have failed Adam from a medical standpoint.

"I didn't know any of that," Henry says, gaze downcast as he hands my phone back. "I must've been too worried about my own name being thrown around. I tried to stay off social media. This does explain a lot."

"But Henry," I say, wincing, "it's also a motive."

His mouth falls open. "You can't actually think Adam would murder Kennedy Russo to get back at her father."

"It doesn't matter if I believe it or if it's *true*, Henry. It matters if the cops find out that Adam blames Dr. Russo and has a reason to want to hurt him. There's no better revenge than taking away someone's child."

"That's just sick," he says.

"Murder is just sick. But if it turns out Kennedy really had a secret boyfriend, and it was Adam..." I shake my head. "Well, then..."

"We're screwed."

I want to tell him *no*, it's not that bad. But sugarcoating this isn't going to help anyone.

"Hayden," Henry says, inching closer to me on the couch. "This is exactly the kind of information I needed. Thank you for telling me, and thank you for not going to the cops with it."

There's something odd about the way he says it. The words slide over me, sticking to me like a fine layer of sand on skin. Making me feel *dirty*.

But I look at Henry with his messy hair and neatly pressed polo shirt, and I know I must be overthinking things. Especially now, as he looks at me with those tired eyes like I'm the only person in his world.

"So," I say, sensing that we both need to switch to a lighter subject, "Bram says you're actually going on the student council retreat?"

He shrugs. "We haven't received approval from the school. Just from Mr. Fuller."

"Why does the school need to sign off?"

"Because of the other parents," he says bleakly. "As soon as they find out we're spending two nights in the same cabin as their precious offspring, they're going to freak out. In which case the school could take our side, since we haven't even been officially named persons of interest. Or the school could prohibit us from attending to keep the peace." He throws a hand up. "And to keep more than four people on the list of attendees."

"This is complete bull," I say, though the frame from the security footage pops into my head: that navy-blue hoodie with the letter *A* trailing behind Kennedy Russo. "I'll talk to Mr. Ortega myself. You guys need student council for college applications. How can he let you sacrifice your futures for—"

Henry reaches for my hand, taking it in his. I'm so stunned, I forget what I was rambling about. I try to swallow, but my throat is dry. He's trying to shut me up; that's all this is. And it obviously worked. I open my mouth to apologize, but he's smiling at me with one side of his mouth, and I can't remember how to speak.

"What would I do without you?" he asks, letting out a soft laugh. He moves his free hand over, cradling mine between the two of his. Excitement and panic clash in me, but then warmth settles in my stomach. I've imagined this moment since I first developed a crush on Henry, back when we were eleven years old. And now that it's actually happening, I can't tell what he's thinking. Is this a *we're good friends holding hands* moment? Or is it something else?

He lifts a hand to brush my hair off my forehead, tucking it back behind my ear. And when his fingers move to my cheek, I'm so still, I'm not even breathing. His fingers slide down to my chin, and his eyes slide down too, resting on my lips.

I'm getting the strong feeling that this is something else, especially as he angles my chin with his gentle touch and leans close enough for me to feel his warm breath on my neck.

But a thump sounds, and our heads wrench apart.

A crash. Glass shattering. And then, an unearthly moan.

12

Henry and I race through the living room and down the hall, checking each room until we find the wreckage. The ornate window of Mr. Abbott's study—arched and filled with over a dozen panes—is decimated. Outside, the agonized sounds continue. Immediately, my mind goes to last year's vandalism incidents. Did someone do more than attack the house this time? Have they hurt Adam or Bram?

But then Henry rushes to the desk chair and leans over, retrieving a football. He slaps it into his opposite palm, his face a mixture of irritation and concern. Then he strides out of the study and around to the French doors. I follow until we both reach the large grassy knoll where the boys used to practice football.

Now, Bram is hunched over Adam, who is writhing around, crying and clutching his bloodied hand.

"What the hell happened?" Henry demands, rushing to them.

"I told him it was a terrible idea," Bram snaps back, attempting to help Adam to his feet.

But Adam wants nothing to do with him. He lashes out with both hands, leaving a trail of blood across Bram's cheek. Henry stops in his tracks, taking in the scene: Adam thrashing around on the grass like a wild animal, his bloodied pulp of a hand. Like an animal caught in a trap.

Bram is undeterred. He tackles Adam, pinning him to the ground and calming him, like one of those weighted blankets. Henry comes around, kneeling in front of Adam and whispering soothing words. I get the impression that the brothers have been through this routine before.

"What happened?" I ask as the boys lift Adam to his feet.

"I've got him," Bram says, walking Adam over to the French doors.

Henry watches them for a moment, waiting. Once they're out of earshot, his head falls in something like defeat. "He manipulated Bram into a game of catch."

"Catch?" The idea is so horrific, it turns my stomach. "But he can barely hold a fork."

"That's why it was idiotic," Henry says, jaw clenched. "Adam's skin isn't healed enough; his fingers barely function. He has another surgery planned for next month! Now, he'll be lucky to keep the surgery date."

That horrible moan repeats in my head. "Is he upset because of the pain, or because he missed the ball?" I ask, indicating the shattered window.

"Oh, I doubt Adam missed the ball," Henry says flatly. "That's what tore his hands up. He tried this with me last week. I finally agreed to a light game of catch, but Adam gets into this…almost *manic* state, where he can't remember his limitations. Or refuses to accept them." He blows air through his gritted teeth. "He probably encouraged Bram to throw harder and harder until his skin broke down. And then he took his frustrations out on the house, which he's been prone to do lately." His brows arch. "Better than on Bram and me, I guess. And if that window is any indication, maybe Adam should give up catching the ball and try out for quarterback."

"Well, you should help Bram," I say, nudging him along. "I'm heading home anyway. I'll help with the mess first. You don't want your dad to find his office covered in glass."

A disappointed look crosses Henry's face. "No, we'll clean it," he says, shaking his head. He gestures for me to walk ahead but, as I pass, reaches for my wrist. "I'm really sorry we can't keep hanging out." His eyes are narrowed, like he's unsure how I feel about his hand gradually sliding down my wrist.

When our palms lie flat against each other, I show him exactly how I feel about it by lacing my fingers through his. "I am too," I say, heat blooming in my cheeks. "But you know where to find me."

He grins. "I do."

Once inside, his brothers' voices ring out from the kitchen. Arguing.

"The doctors don't know shit!" Adam shouts. "Russo paid them off! That bastard made me…*this!*" A sob breaks through. "He made me this. I hope he feels an ounce of what I feel. Now that he's lost everything."

A little prickle makes its way up the back of my neck.

Then a *bang* sounds, like Adam pounding a wall or a table, and Henry begins to lead me past the kitchen to the front door.

"I can see myself out," I offer. "You should go in there. Make him a protein smoothie with peanut butter. It always seems to cheer him up."

Henry takes a breath, staring down the gauntlet that is the doorway to the kitchen. I don't blame him. Giving my hand a final squeeze, he says, "Thanks. I'll see you soon."

"Bye." I stop by the couch to grab my purse, then start in the direction of the foyer. But the instant Henry's figure disappears into the kitchen, I race to the staircase.

Adam Abbott has a grudge against Dr. Russo, and right now, I'm starting to think that it was more than simply a possible motive for murder.

I think he could've actually done it. He may hate Dr. Russo enough to have taken the man's daughter from him.

Henry has tasked me with this mission to help clear him and his brothers. As counterproductive as it may be to search for evidence to support my new theory, I have to know the truth. And I can't ask for Henry's help with this; he can't know that my suspicions about his brother only increase by the day.

I've always done my best to stick up for the brothers because I believed in my heart that they had nothing to do with the accusations regarding Mariana last year. I still want to believe the same about them now, with Kennedy's murder. And if Adam is innocent, I'll do whatever it takes to help clear his name.

But if he did it—if he's the one on the security camera footage, the secret boyfriend, the *killer*—then I'm not sure I want any part of this.

I tiptoe up the ancient staircase, careful with each step. But the commotion in the kitchen has only grown since Henry joined in. Adam accuses them of ganging up on him now. A moment later, sure enough, the blender starts up. I almost feel guilty for my ulterior motive in suggesting the smoothie, but at least no one hears me as I make it to the top of the staircase and slip into Adam's room.

Easing the door shut behind me, I rush to Adam's wardrobe in search of the hoodie. I haven't seen it on any of the triplets since Kennedy's murder, and something tells me there's a reason. The cops think whoever was on that security camera footage was wearing the missing hoodie when Kennedy was brutally murdered. That means her blood would be on it.

If Adam was involved, he wouldn't be stupid enough to leave

it in his room. The detectives could end up with a search warrant, and then it would be over for him. So in a way, finding it here would almost exculpate him, at least in my eyes. And if he had nothing to hide, he could turn it over to the cops and let them test it for DNA. I scrounge around through the messy drawers and haphazardly hung contents of the closet, searching for it.

So far, it's not here.

I move to the bed, dropping to my knees. Wincing, I reach a tentative hand under it and move it around. My fingers light on soft fabric, but when I tug the object free, it's only a wadded-up graphic T-shirt. I feel around some more, finding nothing but dust bunnies and a mini toy car that's probably been down here since Adam was a toddler.

Defeated, I stand up, brushing off the front of my clothes. I get a stab of disappointment at not uncovering the hoodie, safe and sound. I don't like the implications.

I do another scan of the room, and my eyes snag on a familiar spine on the bookshelf.

It's my copy of Mary Shelley's *Frankenstein*, the one I lent to Henry. What's it doing in Adam's room?

I pad over to it, removing the book to find that it's not my copy. *Mrs. Garrett's Class Copy* has been scribbled inside the front cover of this one. Little blue and yellow sticky notes peek out between the pages, and I recognize Adam's messy all caps handwriting. Our assignment last year included annotating our free reading novel. I get a woozy feeling suddenly, remembering that the day we chose our books was the day Mariana died.

The triplets never returned to school after that day—at least not last year. Either Adam worked quickly on this assignment that very afternoon before the accident—which would not have been very *like* Adam—or he continued to read and annotate, even when he knew the novel would never be turned in for credit.

I flip through the pages, reading the passages he's rewritten on the sticky notes, trying to make sense of his color-coded system and the drawings. On one sticky note in particular is a black sketch of a star. Underneath it, the words from the page have been copied: *"Frankenstein! You belong then to my enemy—to him towards whom I have sworn eternal revenge; you shall be my first victim…and in a moment he lay dead at my feet."*

That same prickle I felt downstairs runs up my spine now. I remember this part of the novel. The words were spoken by Victor Frankenstein's creation, the being he formed, only to abandon later. On the note, Adam hasn't merely copied the words in black; he's underlined them in thick marker, red as blood.

At the newly thickened silence, panic surges through me. I should get out of here. For all I know, the boys could already be headed this way. There's a perfectly functional bathroom downstairs, so I have no excuse to be up here.

But the bookshelf is overstuffed, and I have trouble sliding the novel back inside. I try forcing it to no avail. When I attempt to rearrange some books by tugging them out, something slips free onto the wooden floor.

I bend down to pick it up, finding a collage full of photographs.

A prickling sensation runs from my fingertips up to the base of my neck: They're all of Mariana Sanchez.

The photos haven't been pasted on like the olden days. Instead, it's a printed collage with colorful photo frames, graphics of hearts and flowers ornamenting the paper. The edge is torn, like the page has been ripped from a book.

I rush to return it to the shelf, struggling to find its location as my mind grapples with this. Adam has a collage of photographs of Bram's girlfriend—Bram's *dead* girlfriend—hidden in his room.

That's when I spot where the collage came from. It's a hardcover photo album, the kind you can customize online. This one has a title printed on the front cover in the center of a pink heart: *Mariana and Bram Forever*.

Finding this album here is bizarre, to say the least. But there could be a simple explanation. Maybe Bram couldn't bear to have this album in his room, and Adam, not wanting his brother to regret throwing it away for good, offered to store it for him.

Then again, I may be projecting my own history here, considering that in his grief, my dad deleted some of my favorite home videos off the cloud, including the one I used to watch over and over in the months after Mom died. It featured her singing "Daydream Believer" by the Monkees to a baby-sized version of me as I laugh and coo. When I discovered the video was gone forever, I was torn up for days. I almost never forgave Dad for it.

But that was him. Just because Dad wanted to remove traces of what he lost doesn't mean Bram would act the same way in *his* grief.

I want to look at the rest of the pages, but my nerves are crackling; I have no idea what's going on downstairs.

Album in hand, I tiptoe to the door and crack it open. I listen for the sound of voices or the creak of the staircase. Hearing nothing, I flip through the glossy sheets. The title page contains a handwritten note:

To Bram

All my love,

Mariana

This album was a gift for Bram. A handful of pages contain the couple at different events from the period they dated: sophomore year up until the fall of junior year, with one period of separation so short, hardly anyone was aware of it.

Then I get to the pages where Bram and Mariana are with company, namely Adam and Henry. I'm in two of the photos, one after a football game in which our team defeated our rival school, and another in the Abbotts' pool.

My heart is thumping so violently that I almost turn the page and miss it. In the pool photo, we're all floating around on various inflatable toys. I'm on a pink flamingo, laughing with a plastic margarita glass full of Sprite. Mariana is on a massive dolphin, her smile wide as Bram tries to play-tackle her. Henry is in midair, performing a cannonball. I remember that Mrs. Abbott took the photo so we could all be in it—one of those rare occasions when she decided to act the part of the perfect mother, checking to ensure we were properly hydrated and wearing SPF.

Then I spot Adam. Standing on the steps, he's the only person in the photo who isn't laughing. In fact, he looks downright furious.

And he's staring directly at Mariana.

The expression on his face sends a shiver through me. I flip back to recheck the football game photo, and there it is again. This time, Henry must be the one behind the camera because he isn't pictured. We're all smiling victoriously at the camera—all but Adam, who's looking at Mariana with something like disgust.

Or hatred. But why would Adam have hated Mariana?

And if he did, does it mean Adam had a motive to kill not only Kennedy, but Mariana too?

Something Henry said about Adam last winter pushes into my brain. He later denied it, and I forgot all about it. But it's repeating louder in my head now than it ever sounded in real life.

Before I can fixate on those words, though, I snap to my senses, remembering where I'm standing. I stuff the loose page back into the album and jam it back on the shelf. Below, all is quiet. The voices from the kitchen have ceased, and I don't hear the television coming from the living room. It's now or never.

Heart hammering, I descend the staircase and make a mad dash for the front door.

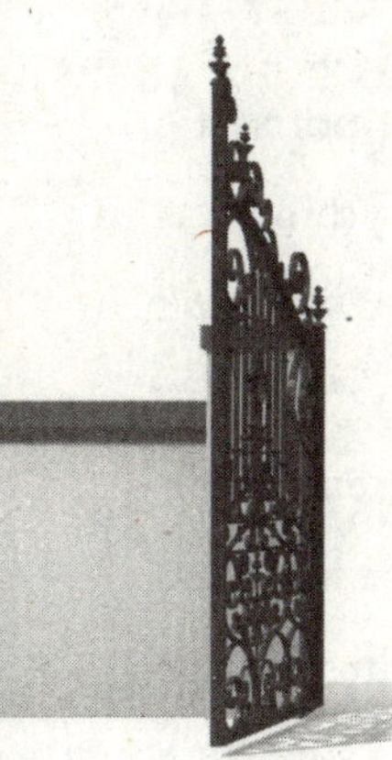

HENRY

LAST DECEMBER

"There is something at work in my soul, which I do not understand."

—*Frankenstein* by Mary Shelley

Henry was in the shed, working on his invention when he got the text from Bram.

It's happening again. Where are you?

Henry growled and tucked the parts and tools back in the box. Lately, with no school and no football, the invention had become more than a hobby—it had become Henry's passion, consuming his thoughts. He truly believed it would change everything.

But these episodes with Adam were becoming a common occurrence. At this rate, he'd never finish it. Tucking the box away beneath a folded blue tarp, he took off for the house.

As Henry made his way up the path to the front porch, he expected to hear shouting and screaming; instead, everything was eerily quiet. His pulse quickened. "Bram?" he called out, swinging the door open.

At first, there was no answer. The boys' parents weren't home. As usual, their mother was at some spa in a far-off place where no one knew of her family's scandal. Their father was off doing damage control, now that no one wanted anything to do with the auto shop chain concept.

Still, the dead quiet wasn't right.

Bram appeared at the top of the landing then. "Hurry," he said before vanishing down the hall.

Henry ascended the stairs, palms sweating now. He started to fear the worst. Adam had never vocalized self-destructive feelings, but he'd been so withdrawn since the accident. So depressed. What if—but before he could finish the thought, he found Bram slumped outside of Adam's room, back to the door.

"He's locked himself inside," Bram said, tossing up a hand.

"Well, is he okay?" Henry's thoughts began to spiral again.

"How the hell should *I* know? He hasn't said anything. He won't open the door. I think I heard him move, though."

Henry let out a breath, relieved. "Maybe we should call 911," he said loudly, only half-serious.

"I already tried all that psychological bullshit," Bram said. "Even threatened to make Mom come back from her retreat. He won't open it." Bram spun around so that his mouth was practically against the door when he yelled, "I really don't want to break down this door, damn it! But I will." He sounded just like their father.

"Before you do that," Henry said, pulling out his phone, "let's try something."

Twenty minutes later, the front doorbell rang, startling both Henry and Bram. It was the first time in over two months that anyone other than the triplets' lawyer had rung that bell.

"Who the hell is that?" came Adam's booming voice.

Bram's face contorted in rage, and he turned to the bedroom door. "You stupid piece of—"

But Henry shoved him toward the stairs. "At least we know he's alive."

"Yeah, but you dragged her all the way up here for nothing."

"It's not for nothing," Henry assured him. "She's going to get him out of there."

"Guess we'll see about that."

When the boys opened the door, Hayden greeted them with a big smile and three brightly colored red-and-gold bags. "Merry Christmas," she said shyly.

"Damn," Bram muttered. "Did he force you over here on Christmas?"

Hayden laughed and pushed past him. "It's not *Christmas* Christmas, dummy. It's the twenty-third. Don't you know what day it is?"

Bram merely crossed his arms and scowled.

"Not much point in keeping track anymore," Henry admitted, scuffing the sole of his shoe against the travertine tiles.

"Right." Hayden blushed rosy pink. "Well, let's see if I can get Adam out of his room."

"What's in the bags?" Henry asked, following her through the foyer.

"You'll see when Adam does." Hayden swung the bags around to her other hand, as if to keep them out of his reach.

"So never then," Bram muttered, following them upstairs.

They reached Adam's door and Hayden knocked twice. "Adam? It's Hayden. I've got a present for you."

There was no answer.

"Adam? Will you please open the door? I just want to say Merry Christmas."

Still no response, but Henry heard footsteps padding around the room, which seemed promising.

Then the music blasted, decidedly not of the Christmas variety.

Hayden sighed and turned to the boys. "I imagined that going differently," she said, trying to speak over the electric guitar. "Like…"

"Like a pretty female version of Santa comes and brings joy to all." Bram smirked, at which Hayden blushed again.

Henry didn't like it, whatever was going on between the two of them. Bram was supposed to be in mourning over Mariana. Though, if Henry were honest with himself—which he didn't want to be—there were other, more complicated reasons he didn't like it. "Maybe we should just go ahead and break down the door!" he shouted.

"Dad will be thrilled," Bram said glumly. "We should give up and let him live out the rest of his life in there."

"He'd starve," Hayden said, nibbling on her lower lip in a way Henry found adorable. "And I hate having failed at this. You asked me over here to do a job, and I want to do it."

"It's not your fault Adam's a bigger asshole than any of us thought," Bram said.

Hayden frowned at him and stepped closer, so she could speak softly. "Have some compassion, please. And a little more patience."

Even Bram's always-pale cheeks flushed pink at this. It had been difficult for the brothers to remain sympathetic to Adam during his spells, considering the emotional toll they took and the way they dragged on. But Hayden was right; Adam was going through something that none of them could possibly imagine.

"Adam?" Hayden called out again. "I'll just leave your gift outside the door here, while I go downstairs and whip up some peanut butter brownies."

Henry's lips quirked up. Those brownies were Adam's favorite, and he'd never be able to resist them.

The footsteps within the room sounded louder now, and Hayden smiled as her eyes flicked to meet Henry's. It was almost too easy.

The door opened a crack. "Hayden," came Adam's voice,

sounding tired and rough. "I don't want to see or talk to anyone. Not now, not ever. So you can take your *present* and your brownies, and get the hell out of our house."

The door slammed then, with a force that stunned Henry more than Adam's words. Hayden stood there, facing the door, her eyes wide and unblinking.

A rage bubbled in Henry's stomach.

But before he could go to her, Bram was there, wrapping an arm around her shoulder. "Don't listen to him," Bram murmured. "We'll let him stew some more. Meanwhile"—he turned his face to the door to shout—"we're going to eat all of Adam's brownies!"

Bram's arm was still around Hayden's shoulders as he walked her through the hall toward the stairs.

Henry didn't like it one bit. None of it. That rage only grew. It wouldn't stay pent up now. He stomped to Adam's door and pounded on it so hard his knuckles ached. "Adam!" he called. "Come out of there right now so I can say this to your face!"

Bram was on Henry in an instant, grabbing him by the shoulder and pulling him back from the door. "Hey! What are you doing?"

But Henry threw an elbow, knocking Bram in the chin. "Get off me! I want to tell Adam to come out here and apologize to Hayden!" He bore his fists and paced around, unable to keep still as much as he was unable to keep quiet. "He had no right to send my friend away when it's *his* fault we're in this situation in the first place!"

"Henry, stop," Hayden said, looking torn between coming closer and keeping her distance.

Bram was rubbing his chin and seething at Henry. "Can you calm down? You're making things worse."

Henry let out a frenzied laugh. "How can I make things worse? How can I screw things up any more than he already has?"

"You don't mean that," Bram snapped, a warning look in his gray eyes.

"Oh, I definitely mean it. We're locked up in here like prisoners because of *him*! And he has the nerve to send Hayden away?"

The door clicked open again, and this time, Adam's face appeared in the opening. "What exactly are you trying to say?"

Henry launched at Adam , but Bram grabbed him. Within seconds, Adam and Bram had overpowered Henry, joining forces to pin him to the ground out in the hall. He struggled, but it was useless.

"What did you mean by that?" Adam asked again, his knee on Henry's stomach.

Henry's glasses were smashed against the wooden floor. "Let me up, damn it!"

"Not until you tell me."

Henry choked out a laugh. "Like you don't know."

"I don't, actually." Adam had Henry's right arm pinned behind his back, and slowly, he began to pull on it. Feeling a shock of pain, Henry let out a cry.

Bram elbowed Adam and shoved him back. "Enough!"

With a grunt, Adam released Henry. Beside them, Bram rubbed his temples like an exhausted parent, the look on his face conveying that things were over.

Once Adam had locked himself back inside his room, Bram went over to Hayden, whose eyes welled with tears.

"I'm okay, I promise," Henry heard her whisper to Bram, who watched her carefully another moment before striding off to his own room.

Henry examined his lenses, finding them smudged but still intact, and put them back on.

"Henry?" Hayden's voice was meek. "Are you okay?"

A wave of embarrassment crashed over Henry. He ran a hand through his disheveled hair, making a poor attempt to tame it. "I'm sorry. I just didn't like him talking to you that way. He had no right."

Hayden took a tentative step toward him, and there was something unfamiliar and terrible in her eyes. Something like fear.

"I'm really sorry," Henry tried again, forcing the rage down, forcing a calm he didn't feel to ease the tension in his chest. "I don't know why I acted like that. Guess he finally got to me." Henry wanted to take her hand, to show her that she could trust him. But her elbows were tucked in close to her sides, and she looked ready to run for the door. "Don't leave. Let me make it up to you? Please? We could watch a movie."

Finally, Hayden's lips curved into a half smile. "You just want me to stay and make brownies."

He grinned back. "I'll help."

She glanced around the hall, as if trying to get her bearings. "Fine. But open your present first." At some point, she'd abandoned

Bram and Henry's bags, and Henry hurried to bring them to the kitchen table.

"Which one's mine?" Henry asked, inspecting one of the bags.

"They're all the same. You'll see."

"Should we wait for Bram?"

"Nah, he can open his later."

Henry liked that response. He liked that he and Hayden were sharing a private moment, apart from his brothers. He removed the tissue paper and pulled out the navy-blue hoodie, holding it up to his chest.

"Turn it over," Hayden said, doing it for him. The letter *A* was embroidered there in white. "I know you guys won't be wearing your letterman jackets much this year. I thought these could keep you warm instead."

With all the vitriol surrounding the Abbott name, Henry's first thought was that the letter seemed in poor taste. If it had been stitched in red, it would've made perfect sense—a scarlet letter fit for a trio of criminals. But Hayden added, "No matter what, you three will always be a team."

Henry felt nothing but shame then. Hayden's words had struck him deep in the gut. Upstairs, he hadn't acted like much of a teammate.

But he could change. He could help Adam, protect him. This sweatshirt would be his reminder that even when he wanted to knock that smug look off Bram's face, or silence Adam's whining and self-pity, the brothers were a team. A team since birth. They would do anything for each other.

Anything.

Henry glanced back down at the sweatshirt in his lap. It was much more Bram's style than his, but he tugged it on and leaned forward to give Hayden a hug. "I love it. Thank you. I only wish I had something for you." He mentally chastised himself.

"I don't need anything. Seriously, you guys have enough to worry about." Hayden glanced at the kitchen window. "Will your parents be here for Christmas?"

Henry tugged on the strings of the hoodie. "They haven't mentioned it. Opening these presents may be the closest thing we have to a Christmas."

"Well, you're all welcome at my house. It's never been quite the same with just me and Dad, anyway."

Henry smiled. "That sounds really nice."

"Hey, Henry?" Hayden asked, her forehead lined with concern now. "What did you mean back there, when you said it was all Adam's fault?"

"Nothing," he said with a headshake. "Just forget about it. I didn't mean anything, and I'm going to apologize to Adam. If he ever comes out of his room again."

Hayden smiled. "Good. I don't like seeing you boys angry with each other."

Henry didn't either. Teammates had to stick together.

13

I can't believe we're not going to the mountains," Sage whines beside me on the bleachers, examining an acrylic nail—pastel pink this time. She pulls out a tube of lip gloss and applies it using her phone's camera while we wait on the gymnasium bleachers for Mr. Fuller and the rest of the student council to arrive.

"At least we get to have a retreat," I tell her, still bitter about her comment to me last week regarding the Abbotts.

She rolls her eyes. "A day on campus is literally the opposite of a retreat. We can't even go outside because it's a crime scene."

"That's not true." Technically, we just can't go into the woods, though they're the closest thing we have to retreat scenery. She's right that the school gym is less than ideal, though. "And hey," I add, "we still get to miss class."

"They should've excluded the Abbott brothers, and everything would've been fine."

I don't bother to argue with her or mention the fact that the police still haven't made any arrests, which means the school doesn't have cause to exclude the Abbott brothers. It's pointless. Plus, I get her frustration; this retreat is the highlight of student council. Sage only has herself to blame, though; it was people like her and her *concerned* parents whose complaining got the whole thing downgraded in the first place. Instead of a three-day mountain experience, we have this one Friday in the gym. The school decided to keep the event close to home, where the whole staff could keep an eye on us.

Classes resumed on Monday, following an assembly in the gym for Kennedy, just like for Mariana last year. Lydia spoke, not only as Kennedy's best friend but as acting student council president. There wasn't a dry eye in the room. As student council president, Kennedy was known by all. She was popular not only because she was pretty but because she was nice to everyone. So even people who didn't actually *know* her felt like they did.

The Abbott brothers stayed home. Adam was already asking to return to independent study, but the boys' lawyer told them it would look like admitting culpability.

So on Wednesday morning, all three of them were back in class. And while gossip is still plentiful, things this time around are very different. There's no taunting, no laughter in the halls. This time, the football players avoid crossing paths with the Abbotts entirely. Everyone is keeping their distance.

Last year, because the circumstances surrounding Mariana's death had been murky, people liked to speculate. They'd trade theories about what happened because they never believed it could happen again—or happen to *them*.

But with Kennedy, it's different. There's no speculating that she was brutally murdered, her body discarded in the woods just behind the school. There's no wondering if someone killed her. Someone *did*, and everyone in this school believes it was an Abbott brother.

And unlike last time, I'm not sure they're wrong.

I keep thinking about the words of revenge spoken by Victor Frankenstein's murderous creation, underlined in red. The page torn from the photo album. Henry's words about Adam last December: *It's* his *fault we're in this situation in the first place.*

"There's no way they'll actually show up," Lydia whisper-yells a few rows behind me in the bleachers.

"And then this will all be for nothing," Liam Yang says.

"And it's like, they weren't even on student council. No one voted for them."

I want to turn around and tell Lydia that she's brand-new to student council and that, technically, no one voted for her to be president. Instead, my eyes remain on the door, like everyone else's.

When Mr. Fuller enters the gym, he stops short and glances around warily. "Uh, is everyone okay? The last time I checked, I wasn't a celebrity."

I'm a bit relieved that he's arrived before the Abbotts. Mr. Fuller isn't exactly intimidating, but he is an authority figure. He'll keep the bullying to a minimum.

"Mr. Fuller, if the Abbotts don't show up, can we still go on the retreat?" Sage asks, her high-pitched voice ringing in my eardrum.

"We *are* on the retreat," Mr. Fuller says, searching for a place to set his briefcase in this wide-open gymnasium. "And we're not staying at the school because of the Abbotts."

"We're staying because someone at this school is a killer!" shouts Liam, inciting a chorus of nervous giggles.

"Speaking of killers," Lydia says.

In the doorway stands Bram, his dark brows slanted, lips downturned in a scowl. He enters, wearing a black hoodie and gray jeans. Henry follows in a turquoise polo and blue jeans. He meets my eyes and takes a step in my direction, and a warmth fills me. The two of us haven't really had a chance to talk since last Saturday. I know he's been too preoccupied with everything else to bring it up, but maybe now, I'll see if we fall back into our normal *friend* swing.

Or if things will be different.

But when Henry sees Sage at my side, he slows again, grabbing the corner of his glasses as he looks for somewhere else to sit. The warm feeling freezes over.

Adam is last, and his attendance surprises me. I figured he'd ignore his lawyer's advice and skip not only the retreat but school entirely. Even more surprising is his green sweatshirt. It's a bright color—bright even for the old Adam—and the hood is pushed back for once, his face on full display. He stares up into the bleachers in an almost combative way, as if to say, *Look at me, all of you. I dare you.*

So that's new.

Now that I can fully observe him without that damned hood, I'm certain Adam is wrong about his looks. Maybe he's paler after all that time indoors. Maybe he doesn't have that too-perfect pretty boy look about him anymore. But he's just as striking as ever.

I expect half the room to up and leave, but everyone remains glued to their seats. Like they can't look away for even a moment. The sophomore class president, Mackenzie Palmer, waves and says, "Bram, over here." She pats the bench beside her, and shrugging, Bram obliges. When Henry and Adam take a seat on the bottom bench, everyone watches with bated breath.

That's when I realize that—terrified or not—every member of student council is going to stick out the day. And more than that, they're going to enjoy it. For once, it's not merely the Abbott brothers' looks making it hard not to stare. That same thrill people get from watching a scary movie is not only keeping them here; it's keeping them riveted. *They like it.*

Having found a place for his briefcase in the corner, Mr. Fuller steps in front of our section of the benches and clears his throat. "Welcome to the annual Silver Creek High Student Council Retreat." Whispers and groans ensue, but Mr. Fuller is undeterred. "The retreat is our official kickoff, now that elections have taken place and class representatives have been chosen. While I know those of you who've been around for a while were expecting something a little different, I'm determined to make this a fun and successful experience. And the main goal of the retreat?" He claps his hands together, awaiting a reply with an expectant grin. No one answers. "Team building, of course!" he answers himself. "Today is about getting to know one another and learning to work together to provide the best student council possible for your school." His smile falters. "Now, we've been dealt an extremely difficult start, and if you need to take time from today to speak with the counselor, please do. But I have utmost faith in your new leader, Lydia."

I glance back at Lydia, who sniffles and pulls a tissue from her backpack.

Mr. Fuller proceeds to divide us into teams for a game involving balancing tennis balls on a person's torso while carrying them across the gym. How this is supposed to help us govern the student body, I may never understand. But a few games and one testimonial given by the junior class treasurer later, it's lunchtime. And Mr. Fuller ordered food from the best (and only) Italian place in Silver Creek.

"At least we're getting *something* out of this," Liam says in the buffet line assembled at the back of the gym. He scoops more than a single portion of spaghetti onto his plate. "The best part of the retreat was always at night, after Mr. Fuller went to bed. Except we're leaving this place at three p.m."

"And heading to the Abbott mansion," Mackenzie says coyly to Bram, who's slouched behind her in the salad line. "Right?"

Bram tilts his head at me with a *this girl can't be for real* look.

"What?" Mackenzie asks innocently. "I heard your parents are never home. The place is huge. It's the perfect venue to end the retreat, without Mr. Fuller or any adults."

Sage cuts in front of Bram to grab the salad tongs. "The whole reason we're here is so adults can keep an eye on us."

"I don't care," Bram says, his plate still empty, though he's nearly through the buffet line. "Come over. Don't come over. Either way, there will be no refreshments."

"I can take care of that!" Mackenzie says, smiling brightly.

"Maybe we should ask Henry," I say, searching for the sensible brother. I spot him, seated on the benches with Adam and a couple of sophomore girls.

"Oh, what is it, Hayden?" Lydia asks. I flinch, because I didn't even know she was behind me in line. "You're not scared of them too now, are you?"

I grab a piece of garlic bread. "Of course not," I say quietly, so the others can't hear. "But you are. So why would you want to go to a party in their big scary mansion?"

"They won't kill us in their home," she says. "Too obvious. But we should all be careful. Because tonight they could be seeking out and marking their next victim."

It makes my blood boil, how these people can be so hateful, so mean and exclusive for an entire year. Yet the second they catch the scent of something exciting—something that can breathe life into their mundane existences, maybe even give them something new to gossip or post about—*oh, did I ever tell you I was in the house of a murderer?*—they flip a switch. I'd like to throw my plate full of pasta in Lydia's face. But I resist, instead picking up a plastic fork and a napkin. "Sounds thrilling," I say, walking off in the direction of Henry and the others.

But sitting with the boys and their new friends doesn't fare much better. Everyone is talking about tonight's party. No one seems more excited than Adam, who almost looks like his old self here, in his element, surrounded by admiring girls.

"What do you think about all of this?" I whisper to Henry, who's seated beside me.

He shrugs. "I mean, our parents won't be there. And it's just student council. It's not like they're going to go savage and wreck the place. How bad can it be?"

Something about the way he says this—the clear and obvious hope—twists at my chest. I see that hope in Adam's demeanor too. Both boys are so ready and willing to place it in the wrong hands.

Because these people—the student council members—might not wreck any possessions or valuables in the Abbott house tonight. But I have a strong feeling something will end up broken.

14

There are no streetlamps on the road outside the Abbotts' wrought iron gate, so I use my phone's light as I approach on foot. A few cars are already lined up along the road, and another rolls up behind them, shutting off its engine.

Lydia gets out quickly, locking the door three times, apparently for good measure. "Hayden, wait up!" She hurries to my side, shivering as she looks up at the gate, where three enormous ravens are perched atop it, silhouetted in moonlight. "This place is creepy as hell. Why have we never had a Halloween party here before?"

"Because everyone at school is horrible to the Abbotts."

She keeps her gaze on the birds. "Maybe we wouldn't be if they hosted more parties."

"Glad that's all it takes to assuage your fears about them." I start to push the gate open. "You know, you can move your car inside if you want. They've got plenty of space to park on the property."

Lydia laughs. "Oh, sure. I'll just lock myself *and* my car inside. Make it so I have absolutely no escape when they try to murder me."

"You're the one who said they'd never try to kill us tonight." We start up the winding path to the mansion beneath the bony branches of the birch trees.

"Yeah, but then I started thinking. They could drug one of us, keep us locked in the basement, tell everyone else we went home. Leaving my car in a visible spot could be the only clue they're lying."

"Good thinking."

"Thanks."

"How are you feeling about being president?" I ask, desperate for a change of subject.

"I mean, overwhelmed," she says, her voice shrinking. "I only ran for VP because Kennedy said there weren't any cool people on student council this year—no offense."

"Why would I find that offensive?" I mutter.

"She wanted me to do it with her, and now that she's not here, I'm all by myself. Completely alone."

"Completely."

"But I mean, I'll be okay. I'll handle it," she says as if it were the bravest act ever undertaken by a high school senior. "And I guess it'll look good on a college application." She stops in her tracks, chin tilted skyward. "Damn."

Ahead lies the mansion, its turrets and pointed arches towering over us. Its face is blanketed in moss, like it's been hidden back here behind the trees, asleep for centuries.

"Yeah," I say, the sound of music already drifting out as we make our way up the stone steps of the porch, ornate railings weathered and woven in vines. Taking hold of the brass knocker, I hit it twice before opening the door myself. We follow the voices to the kitchen, where someone has set up a drink station.

Immediately, I notice a sullen-looking Bram across the kitchen. He leans against a cabinet, nursing a red Solo cup. He's dressed in a fitted black T-shirt, and my eyes roam to his bare, toned arms. When he spots me, his lips curve in the faintest trace of a smile.

"Girls!" Liam says, raising his own plastic cup. Beside him, a couple of other guys are cracking open beers. "Help yourselves to a drink. We were just about to go on a tour of the castle. Weren't we?" He grins at Bram.

"No," Bram says flatly, "we weren't."

"Aw, come on. Show us the cellars where your ancestors used to torture people."

At this, Bram's face lights up, almost imperceptibly. "You've twisted my arm," he says with a shrug. "Though it's technically a dungeon, not a cellar. Follow me." He starts walking, then pauses, tilting his head thoughtfully. "Maybe we can put one of you in the iron maiden."

"Bram," I scold. "Stop it."

Liam turns on me. "Hey! You're killing the vibe here."

I roll my eyes. "His ancestors didn't torture anyone."

"How do we know that?" Bram turns, eyes glinting with amusement.

"How do we know your ancestors, the *auto repairmen*, didn't torture anyone?" I push past the other boys to grab him by the arm. He doesn't resist, and once I've dragged him along into the empty formal dining room, I release him. "You are doing nothing to help yourself."

He lifts both hands in surrender. "That guy was the one who said the thing about my ancestors."

"You don't need any more of a bad family rap than the one you have. Where are your brothers?"

Bram takes a swig of his drink. "Am I my brothers' keeper?" He smirks, but his eyes tell a different story.

"What's wrong?" I ask.

"Nothing's wrong," he says, waving a hand. "Everything's great. It's a party."

"Bram, how many of those have you had?" I gesture to the red Solo cup. "And what is in there, exactly?"

"A *secret* family recipe. Come on, I'll make you one." He motions me along.

"No," I say, but he's already halfway to the kitchen. Rather than follow him, I take the other door that leads to the living room. People are trickling in, and so far, to my relief, everyone seems to actually be on student council. I wonder if Sage will show up, or if she's still convinced that one of the Abbotts is a killer.

At this thought, I start to scan the room for Adam with more urgency. For some idiotic reason, Lydia's deluded basement-prisoner scenario trickles into my head. I need eyes on Adam.

Instead, I spot Henry over in the corner. He's laughing, red cup in hand as he talks rather closely with Mackenzie. A wave of heat streaks through me. He's probably the reason Mackenzie wanted to invite everyone over here. And *she* could be the reason Henry was so willing to say yes.

Maybe it's stupid that I ever thought something was going on between Henry and me. We've been best friends since we were kids, and that's the way things will stay. I attempt to back out of the room, partly because I don't want to interrupt their conversation, and partly because I'm suddenly finding it hard to breathe. But Henry meets my eyes over Mackenzie's shoulder. "Hayden!" He breaks into a smile, pinching the corner of his glasses between two fingers the way he always does, and I get a flutter in my stomach.

"There you are," I say brightly, like I only just noticed him.

Mackenzie turns around and gives me a look like I have a lot of nerve showing up at this student-council-members-only party. Even though this is my fourth year on student council and only her second.

To my delight, Henry presses past her to pull me into a hug. It's been less than a week since he took my hand on the couch, but he holds on to me like it's been much longer. I breathe him in, the familiar herbal yet clean scent replaced by the citrusy, warm alcoholic notes of whatever he's been drinking.

I let go sooner than I'd like to, only because I sense Mackenzie still beside us. "I can't believe you got these guys to host a party," I tell her.

"I have my ways," she says in a flirty tone. A new song starts up, and Mackenzie swings her hips. Raising her red cup in the air, she moves with her eyes shut.

I make eye contact with Henry, and we choke down laughter. "You're not dancing," I say, trying and failing to imagine it.

"And you're not drinking," he says. "Maybe if we were both—you know." He tips his head in Mackenzie's direction. "We'd both be dancing." His brows arch mischievously, and I doubt I'd need even a sip of liquid courage to dance with Henry if he took two steps closer.

"Hey," comes a deep voice. I turn to find Bram behind me, holding out a red cup. "I used my dad's bourbon, not whatever cheap shit the rest of them are drinking."

"Thanks," I tell Bram before turning to Henry. "Problem solved, I guess?"

Only Henry's smile has faded, his gaze locked onto his brother.

"Rich people are *weird*," Mackenzie says, dancing up close to Bram, who takes a step backward. "This cheap drink tastes delicious." She downs the rest of it, then trots off, presumably in search of a refill.

I sip Bram's concoction, which burns my throat on its way down. I cough, and Henry pats me on the back. "What the hell did you give me, Bram?"

He laughs. "Oh, sweet Phil." He reaches out to wipe something that I apparently spit onto my chin. "You don't have to drink it."

My face ignites. When he tries to take the cup from me, I pull it out of his reach, even though I have zero intention of taking another sip. "I'm not sweet," I protest.

"No, of course not." Bram bites his lower lip and puts on a faux serious face.

At my side, I can practically feel Henry stewing. Despite the blaring music, the silence among the three of us is mind-shattering. I have to end it. "Where's Adam?" I ask, trying to sound casual and not like I suspect he's off with victim number three at this very moment. "Did he decide not to come down?" That wouldn't surprise me at all.

"Oh, he came down," Henry says, eyes swinging to the French doors. "He seems to be back to his old self. He's outside, showing Ella—or Emma?" He shrugs. "He's showing some girl the gardens."

My throat goes dry. "It's Emma," I grit out. And she's only a freshman. "Maybe we should go check on them."

"Check on them?" Bram is smirking again. "You want to disturb Adam the first time he's not mopey and insufferable in a year?"

"I'll come with you," Henry says, all too eager to leave Bram behind.

Or maybe he offers to accompany me because he *knows*. About Adam. *It's* his *fault we're in this situation in the first place*... Last December I asked Henry what he meant by that, but his response was vague. And then last week, when I asked if he thought Adam might have said something incriminating to the doctor, he practically hung up on me. Could Henry also be worried about what Adam might do?

He passes me, his fingers brushing mine. It's a subtle gesture, not meant for Bram to see, but my hopes soar. Could it mean he doesn't regret last Saturday and whatever nearly happened between us?

He leads the way, and we pass Lydia in the formal dining room, talking to Liam. Her eyes are glued to an antique clock as she asks, "Can you believe this place? How much do you think something like that is worth?"

I glance at Henry, who doesn't react. Maybe he wasn't listening, or maybe he's choosing to ignore her. When we make it outside, Henry stops to look at me in the moonlight. "What's going on?" he asks. "Is this about the other day? Adam's breakdown?"

"Sort of," I say, unable to look him in the eye. "Henry, after our talk last weekend about Adam, I started thinking again about last December."

"Last December?"

"When you and Adam got into that fight, and you said your whole situation was his fault."

Henry lets out a puff of air. "I thought we went over this. I was mad, so I said it. I didn't mean it. Well, maybe a little."

"Really?" My heartbeat quickens.

"Of course. Bram and I wanted to force the school board to actually make a ruling. We'd done nothing wrong. But Adam said he couldn't face everyone, and"—he shrugs—"we were sort of guilted into staying home with him. Our parents agreed with him, saying it was all for the best. I got stir-crazy, that's all. I wanted him to fight, like he would've done before the accident. But I expected too much."

"Right." For a moment, I feel better. But then I remember that photo collage of Mariana, Kennedy's body lying in the woods, and the possibility that Adam had motive to hurt both girls. We have to find him. "Still," I say, "after that breakdown, we should make sure he's okay."

Henry examines my face for another moment, unconvinced. "I'm sure Adam is fine," he says, taking my hand in his. Everything I felt on Saturday comes rushing back. His fingers thread through mine, the warmth of his hand radiating up my arm.

"Adam never turned the lights on back here," Henry says, peering out into the darkness. Releasing my hand, he moves to the electricity panel and pulls a few switches. "Damn. It won't turn on."

"But the electricity isn't out," I say, looking through the glass of the French doors at the lit rooms.

"No, it's not."

A shiver runs over the back of my neck. Did Adam sabotage the lighting out here?

I follow Henry, our pace quick over the path. As we reach the pond, my phone dings in my back pocket. I stop to check it, hoping it's Bram reporting that Adam is back inside the house and Emma is safe and sound.

But it's an Instagram notification. A DM from Desiree Watts, containing nothing but a link.

When I click on it, I'm sent to a post on Lydia's account. It's a photo of a gold bracelet, little pom-pom charms bookending a series of dangling letters that spell out the word *CAPTAIN*. The post contains a caption:

> Never thought I would be awarded cheer captain under such terrible circumstances. Rest in peace, Ken. We love you

"Coming?" Henry asks, stepping out onto the bridge.

"You go ahead," I say. "Find Adam." As his footsteps trail off, I read the message again, wondering what I'm missing. Sure, it's in poor taste to post something like this now. But Kennedy was cheer captain, so when she died, the position went to Lydia. Much like the student council president situation. Lydia was always the default after Kennedy.

When I reached out to Desiree, she told me she had nothing to say on the matter. So why is she sending me this cryptic link?

Frustrated, I message her back. Sorry, I don't understand.

I expect her to ignore me, the way she did last time, and look up, remembering that I told Henry to go on.

It's starting to get cold, and I'm wearing denim shorts and a tank top. I didn't plan on being outside tonight. "Henry?" I call out. But the only response is another ding from my phone.

Desiree again. It's all she ever wanted.

I stare at the words, trying to make sense of them. All Lydia ever wanted was cheer captain? Is Desiree saying what I think she's saying?

Another sort of chill runs through me. Maybe this is the reason Desiree didn't want to talk last week; she's afraid of Lydia. But could she really think Lydia did something to Kennedy in order to take cheer captain from her?

I start to mull over everything Lydia told me at her farm on Saturday. That she thought Kennedy had a secret, and that it might be drugs, so she followed Kennedy. Lydia said she was worried about her best friend. But what if there was another reason she followed Kennedy? What if Lydia was hoping Kennedy was involved in questionable—or even *illegal*—behavior, so she could catch her in the act? Then the cheer captaincy would be all hers.

And president of the student council, for that matter. Lydia said she never wanted the position, but she admitted it would look good on a college application. What if her plan was to catch Kennedy and depose her, but the plan failed? So she resorted to other measures. Bloodier ones.

It's a stretch, for sure. And I know Desiree even less than I know Lydia. Still, Desiree is the first person from school who hasn't tried to pin this murder on an Abbott brother.

At the thought, I remember that I'm supposed to be looking for one of those brothers right now. Instead, I'm standing in the dark, my only source of light this phone and the wash of moonlight trickling through the foliage. "Henry?"

I take a breath and click on my phone's flashlight. The gardens are expansive, containing a literal hedge maze. It's easy to get lost even in broad daylight. "Adam?" I try as I find footing on a cobblestone path. The overgrown grass and flowers tickle my ankles. "Emma?"

Something scratches my bare arm, and I jump, causing my nearly full drink to splash over my shirt.

Letting out a growl, I abandon the drink on the path and shine my light at whatever brushed me. I find myself at the opening of the hedge maze. Tilting my phone, I let the light cascade down the dark corridor. As much as I want to avoid it and keep walking, it's exactly the type of place Adam would take Emma—maybe even lure her—in an attempt to impress her. Unlike me, the boys have been through this maze thousands of times and have memorized the way.

"Henry?" I call out again. But there's no answer, so I call him on my phone. He doesn't pick up. In fact, I don't even hear the ring. Maybe Henry and the others went a different route and are already back inside.

It's stupid of me to worry about Adam. I know him.

And yet…I can't ignore what he underlined in *Frankenstein*. I can't ignore his hatred of Dr. Russo.

Or that photo collage hidden in his room.

My heartbeat is like bullets firing in my chest. I take one step closer when a voice calls out, "What are you doing?"

I spin around, shining my light into the figure's face.

"Stop that!" the voice squeaks now. I lower the phone and squint into the dark to find Sage shielding her eyes.

"You came," I say, not quite believing it. After all, Sage's family is convinced that the Abbotts had something to do with her cousin Mariana's death.

"Yeah, and then you weren't even there. The broody one said you were out here. What the hell are you doing?" She glances around the gardens, shoulders tucked in close.

"Uh..." I can't admit to Sage that I'm searching for Adam because I might not trust him. I can't tell her I might agree with her and the rest of this town that he's dangerous. "Hedge maze hide-and-seek. Henry's out here somewhere."

She stares at me like I've lost my mind.

"I'm surprised to see you," I say, leading her away from the maze.

She crosses her arms. "I've been a dedicated member of the student council since freshman year. I'm not going to miss our first party just because some of the members might be murderers."

"Right," I say, looking down at my shoes as I scrounge for words. "Do your parents know you're here?"

"Of course not. I'm risking everything to be here."

"That's uh...so *brave* of you." Or is it? A little insect of suspicion buzzes at my ear as I recall how devious Sage could be back in elementary school. Righteous acts like writing *Todd Ellison still wets the bed* on the whiteboard while everyone was at recess, in retribution for him calling a girl in our class a "fatty." At the time, it earned my admiration and made me want to be Sage's friend.

But now, my defensive instincts are kicking in. She'd better not be planning some way to humiliate the brothers in front of the entire student council.

"Yeah," she says, "but necessary, you know? Without Kennedy here, I feel like I should keep an eye on things. Lydia is so green. She might need my help."

I resist the urge to remind Sage that it's a party and not a gathering in the Situation Room. "Good thinking." Except I'm now realizing that Sage lost the student council president race to Kennedy; she probably can't help but feel jealous that Lydia gets to slip in and take it. "Just uh, be careful with Lydia," I say before I can help it.

"What do you mean?"

"I just mean that she's been through a lot. Don't say or do anything to make her feel…threatened."

Sage shrugs. "I was only going to help."

I nod. "I know you were." I start to wonder if I should head back inside with her when I hear something. Voices from somewhere deep in the maze. Sage perks her head up like a bird on alert. "Oh," I say, "Henry and the others must've given up on me. I'll go get them." I nudge her along toward the path. "Be inside in a sec."

"You better be." Resignedly, she hurries back toward the bridge.

I turn to face down the maze again. Ducking inside, I try to recall the times we used to play here as kids. The first turn is a left; I know that. But at the fork, my memory goes hazy. One way dead ends immediately, while the other takes you on a twisty adventure to nowhere. The third option leads you closer to the exit.

I inhale a breath and choose the path to the right. At my first step, a heavy hand falls on my shoulder.

15

I scream and jab an elbow back, nailing my attacker in the stomach.

There's a groan. "Damn it, Phil."

I whip around. "Bram? Why the hell did you grab me?"

"I didn't grab you! I touched your shoulder."

I wince, the incident replaying in my mind. "Sorry, it was instinct. You could've said you were behind me. What are you even doing out here?"

"It got loud." He stops fussing with his injury to rub his temples. "When are these people leaving?"

"The party just started. And you guys told them they could come over."

"Yeah, well, Adam and Henry aren't in there. And I'm not exactly the life of the party."

"No," I say, "you're not."

His head falls back. "And that Mackenzie girl won't stop talking. Please come inside and make her stop."

"I can't. I never found Adam. And then..." This part is even more embarrassing to admit. "I lost Henry."

"Maybe he's avoiding you," Bram says without hesitation.

I clench my molars. "What's your problem?" I ask, the anger in my voice letting him know he's gotten to me. "You're always a jerk, but you're not usually this...*mean*. And you definitely don't drink. Tell me what's going on."

He backs up, his spine grazing the hedge wall, crossing his arms. "Nothing's going on."

"I don't believe you. You've been self-sabotaging all night, making yourself look like the asshole these people think you are."

He straightens now, talking a step toward me. "I am *exactly* who these people think I am," he says, each word spoken like a slap.

"That's not true," I argue, but he takes another step toward me, and I have to force myself to hold my ground.

The moon's glow hits his face, casting shadows, highlighting sharp planes. "You have no idea what you're talking about," he says in that same bladed tone.

"I know you act like a jerk, but you care about people."

"People like you?" he asks, his gray eyes dark and unreadable.

A lump forms in my throat, and I try to clear it. "People like your brothers."

"Oh, like my brothers." He laughs, but the sound is frayed. His face falls into shadow again, and when I take a step closer, I see his lips are contorted; he looks devastated.

"Hey," I say, moving to him, reaching up to cup his rough jaw with my hand. "What happened? You're worrying me."

He lets out a breath, and it's sweet and smoky from the liquor. "Don't worry."

"Then talk to me."

"I don't feel much like talking."

"Then," I start, failing to find the words. Instead, I close the gap between us, wrapping my arms around his waist to pull him into a hug. "It's okay," I whisper, letting him enfold me, letting his head rest on mine. The moment from last year in Bram's closet pushes into my head, and my body heats in response. But I ignore it, because Bram relaxes into me, letting go of whatever burden he's been carrying.

He lifts his head for a moment to examine me. "You really must've liked that drink I made you. It smells like you took a bath in it."

"More like I spilled it all over myself trying to walk in the dark." His chest rumbles with a silent laugh.

"You're deflecting," I say, looking up into his miserable eyes.

He bites his lower lip, and his hands drop to my hips. When he speaks, it's in a resigned voice. "Right before the party, my dad called me from Bali or wherever the hell he is. Apparently, the cops have new evidence. It's not looking good for me."

"But how?" I ask, inching back, my hands sliding from his spine to his sides in the process. "*You* didn't do anything wrong."

"It looks like I did. This evidence, it's pretty damning."

"What do they—"

Leaves rustle in the maze, somewhere back in the direction of the house. I pull away from Bram and hurry toward it, turning the corner.

At the sound of my footsteps, the figure halts. Adam turns around, and by the look on his face in the moonlight, I know he saw everything.

"Adam," I try, but he's already barreling back to the house. "Adam, wait!"

He continues striding ahead, not stopping as he calls back. "You know, he told me!"

I struggle to keep up without tripping over something on the overgrown path. "Who told you? Bram?"

"No," Adam says, his voice ragged from the physical exertion as he reaches the pond. "Henry." He's still moving too fast across the bridge.

"What? Adam," I shout, winded myself now, "will you please slow down?"

He comes to a stop with his back to me. "Henry was furious with me. He told me how he finally got up the nerve to make a move with you. How he held your hand? How he thought everything was going so well, and how you two almost kissed? And how *I* ruined everything with my episode. Guess he was delusional, huh?"

"No, Adam," I say, venturing a step closer. "He wasn't delusional. I did want to kiss him." I wheeze in a breath. "Bram was just upset. Please don't make a big deal out of this. What you saw back there was nothing."

"Oh, I know exactly what it was."

"No, you—"

"I do," he spits, turning on me so suddenly, with such ferocity that I flinch. "I do know. Because it's who Bram is. It's what he does."

When I only gape at him, terror and confusion tangling in my chest, he smiles. It's ghastly, and not in the way Adam might think. It has nothing to do with his scars and everything to do with the malice in that grin.

"Don't you see? This is what Bram does. He steals girls away from the boys who actually love them."

"No," I protest. "Bram isn't—"

But Adam is already clomping away from me, leaving me out here in the dark.

ADAM

LAST OCTOBER

"If I cannot inspire love, I will cause fear."

—*Frankenstein* by Mary Shelley

As he left Henry in the auto shop, Adam continued to hear the voice whisper in his ear.

Bram had never returned down the path, which meant he and Mariana were up at the house doing God knows what. A gust of fury tore through Adam then. He glanced back at the auto shop; he should've felt bad about making Henry work on the car alone. But the voice and the fury grew louder, drowning out everything else. He had to go through with his plan today. That's what the voice kept repeating. It insisted.

He got out his phone and typed a text. Need to speak with you. It's urgent. Don't tell Bram. Meet me at Creek Bridge. He sent it, nerves crackling as he waited. A moment later, he saw that the text had been marked *read*.

So he'd done it. He'd obeyed, setting the plan into motion. Surely, he'd be rewarded for it.

The response came then. What's this about?

Please just come, Adam typed out, his fingers starting to feel sticky, either from the nerves or the afternoon heat. I'll explain everything

The wait for a response this time was excruciating. I'll head over

Adam felt a victorious jolt, followed by a swell of terror. He took off, out the gate and down the road, up the path to the creek. When he reached the long rickety wooden bridge ten minutes later, he paced, hoping she'd really come. He wondered what excuse she'd used to get away from Bram. He wondered if she even had it in her to lie.

But sure enough, he saw her coming down the path. Dread filled his stomach then.

He thought suddenly only of Bram, and doubts flooded his head. He couldn't do this, not to his own brother.

But the voice whispered, *He did it to you first. Stick to the plan.*

Mariana approached the bridge, and as the wind whipped through her curls, she reached up to tuck a ringlet behind her ear. Adam thought she was the most beautiful thing he'd ever seen. He'd longed to touch those dark curls, the smooth skin of her cheek.

She pouted, her pink lips forming a perfect heart. "What's going on, Adam? What is it you couldn't tell me up at the house?"

"It's about Bram," Adam said gravely.

Mariana's brown eyes widened. "Is he okay?"

Adam was both hurt by the way she reacted over Bram and guilt-stricken; he hadn't meant to cause panic. He'd meant to cause a very different sort of feeling. "Yes, he's fine. But Mariana…" He thought about taking her hand then, as a gesture of support to help her through the news. Only it wasn't the right time. It would be soon, but not yet. "This is hard to tell you. But it wouldn't be right keeping it from you either."

"What is it, Adam?" Mariana asked, her skin blanching.

"I saw Bram in the woods on our property last week, and he was…" Adam licked his lips. Once it was out, there'd be no going back. "He was kissing someone."

"Kissing someone?" Mariana's brow furrowed.

Adam nodded. "Another girl."

She looked stunned. Those dark eyes went wide, long lashes still. She took a step back, her foot hitting a gnarled tree root. When she teetered, Adam had no choice but to reach out and take her by the waist. But she looked disoriented as he righted her. "Sorry," she mumbled. "I, uh… Are you sure it was Bram?"

"Yes, I'm sure. He was there on our property."

She blinked as though she'd just woken up. "Who was it?" When Adam failed to respond, she asked again. "Who was Bram kissing in the woods, Adam?"

"I don't know," he admitted. "The sun was going down."

That evening, between the blinding rage at finding his brother with a girl who was not Mariana and his poor view of the couple between the trees, he couldn't tell. His brother's head had been covering her face. He'd seen her hair though, a ponytail draped over one shoulder. In the fading light, he saw that it was light in color, long and straight.

Mariana's hair was dark. It was short and curly, never tied back but always untamed and free.

When a branch had cracked under Adam's foot, he'd spooked and returned to the house. On the way back, he'd doubted himself. Maybe it had been Mariana he'd seen in the woods with Bram. Girls changed their hair all the time.

But when he'd come inside, there was Mariana, waiting for Bram on the couch.

The rage doubled its force then. Adam had thought to confront Bram immediately. But before he did, the first inkling of the plan crawled its way into his brain. If he could be patient, everything would work out. For him and for Mariana.

Now, Mariana looked anything but pleased. "I think I can guess who it was," she said as tears streamed down those perfect soft cheeks, dripping onto her rosy lips. Adam wanted to ask who, but as the tears continued to mar her lovely face, he reached out to wipe them. And when he offered her a hug, to his surprise and delight, she fell into his embrace. "I don't know what to do," she sobbed into his chest.

"I'm sorry," he said, stroking her back. He allowed his fingers to move up into her curls the way he'd daydreamed. "It's an impossible decision. But it's the only decision, really. Deep down, you know that."

"You mean break up with him?"

"Of course." Adam frowned. "He's my brother, Mariana. I love him with everything in me, but I can't stand by and watch him mistreat you. He isn't valuing you the way you deserve."

Mariana was close enough that he could hear the sound of her swallow. "You're right."

"I wish I weren't." He held his breath now, waiting for her to say it, allowing his hopes to rise.

"I'm going up to the house," she said, glancing behind her at the path. "I'm going to break up with him."

"I am all in a sea of wonders.
I doubt; I fear; I think strange
things, which I dare not
confess to my own soul."

—*Dracula* by Bram Stoker

16

Bram's voice calls after me through the gardens, but I don't stop. Instead, I follow Adam over the path and inside the house, through the laughing and dancing student council members in the living room. He stops in the kitchen, where to my shock, Emma the freshman is perched on the counter, sipping from a red cup. My relief is tempered by a hot wave of embarrassment. I can't believe I ever worried Adam would hurt her. That I let my imagination—no, *Lydia's* imagination—get the best of me.

"Adam, can we please talk?"

His back is to me, and he's helping himself to a drink. "Go ahead, talk."

"Somewhere more private, please."

"Oh, you don't want to talk about what you were doing out there in front of"—his finger does a turn of the room, brushing over Emma, zigzagging past a couple of girls over at the kitchen nook, and finally landing on the doorway—"*him*?"

My heart plummets. Henry stands there, brows angled in confusion.

"What's going on?" he asks, crossing the kitchen and parking himself between Adam and me. "What's he saying to you?" He peers down at me with concern, like I'm a lost kitten in need of protection.

"Yeah, Hayden," Adam taunts. "What am I saying to you?"

"Nothing. Just—I need to talk to Adam. Somewhere else."

"Aw," Emma complains. "Adam was going to fix the lights, so we could do the maze."

"He can fix the lights in a minute," I say. "Please, Adam."

"Fine," he says, topping off his drink with vodka. "Let's go talk." He plods out of the kitchen.

I offer Henry an apologetic look. "I'll be right back. It's about… you know." I tilt my head in Emma's direction, as if to imply that Adam and I need to discuss our murder investigation, away from others. Henry nods, looking torn about letting me go. As I follow his brother out the door, I realize with a sick twist in my stomach that I've just lied to the boy I love.

Out in the living room, I catch Bram in my peripheral vision. He's leaning with an elbow on the grand piano, watching us.

Upstairs, Adam closes the door to his room behind us and gestures to the desk chair with a great swoop of his hand. "Have a seat."

"Okay, I just want to—"

"No, you're going to listen," he says. "Because it's the only way to save yourself."

I bristle and want to ask what he means by *save yourself*. But I consent, noting the fist-sized hole in the wall above the chair before sitting down.

Adam knocks back his entire drink in front of me, then plops onto the edge of his unmade bed. "I guess the story starts back in sophomore year," he says thoughtfully. "I met a girl named Mariana Sanchez, and she and I started hanging out. I'd never met anyone like her before. I was even planning on asking her to the fall dance. And then, two weeks before the dance, Bram asked her out. She said yes and then acted like I never existed." His words are starting to slur. Before tonight, I've never seen one of the triplets drink alcohol, and now Adam's suffering the effects of that moronic bad boy display he just put on for me. He starts to crush the plastic cup in his grip, as if blaming *it* for his current state.

"He didn't even ask her to the dance," Adam continues. "Just brought her here to the house. Called sitting on the couch a date. I'd planned on taking her on a road trip to see all the flowers in bloom. I'd planned a lot of things for us, mostly outdoors, because Mariana loves to get out of the library and be in nature. The first time I met her, she had a wildflower tucked in her hair." His fingers move to his ear, gaze veering from the floor to the window. "But Bram didn't care about what she wanted. He stole her away and stuck her in this damned museum."

Something about Adam—about the way he tells the story—seems off to me. There's a shiny, almost maniacal look in his eyes. I don't know what to believe. Still, my heart breaks for him. He doesn't shed a tear, but I feel his pain. "That's terrible, Adam. I'm so sorry."

"Oh, I'm just getting started." His lips curve as he stares into the crinkled, empty cup. "They were together for a whole year before I found out what he was doing behind her back."

He looks up at me, and when his blue eyes meet mine, fear lances through me, so sharp and acute that my upper body goes numb.

"Bram was cheating on Mariana. He stole her from me, and then he couldn't even stay faithful to her. He couldn't be content with the *one* thing I wanted more than anything."

I try to swallow. "No," I say, "he wasn't cheating. You're wrong."

"I *saw* him. I saw her too." He smiles, and suddenly, I want to get up and get out of this room. I want to run down the stairs, out the front door, and never face him again.

That day with Bram in his closet by his painting—or later, when he chased me into the woods—flickers in my mind like a fire, growing and consuming my thoughts. Heating my body to such a degree that I can't take it. I don't ask who the girl was. I *won't*.

Adam didn't see us that day. He couldn't have.

"The day Mariana died, I told her the truth about Bram."

No. I feel dizzy. Adam, his smashed cup—they're coming in and out of focus. Even his voice is deep and distorted, like it's been altered by one of those voice changers.

"She said she was going to break up with him," Adam says, almost a bittersweet note to his now-warped voice. "An hour later, Mariana was dead."

17

I thought you had no memory of what happened that day," I say quietly, my mind still reeling.

Adam's glassy eyes spark now. "I remember everything up until Creek Bridge, when I told Mariana about Bram. After that is when things go hazy. I don't remember her getting in the car. I don't remember who finished working on it. I don't remember how I got my injuries. It's all lost up until I woke up in the hospital and they told me she was gone."

I still hear the pain in his voice. But it's a conveniently small window of time to have forgotten. "I don't believe you," I say.

"That's because you can't accept the truth. About Bram. About yourself. You fell into his trap the same way Mariana did."

"No, but you—you're saying Bram *killed* Mariana?" My brain feels like it's about to explode. "*That's* what you meant when you said it's the only way to save myself? The only way to save my life?"

"What? No." Adam sobers suddenly. He looks at the crushed cup in his hand and tosses it onto the floor. "No, I..." He shakes his head. "I'm talking about this *power* he has over you. You have Henry, a boy who loves you, right in front of you. Just like Mariana had me." He glances at the bookshelf, and I don't have to wonder why. "I know you love Henry—I've seen the way you look at him. But you're going to lose him and regret it forever. All because Bram takes some sick pleasure in stealing girls away and draining the life out of them."

"No." I shake my head. "Bram never did that." But I no longer believe this, nor do I think that Adam is inventing this tale about Mariana.

I think of the camera footage, of Bram's words outside. *This evidence, it's pretty damning*. Maybe damning because Bram did exactly what the cops think he did. He was seen in the woods with Kennedy, though he denies being there. And yet...he was the first on the scene. He discovered the body. What if Lydia's theory about Kennedy dating an Abbott in secret was reality? If Bram was dating Kennedy and she wanted to end things, maybe Bram couldn't accept it. Just like when Mariana tried to end things an hour before she died.

"I don't feel very well," I say, trying to stand up and knocking my elbow on the armrest.

"Damn it," Adam says, crossing the room. "Here. Let me—" But

I wave him off, and he takes a step back. He stands in the middle of his bedroom, wringing his hands. "I'm sorry, Hayden. I didn't mean to upset you. I do care about you. It's only that I care about Henry's feelings too."

"But I—In the garden tonight, I never did anything with Bram."

He doesn't argue, but his gaze falls to the floor. My stomach clenches. He thinks that I have singlehandedly come between all of them. And if he told Mariana about another girl, I have to assume he'll tell Henry about the garden. Despite the fact that *nothing* happened out there.

And I'll lose him before he was ever even mine.

"Please, Adam," I say, my voice breaking. I want to tell him about everything I've kept secret on his behalf. All of my suspicions this past week that I've kept locked away. But of course, doing so would be ludicrous. "He mentioned a call with your father," I offer.

Adam's eyes snap to mine. "What call?"

"He didn't tell you?"

Adam neither confirms nor denies. Instead, he presses his lips flat and begins pacing the room.

"I'm not sure," I say. "He was telling me about it when you walked up. That's all that was happening. Talking. And he was upset, so I tried to—I hugged him. Maybe that was wrong, but he had no one else."

"He had me and Henry," Adam says, but his tone lacks conviction. This whole situation, this case, it's caused even more cracks in their relationship than the ones that already existed.

"I asked you last week if you thought Bram was seeing Kennedy in secret before she died. You lied to me."

He tries to protest, but I don't let him.

"You think he did something to her, don't you?" I ask. "Just like you think he did something to Mariana."

"No, I don't," he says firmly. He's bent over me now, teeth gritted. "And you're not going to say anything about this to Henry or Bram. Got it?"

I hesitate, then clench my jaw and work up my nerve. "Tell me where you were during the fire alarm, and we've got a deal."

He sneers. "You don't exactly have the leverage to be asking questions, do you?"

"Tell me why you never came to class, and why you weren't outside during the emergency drill. Then I'll keep quiet."

He grunts and punches into his bed with his good hand. The mattress takes the brunt of it, but there's a crack as the base of the bed buckles under the force. "Fine. But it's not going to make you feel better about Bram."

"Why not?" I ask, my pulse racing.

"Because I was helping *him*. He asked me to play lookout, while he pulled the fire alarm."

"What?" My spine stiffens against the chair back. "Why would he pull the fire alarm?"

His lips press flat together. "Why do you think?"

And then it's obvious, isn't it? To cause a scene. Chaos. So everyone would be scrambling around, distracted. So teachers wouldn't have time to take roll properly. So no one would notice that he and Kennedy were the only ones missing when she was killed, because *everyone* was out of class. Everyone was outside.

Except he didn't count on one thing: the security cameras.

"Did you see him take Kennedy into the woods?" I ask, my voice weak.

Adam shakes his head. "I went and sat in the car for the rest of the period. If you'll remember, I wasn't in the best of spirits after the little incident in the cafeteria. The school has footage of me walking out the front door. But the cops are saying my head was down, and because of the hood, they can't confirm my alibi."

So the exact kind of footage they're trying to use against the brothers, they refuse to use in their exculpation. "And you really don't know what this evidence is that the cops now have against Bram?"

"No, but I'll find out soon enough. We've got a meeting with our lawyer tomorrow, after my dad gets back from his trip."

Of course. Even in the midst of all this drama, Mr. Abbott can't be bothered to stick around. "Why *is* your dad on a trip right now, Adam? You obviously need him."

"Apparently, it's business this time. We're about to spend our entire fortune on lawyers, so for the first time in his life, he actually needs to find a way to pay bills. The auto shop is obviously never going to bounce back."

I think of Dr. Russo's lost investment and wonder if Adam knows the extent of the damage his father has caused. "And your mom?"

He lets out a soft, vacant laugh. "Couldn't cope. Loves the

spotlight but not the unflattering sort of lighting. And I think… They haven't said anything, so don't tell Henry. But I think they're separated. They've been arguing a lot more this past year. She hasn't been around in ages, and she let the place go to shit. Not likely she's coming back here." He gnaws on his lower lip. "I think Mom blamed Dad for letting Dr. Russo butcher my face. For allowing one of her beautiful boys to turn into *this*." He points at his scars, a sardonic expression on his face that warps into a grimace. "For letting the family name get dragged through the mud. So all of this with Kennedy—it's just added stress."

"I'm really sorry, Adam," I say, not knowing how to comfort him.

He shrugs. "You of all people don't need to feel sorry about my parental situation."

"But I do."

"Yeah, I know." His eyes flick up to mine. "I won't say anything to Henry."

"Because nothing happened with Bram," I say, indignation coating the words, even though I'm no longer convinced they're true. "I won't tell Bram about your vodka-infused rambling. I know that's all it was."

I say this to reassure him. I say it to reassure myself.

But as I get up and leave Adam's room, I know that it's the biggest lie I've told all night.

I want to get away from this place, to leave the party without having to look Bram in the eyes ever again. But Henry is at the bottom of the stairs, concern still etched on his brow.

"Is everything okay?" he asks when I reach him.

"Yeah, but I'm not feeling great. Think I'll head home."

"You drank that stuff Bram made you," he says, reaching out to touch my arm. His hand slips down to take mine, and for the first time, he seems at ease touching me. Like whatever happened on Saturday marked a change between us, a change that I've wished for since we were in middle school.

It would be easier to lie and say yes, I drank that horrible drink. But I don't want to continue down this path of untruths with Henry. I look into his eyes, and the last thing I want to do is come clean about this. To come clean to myself, once and for all. "It's Bram," I say, and Henry's eyes narrow. "Something happened, and I…" *I don't want to lose you. I don't want this moment with you looking down at me, your hand on mine, to be the last.*

"Yeah, I know," Henry says, his expression dimming as he lets my hand fall.

"You do?" If he knows, why is he even standing here, talking to me?

"Somehow, Sage got the video. She posted about it on Instagram a few minutes ago. It's all anyone's talking about." He gestures to the rest of the room, where sure enough, every eye is on a phone screen. Some people are laughing nervously; some are looking up from their screens to stare at Henry and me.

"Sage?" My insides go hollow, everything shelled out and replaced by horror. Sage must've stayed when I told her to go back inside. She must've followed Bram out there to the hedge maze and somehow recorded us together.

I scan the room for Bram, but he's not here. I need to know how bad it looks. Palms sweaty, I pull out my phone and navigate to Sage's post.

What I find is far worse than I imagined.

It's not a video of Bram and me in the garden. It's a clip, shot within Silver Creek High's school hall. The footage is shaky, like it was recorded on someone's phone, and this time, there's no mistaking the subject. Bram is standing in his black T-shirt. He glances from side to side, then reaches out and pulls the fire alarm. The last thing the camera captures is him racing out of the frame, in the direction of the back doors.

The caption on Sage's post reads like someone reached straight into my head, removed my thoughts, and pasted them onto the screen:

Still having doubts about whether or not Bram Abbott killed Kennedy Russo? This was recorded minutes before she was lured outside by the sound of a fire alarm and murdered.

18

In the morning, feelings of guilt, embarrassment, and fear rush back before my eyes are even open. I see the garden behind my closed lids, hear Adam's horrible tale all over again, remember Sage's social media post.

Last night, Sage left the party immediately after posting. That must've been her plan all along, the one I'd predicted. To stay long enough to witness Bram's undoing and then skip off into the night.

Bram had locked himself up in his room, so it was up to Henry, Adam, and me to send everyone home. The house was in shambles, disproving Henry's assumptions about student council members not partying too much. I offered to stay and help clean up, knowing Mr. Abbott would arrive today. But they told me to go home, and though I said I'd be fine, Henry insisted on walking me because of the late hour.

He held my hand the whole way home. After everything with Sage's post, I didn't have the heart to mention the whole Bram situation. Dad was waiting up for me, so there was no possibility of a good night kiss at my front door. Which is just as well—I won't kiss Henry until I've come completely clean about my history with Bram.

Bram, who may be a killer.

Though my mind—or maybe my heart—refuses to accept this. Sure, Bram is gorgeous and has never had an issue getting attention from girls. But I can't wrap my head around this girlfriend-stealing monster that Adam has painted him as. *I know* Bram. I keep going over everything that happened with him last year.

Did he lure me into his bedroom? No. *I* asked to see his painting. Maybe, subconsciously, I wanted something to happen. But that's just as ridiculous. There was Mariana, of course. And even back then, I had a crush on Henry. I asked to see Bram's paintings as a friend. And in the garden last night, I was trying to comfort my good friend—or someone I *believed* was my good friend.

Now, I sit up in bed and check Sage's post again, hoping that the school or the police have taken it down. But it's still up, its views upwards of one hundred thousand, with hundreds of comments. Despite feeling torn, I recall the scared look on Bram's face last night in the garden, and my heart twists for him.

I text Sage, asking if she wants to meet me at the coffee shop in town to get started on our English papers. Our rewrite deadline was extended on account of the murder. She responds immediately:

Don't need help but always need caffeine

An hour later, I arrive at the shop dressed in jeans and an oversized sweater, my backpack heavy with the weight of my laptop. Sage is already there, wearing a cute floral sundress and a cropped white cardigan. She has headphones on and a latte on the table as she types away.

I wave a hand in front of her, and she removes the headphones. "Oh, hey."

"How's the paper coming?" I ask, setting my things down across from her.

"Fine, I guess. Mrs. Lieu's grading rubric is a complete mystery. So who knows?"

I open my laptop and take a seat. I'd planned on making up a question about my paper topic, just to ease my way into the real reason I asked her here. But I get as far as pulling up a blank document, typing out my title, and messing with the font before blurting out, "I wanted to ask about your post last night."

Sage's lips purse. She leans back in her seat, crossing her arms. "I thought it was a bit weird, you asking me here. I don't think we've done homework together since sophomore year. You're not even going to order a drink before you give me the third degree?"

I glance up at the counter. "Fine." I grab my wallet, hoping she doesn't pack up and slip out before I finish ordering.

But when I return a few minutes later, she's still at the table, though she's not typing quite as furiously. "Sage, how did you get that video of Bram? Did you take it?"

"I can't share my sources," she says without looking up from the screen.

"Because your source is a complete idiot for sharing it with you instead of the police?"

Her head tilts. "Let's just say a friend may have been excused from class to go to the bathroom, but they were actually hiding out and recording a cute little video for social media. And then that video got more interesting when this friend spotted shady behavior down the hall. Oh, and this friend may also want Bram to go down for his crimes as much as my family does."

Which of Sage's friends would hate Bram enough to want the footage leaked?

Immediately, I know the answer. *All of them.*

Though Adam's injuries cast him in the spotlight last year, the fact that Mariana had been Bram's girlfriend was never forgotten. "You should let the police handle it," I say. "If they thought Bram was guilty of something, they would've arrested him."

"Oh." Sage finally glances up with a devious grin. "That's coming. Soon, now that the public has the video footage. They'll be putting extra pressure on the detectives to make an arrest."

My jaw clenches. "You have to take that post down."

"Why would I do that? I'm finally getting people to call in to the station. Finally, others are helping with what my family has been trying to do for a year."

"Please, Sage. Bram is my friend."

"Is he?" she asks condescendingly. "Deep down, I don't think you believe that."

"He didn't do this," I plead.

Her expression softens, no longer self-satisfied and victorious. Instead, I see pity as she picks up her coffee. "We both *know* you don't believe that."

And though I should try, I can't find the words or the will to argue. Instead, I say pathetically, "We used to be friends, Sage. Can you take it down for me?"

She sips her coffee, and for a moment, I think she's going to comply.

But then she sets her cup down and looks me in the eye. "We stopped being friends because my cousin was murdered, and you took *their* side, not mine. Or have you forgotten?"

She pulls her headphones back on, ending the conversation.

BRAM

LAST OCTOBER

"The last I saw of Count Dracula was his kissing his hand to me, with a red light of triumph in his eyes, and with a smile that Judas in hell might be proud of."

—*Dracula* by Bram Stoker

"There you are," Bram said, finding Mariana on the path up to the mansion. Her curls were windswept, and when he got closer, he saw that she'd been crying. "What's wrong?"

When he reached for her, she shrank back. "Stop, Bram."

"What happened?"

She sniffled. "I can't be with you anymore."

Bram stood there in the mottled shade of a birch tree, stunned. "Okay," he said, the word stretching like the shadows of the branches on the path. "Are you going to tell me why?"

"You already know why," she said, wiping at her nose. A leaf had fallen into her hair, and Bram had to resist the urge to tug it free.

"I'm lost here, Mar. Can you tell me where you went?"

"I just had a little talk with someone who put things in perspective."

Realization struck Bram, and a hot fury rose within him. "Mariana, it's not what you think. She's a liar."

"She?" Mariana laughed, but tears streamed down her cheeks. "So you admit there's someone else."

"No! I don't know what she told you, but you can't trust a single word out of her mouth." He was speaking so fast, the words knocked and skidded into one another.

Mariana shook her head. "I don't want to talk about it."

"Mariana, please," Bram said as she brushed past him on the path.

"I'm just grabbing my things, and then I'll head down to the shop. Hopefully, my car will be done soon, and I can get out of here."

"Will you just listen?" he called after her, hating that she was hurting. Hating that he'd let things spiral so far out of control. "She's crazy!"

But Mariana only quickened her pace, as if she couldn't wait to get away from him.

Bram watched her, that fury bubbling over now. He couldn't follow her, not now. By the looks of her, she would only run. Or maybe even scream.

Instead, he trekked on in the direction of the auto shop. But before he reached the fork in the path, his phone dinged. He looked at the screen and saw that it was *her* again.

Our usual spot?

Bram wanted to throw the phone, to smash it into a million pieces. They didn't have a usual spot, but he knew she meant the woods on the Abbott property. It was the place she'd first tried to kiss him.

After he'd rejected her, she'd gotten angry. She'd been bombarding him with texts ever since. And now, she was clearly lying to Mariana, telling her that Bram was cheating on her. If he'd only been up-front with Mariana about everything since the beginning, she never would've fallen for it.

Normally, Bram would ignore the text or tell her to leave him alone. But right now, as his blood pulsed like fire in his always-icy veins, he had some things to say to *her*.

I'll be there in ten minutes

Bram made it to the woods in six. The canopy of trees was thick, allowing only a circle of light to trickle through. As he waited for *her* to show up, pacing the forest floor, he thought about Mariana and how heartbroken she'd looked. He felt terrible. Maybe he hadn't done what she'd accused him of, but Bram had been lying to Mariana for a long time. And in a way, he'd been unfaithful. Maybe all of this was for the best.

Regardless of what happened to Bram and Mariana in the future, though, he needed to do something about *her*. *She* had caused Mariana pain, and he suspected she relished in it.

He wondered what he could do to her, to stop her once and for all. To inflict pain on her, the way she had on Mariana.

She was late now, by four minutes. Bram thought he smelled smoke in the distance, a firepit in one of the neighbor's yards, perhaps. He continued to stew, his mind covered in black and red, as if he were seeing blood painted onto a black canvas.

A sound like a thunder crash came then, so loud the birds cried out and abandoned their perches. Bram dropped down, thinking he was under attack, clutching his head. And then he couldn't hear anything, deafened by the noise.

But Bram had his sight. And as he carefully lifted his head to look through that hole in the canopy of trees, he saw that the sky was lit up in reds and oranges, the gray of smoke.

The sky itself was on fire.

19

I wake in a panic, not knowing where I am or what day it is. It's pitch dark. I can't see a thing, but I feel the blanket over me and the cushions and remember that I was with Henry, on his couch. He invited me over. Apparently, the meeting with Mr. Abbott and the lawyer hadn't gone well. Mr. and Mrs. Abbott took off again immediately afterward, checking into separate posh hotels in Stowe to avoid not only the local press but each other. Bram and Adam were holed up in Bram's room, coping via a video game marathon, and Henry needed a friend.

We talked for a while, and then he put a movie on. For once, we watched in silence, all of our words spent. I remember resting my head on his shoulder at one point, but I'm alone now. Warmth fills me, knowing he must've brought me this blanket before heading to bed.

But the feeling turns to panic when I think of Dad. He must be worried out of his mind, especially considering the recent murder. I have to check the time, but my phone is lost somewhere in the dark.

Standing up, I feel around on the couch, then move to the end table. With no luck, I head toward the wall in search of a light when my right shin crashes straight into something. I cry out as sharp pain radiates up and down my leg.

I fall back onto the couch, still caught in the dark as my shin throbs.

A light clicks on, and my bleary eyes struggle to adjust.

"I came down to get some water and heard a noise," Bram calls from the doorway. "Are you all right?" I turn and blink a few times to watch him cross the room toward me in a fitted black T-shirt and dark sweatpants.

"Yes," I say, my voice too high-pitched. "I'm fine. Just couldn't see."

But he rounds the couch, advancing on me. I shrink back, Adam's words blaring in my head. *She said she was going to break up with him. An hour later, Mariana was dead.*

He stops suddenly, his eyes flooding with hurt before lowering to the rug. "You're afraid of me," he says with none of his usual humor.

"No, I'm not," I lie.

"Then let me help you." He waits for me to answer, unconvinced. He doesn't take another step.

Nodding, I start to lift the hem of my jeans. "I'm sure it's nothing."

Bram moves to kneel in front of me, his hand brushing mine as he takes over, rolling up the leg of my jeans past the knee. Sure enough, there's a large gash where my shin met the sharp edge of the wrought iron coffee table. The area is already starting to swell, and blood has seeped into my jeans. Bram's fingers graze my ankle as he looks up at me with sleepy eyes. "You've made a mess of yourself, Phil."

"I told you, I'm fine."

Ignoring me, he gets up and ambles from the room, returning a minute later with a first aid kit.

When I try to take it from him, he slings me an annoyed look. "Why are you acting like I'm going to take the antiseptic and find a way to kill you with it?"

"I'm not. I just don't need any help."

"You were there for me Friday night," he says, already finished cleaning the wound and moving on to the gauze. "Let me be there for you."

"Friday night was a mistake."

Bram's head draws back, his eyes flicking up to mine. "Why is that?"

"Because Adam thinks something happened between us," I say, pulling the blanket up to neck level, "and I think he might tell Henry."

"So"—he clears his throat, eyes back on the bandage—"you and Henry. You're..."

I shrug. "I don't know. Maybe." Nothing happened between Henry and me tonight, apart from my falling asleep on his shoulder. There was no more hand-holding, no kiss to solidify whatever inklings I've had. We just talked, like old times.

Bram rises, saying only, "Let's get the place a little warmer," before moving to the ornate wood-burning fireplace in the corner. He works on it, leaving me to wonder if he even heard what I said about Henry. Once a fire is blazing, he takes another match and lights the votive candles on the black console and the coffee table. Then he dims the main light in the room to near black and kneels again without making eye contact.

"How are you doing," I ask, "ever since…you know, Sage's post?"

"I'm not in jail, so I guess I'm doing pretty *swell*. Sage's post is down."

"It is?" Did she take it down because I asked her to?

"Our lawyer got the police involved. They had it removed." Guess that answers my question. He finishes up the bandage and rolls my pant leg back down. "All done." Only he stays kneeling there, staring off in the direction of the doorway. "Go ahead. Ask."

I hate it when he knows what I'm thinking. I nearly deny having questions. But they're too burning, like the hot coals from the fire sitting in my back pocket, trying to scorch right through the layers of fabric and skin. "Why did you pull the fire alarm?"

Bram rubs the back of his neck. "I can't tell you that."

"Why not?"

"Because I promised someone I wouldn't. And like I said during your last interrogation, I don't want to lie to you."

"You put your face on camera," I say, my tone admonishing.

"That's not accurate," he says, trying to lighten the mood. "I didn't know someone would be hiding out, recording me from behind the drinking fountain nook."

"You weren't even disguised, just wearing a stupid T-shirt. Even if a girl *hadn't* been murdered, you could've gone to jail!"

"These are all extremely good insights, Phil. Do you think I would've chanced it if I'd planned on killing a girl afterward? Also, thank you for noticing my T-shirt." He gestures to the one he's wearing now. "If you'll remember, I told you and the cops that I left my sweatshirt in the cafeteria at lunch. The timestamps *prove* that I didn't have it anymore when the second video was taken. So I couldn't have been the person caught on it with Kennedy."

"That doesn't mean you didn't kill her," I say without thinking.

Bram presses his lips flat. "Huh." He nods and starts to get up. "Okay. Well, I appreciate your trust in me."

"Just wait," I say, still letting my mouth work in isolation from my brain. Because trust is the last thing on earth I have for Bram Abbott right now. He scowls, considering my request for a moment before moving with resigned sluggishness. Once he's seated on the couch beside me, I turn to face him. "You want to know why I lost trust in you? Because Adam told me about Mariana. That you stole her from him—"

"*Stole* her?" His head wrenches back. "I don't know what you're talking about."

"And Adam thinks that you were cheating on her with *me*. All because of that day when you and I..." I can't say the words.

"What?" Bram's face pales. "Oh, no." He slumps against the backrest, rubbing at his temple. "It was *him*. It was Adam the whole time."

"*What* was Adam?"

"I assumed it was Kennedy."

"I'm lost," I say, my frustration growing.

Bram sighs. "Last year, Kennedy tried to come between Mariana and me. She harassed me, threw herself at me—it was like an obsession."

"What?" Kennedy had feelings for Bram?

He rubs at his face, eyes combing the room as if in search of answers. "Adam must've seen us together and misconstrued everything. He must've told Mariana there was someone else. That's why she broke up with me."

My chest lightens a little. The girl in Adam's story wasn't me. It was Kennedy.

Still, I'm not sure I buy Bram's version of events.

I think back to that day in Bram's closet two summers ago, when I let my hands slide down to his wrist. When he looked me dead in the eyes, like he was trying to read my thoughts, and all I had in my twisted head was that I wanted him to kiss me. About how his hands moved to the small of my back, and he read those thoughts with deadly precision.

How his lips met mine, hands pulling me in, crushing me against him.

How, for a second, I lost myself in him, and it was everything I wanted.

How I regretted it immediately, feeling terrible for Mariana. Thinking of Henry.

I pulled away and fled the closet, Bram's room, the mansion. I ran to the woods on the Abbott property, but Bram caught up with me.

"I'm sorry," he said, out of breath. He dug the fingers of both hands through his dark hair. "I thought it was what you wanted."

"Why would I ever want *that*?" I yelled, knowing with my entire being it was a lie. "You're with Mariana!"

Bram shook his head. "No, I'm not."

"What do you mean?" I asked, stunned as much as relieved. And there was another feeling matted up with the others, one I couldn't quite pinpoint.

"We broke up."

"Why? What happened?"

"I don't want to get into it. But we're not together," he said, nearing me cautiously. "It's over. So you and I—"

"I can't," I cut in. "I shouldn't."

"Because of Henry," Bram said, his gray eyes pained. "You're in love with him."

I couldn't deny it. I'd never said it out loud before, but at the time, I believed it.

I still believe it, I think.

"Look, I had no idea that Adam liked Mariana," Bram says now. "She never even talked about him, and he never told me." His lips twist, gaze drifting away from me, like he's trying to conjure up some memory. "I knew they were weird around each other. But Adam has that effect on some people. He's loud and forceful where Mariana was quiet and gentle—she worked at the library, for God's sake. I just assumed they didn't like each other. Honestly, it was one of the reasons I was thinking of ending things with her."

"Like you did the first time," I say quietly, remembering that day in the woods, the summer before last. I thought I'd have more time to think about that day, to think over Bram's words. *So you and I...* But then a few days later, he was back with Mariana. "You never did tell me why you two broke up that first time."

Bram flushes. "Because it was humiliating." He runs his finger over the now-faint white line that used to be a scratch on the back of his hand. "Mariana asked me point-blank if I had feelings for *you*," he says, voice rough, "and...I didn't know how to answer that. I just knew I couldn't lie to her. So we broke up."

My heartbeat accelerates. It's pumping furiously in my chest, my head, my hands. Everywhere.

"I let myself hope you felt the same way, and then that day in my room with the painting and afterward in the woods...well, you made it pretty clear that it wasn't ever going to happen. So I told Mariana that, no, I didn't have feelings for you, and she took me back. Only that time"—he twists his lips—"I *did* lie to her."

"Bram," I say, heat fanning up my neck, "you don't know what you're saying."

"I do." He's looking at me like *I'm* the one who's confused. He shifts closer to me on the couch until our legs touch. "I was so sure you wanted me to kiss you that day." He pauses, as if replaying the moment in his mind, and my face heats. "Why didn't you kiss me back?"

I avert my eyes to the coffee table. "I told you. I thought you were with Mariana."

"You know what I mean. In the woods, when I told you that was over."

My chest is tight, my thoughts all scrambled. "Because you're my best friend."

"That's what you say about Henry too."

"Yes, but—"

"But with Henry, it's the truth," Bram cuts in. "You two are friends, always have been, always will be. For you and me, it's not true, Hayden." He reaches out slowly to cup my chin, gently tilting my head until I look him in the eyes. I can't help but notice that for the first time in ages, he used my real name. It sounds strange and intimate all at once, like he's broken me open. "You and I are *not* just friends. And I think you know that."

I swallow, the sound like a blast. "You're trying to mess with me," I breathe, my face only inches from his. "You love messing with me."

"Yes," he says unabashedly. "It's one of my favorite things. And I would like to continue doing it forever."

I glare at him, but I don't pull away. "Adam says that Henry loves me. You would do this to him? The way you did to Adam with Mariana?"

Bram's jaw clenches. "I didn't do anything to Adam," he grits out. "I told you, I didn't know about his feelings for Mariana." He lets out a breath through his teeth. "It explains a lot, though, about his state of mind this past year. His depression. He was dealing with a lot more than physical injuries."

He's right about that. The photo album in Adam's room was there because he missed Mariana. Whether their connection was all in his head or not, Adam has been torn up about losing the love of his life.

"As for Henry," Bram continues, "look, naturally he thinks he's in love with you. Who wouldn't be? Maybe he won't see it at first, but he's not the guy for you. And you are not the girl for him."

"Because I'm the girl for *you*," I say, only it fails to carry my intended sarcasm.

His gaze slips from my eyes to my lips, then down to my throat. "You didn't do anything wrong Friday night, if that's what you're worried about." He lets his hand fall from my face, and I hate myself, because I immediately want it back. "If Adam tries to make something out of this, I'll back you up."

"I'm not sure how much your word counts in a situation like this, but thanks."

"I only want you and Henry happy. You did nothing wrong in the garden, but I do think…" he starts but stops himself.

"What?" I press. "Tell me."

He bites his lower lip. "I think it's—nothing. It's nothing." Only the way he looks at me is the complete opposite of *nothing*.

"Tell me about the fire alarm," I whisper, my full voice trapped inside me.

"Like I said—"

"I can't trust you if you don't tell me," I interrupt.

His smirk is joyless. "That's not exactly how *trust* works."

"You want me to give you so much, Bram. But you won't give me a thing."

He hesitates, as if this thought might have resonated with him. "You don't actually want to know the answer to your own question. That's the truth."

"Tell me anyway."

He inhales, long and slow as he deliberates. "You might want to talk to the *love of your life*," he says, the words doused in irony, "since he's the one who asked me to pull that alarm."

"Henry?" My thoughts spin, everything colliding to a halt. "No—why would he do that?"

"I'm not sure. After the cafeteria, he wanted to talk. He said he needed me to do something for him. He said he'd taken care of the security cameras, figured out how to disable them remotely. I just had to pull the fire alarm and ask Adam to play lookout."

"What? But the camera—"

"He must've only managed to disable the indoor cameras. He either forgot about the ones at the back and the front of the school, or he didn't realize they were on a separate circuit. All he would tell me was that he was going to do something that would change all of our lives for the better. And I was too worried about Adam to ask questions. So before following Henry's orders, I went and found him, which was lucky because he was about to do something stupid, like vandalize Todd and Neil's lockers. He was really upset, but I managed to calm him down. Then I told him to play lookout while I pulled the alarm, just like Henry asked."

I can only stare. "And you just...did it?"

"It was Henry," Bram says, shrugging. "Sweet, smart, innocent Henry begged me to do this. I never thought any actual harm could come of it. I didn't think about cameras or consequences. It was my brother—the most sensible of the three of us. So yeah, I just did it."

Why the hell would Henry ask Bram to pull the fire alarm? "You didn't see Henry afterward?"

Bram shakes his head. "I started toward the back doors, so I could blend in with everyone else during the drill. But I noticed Adam wasn't coming, so I went looking for him on campus. With his state of mind and everything, panic took over. I had no idea what he was capable of. I finally found him in the car and sat with him the whole period."

Something isn't clicking yet. "How did you end up in the woods with Kennedy's body?"

Bram rubs at the back of his neck. "When everything happened with Mariana and the town turned against us, Kennedy stopped harassing me. I didn't see her or hear from her for a whole year. But the second she saw me back at school, it all started up again. Her texting me, sneaking onto our property, vandalizing shit to get my attention. She even showed up here in the house once. In the *house*. She was so aggressive, I had trouble getting her off me without hurting her. I was so upset, I said some of what I'd wanted to say. But not all of it. She'd caught me off guard, so I didn't have a chance to really sort out everything on my mind. About Mariana." His eyes go from angry to sad and distant, his mind seemingly just as trapped as his physical body, in this house, since Mariana died.

"Because in a way," he continues, "I blamed Kennedy for what happened. If she hadn't lied to Mariana, maybe Mariana wouldn't have been in the wrong place at the wrong time—I don't know. Anyway, the morning Kennedy…*you know*, she texted asking me to meet her in the woods behind the fields after school. Obviously, I wasn't going to meet her. There was no way. But then, the whole time I sat with Adam in the parking lot, I thought about what else I wanted to say to her. I'd planned to tell her it was never going to happen and to double down on reporting her stalking to the cops. And then, when the bell rang ending school, I left Adam in the car and went to the woods to finally confront her. Only instead of having that conversation, I found Kennedy dead."

A chill runs up my spine. "So then, Kennedy's phone—the one with her text messages to you—the cops must have it, right? They know that she texted you to meet her in the woods?" The very place she was killed.

"They haven't mentioned it," Bram says. "But yeah, I assume so. They'll toss it into their growing pile of evidence against me."

Only he wasn't even there when Kennedy was murdered. He was with Adam in the car, each one the other's alibis—alibis they couldn't share because of the parts they played in pulling the fire alarm.

A third person—a person wearing the exact hoodie I gifted the Abbott brothers—took Kennedy out to the woods where her body was discovered, only minutes later.

There's only one other person who could be in that video.

"The companions of our childhood always possess a certain power over our minds which hardly any later friend can obtain."

—*Frankenstein* by Mary Shelley

20

I need to get home," I tell Bram when I finally check the time. It's 2:14 a.m. Dad must be worried sick.

"Henry took care of it," Bram says in a calming voice. "I overheard him calling your dad and saying you'd fallen asleep on the couch. Like a perfect gentleman."

"And my dad was okay with that?" Even after his little warning about them in my room after Kennedy's murder? And the way my questions about the Abbott-Russo feud seemed to freak him out? I guess Dad meant what he said about not believing the rumors. He really trusts Henry.

For the first time in my life though, I'm not sure I do. Henry hasn't been forthcoming with me about any of this. He wouldn't tell me where he was during the "fire drill." He must be the person who headed into the woods with Kennedy, yet he never admitted it.

My stomach starts to turn. After Mariana died, Henry's name wasn't thrown around by the public nearly as much as his brothers'. He wasn't the boyfriend. He wasn't the brother who was there at the explosion.

Yet Henry *was* on the property that day, working on Mariana's car.

And he might've been the brother in the school security camera footage with Kennedy.

It can't mean what I think it means, and yet, goose bumps prickle up my arms.

"Here." Bram reaches for the blanket, draping it around my shoulders. "You should get some more sleep."

I shake my head. "I don't think I can." I keep thinking about Lydia's suspicions, that Kennedy was seeing an Abbott brother in secret. Maybe Kennedy was acting weird because she liked Bram, and he never reciprocated. It could account for her sneaking onto their property and acting secretive.

But what if that isn't the only explanation? What if, after so much rejection, Kennedy switched her sights to Henry?

"Bram," I say, tugging the corners of the blanket in front of my chest, "you seem so sure that Henry isn't for me. Is that because…? Did something happen between him and Kennedy?"

Bram's eyes widen. "What? Between Henry and Kennedy? I-I don't think so. I really don't think so."

"You don't tell each other everything, though."

"No, but..." Bram doesn't finish the statement, and a forest of dread crops up inside me.

Somehow, I need to get ahold of Henry's phone. If only to disprove this wild theory that's spinning through my head.

"I can drive you home," Bram offers. "Or..." He averts his eyes. "I can get Henry to drive you, if you'd be more comfortable."

"No," I say quickly. "I don't want to go."

He nods and gets up, but I reach out to touch his arm. "Will you stay up with me for a bit?"

The barest hint of a smile slides onto Bram's lips. "Yeah, of course." He lowers back down and picks up the remote, scrolling for something to watch.

"I'm sorry," I say, my eyes on the television screen now.

"Sorry for what?"

"For not trusting you."

He laughs. "Nobody trusts me, Phil. It's not like you're the first person to decide I'm dangerous."

Bram *is* dangerous, that's certain. But only in that I can't trust myself around him. I'm confused about my own feelings. "*I* trust you," I say, offering him a small smile. As his eyes meet mine, though, even sitting beside him on the couch feels different than it has in the past. "And I'm going to help you." I turn to face the screen again. "I won't let you go down for something you didn't do."

Except if Bram continues to hide the truth from the cops to protect his brothers, there may be nothing I can do. I think about telling him my plan, enlisting his help. It would be easier to get

Bram to swipe Henry's phone. But would he help me? If it meant betraying Henry?

I already know the answer. Bram pulled the fire alarm for Henry, after all, no questions asked. He has continued to keep the whole truth from the cops to protect Henry. There's no way I can include Bram on this.

Which means I'm on my own.

When I wake again, I wake curled up on the couch with the blanket draped over me, my head resting on a throw pillow. Only I'm not alone this time. Bram is slumped over at the opposite end of the couch. I can't help but look at his sleeping face, those sharp, beautiful features softened by the wash of blue light streaming in from the stained-glass window. Almost angelic, if I didn't know him to be a wicked pain in the ass.

The moment I start to get up, he stirs, reaching for the side of his neck. "Holy hell," he grumbles.

"That didn't look very comfortable," I say.

"It wasn't."

"You didn't have to sleep down here."

He shrugs. "I didn't want you to wake up alone in this weird place again. The first time you nearly got killed."

"I did," I say, though my leg barely hurts anymore.

Bram rubs his arms, the cold having apparently gotten to him. I slide closer on the couch, offering him half my blanket. He accepts, and I can't help but think how natural it would feel to rest my head on his shoulder.

My arm brushes his bicep, which is shockingly cold. "What happened to the fire?" I ask, glancing over at where the blackened logs sit.

"I got up at some point and put it out. We've had our share of fire mishaps."

This is true. Still, the feel of his frigid arm brings another thought to mind. "You never found your hoodie?"

"No, I'm sorry," he says. "And not just because it was a gift from you. I'm sorry because having lost it makes me look like a murderer."

A laugh escapes my lips, but I ram my shoulder into his arm. "You can't joke about this."

"It's either joke or despair," he says glumly.

"Did you check the lost and found?"

An amused smile lights his face. "Do I look like I'm in third grade?"

"Not even a little," I say without thinking, and the back of my neck heats.

He laughs softly, slipping out from under the blanket. "I will check the lost and found this week, okay? You want coffee?"

"Sure. I'll come help." I start to fold the blanket and fluff up the throw pillow, my thoughts on the missing hoodie. On whether or not someone could've taken it and made it look like Bram was with Kennedy before she died. I think of Lydia, who, according to Desiree, wanted the cheer captaincy more than anything. Lydia, who, without Kennedy around, now not only has that captaincy but is president of the student council.

A few minutes later, the coffee is brewing, and Bram and I are scrambling eggs on the stovetop.

Henry wanders in wearing pajama bottoms and a T-shirt, his hair messy. It's a good look on him as he nears us to say hi with a sleepy smile. "I see Mom hired the kitchen staff back."

"Except no one on staff bothered to do the shopping," I say, pouring him a cup of coffee. "So we can only make eggs and toast."

"Sounds perfect," Henry says, taking his coffee over to the kitchen nook. "Though the market remains a challenge, seeing as how we're banned from town and Uber Eats won't deliver up here."

"I'll go," Bram says. "I don't care what that idiot Mr. Swanson says."

"Bram," Henry says in mock surprise, as though he's only now noticed his brother's presence. "You're up early."

"This toast would be so much tastier with apple butter," Bram says. "Why don't you head over to the orchard and pick some apples?" he suggests, his eyes devilish.

Henry gives him a bored look. The apple orchard is all the way at the tail end of the property, a twenty-minute walk.

"Apple butter actually sounds really nice," I say.

Henry's eyes widen. "You're kidding, right?"

I offer my sweetest smile. "And if you get enough, I could make muffins later." I know I'm pushing it, but if I could get him out of the house for forty minutes—without his phone—I might be able to put the Kennedy-and-Henry theory to rest for good.

Henry looks to Bram now, who says with a shrug, "Hey, your girl wants apples."

My face ignites, and Henry goes just as red as he brings his mug to his lips.

"I can go," Bram offers, "if the walk is too much for you." He makes to pass Henry the spatula, and I consider throwing my coffee into his smug face.

"I'm happy to walk." Henry flashes his brother a caustic smile as he waves off the spatula and slides out of the nook. "Apple butter it is." He looks around as if missing something. When he pats his pajama pants, I double-check that they have no pockets. Zero pockets means zero phone.

I race to the cupboard where the family hangs the grocery bags. "Here," I say, yanking one down and pushing it at him. "To carry the apples in."

"Thanks," he mumbles, unable to make eye contact with me. Which is perfect, because I can't have him asking me to join him on this walk.

He wanders out, and I breathe a sigh of relief. But I quickly turn on Bram. "What the hell was that?"

"What was what?" he asks, scooping some eggs onto a plate, only the hint of a smirk on his lips.

"You know what," I snap. "That wasn't nice."

"I'm not nice," Bram says flippantly. "You remind me of this fact all the time. And yet, you know I'd walk a few state lines to get you those damned apples."

My stomach swims. Somehow, I do know. I know that Bram would do a lot more for me than trek far and wide for fruit. "I've got to call my dad," I say, leaving my coffee on the counter.

I hurry out the kitchen door and upstairs to Henry's room. I have to be quiet; Adam's room shares a wall with this one, and he's in there now.

To my dismay, Henry's phone isn't there on the bedside table.

I check the wrinkled bedsheets and the desk. I even root around in the drawer, but it's nowhere to be found. When I start to wonder if he somehow had the phone on him after all, I spot the desk chair, rolled over to the corner. My spirits soar. The phone is resting on the seat.

I tiptoe over, finding it locked. Fortunately, I know Henry's passcode. He had a phone long before I did and let me use it often to call my parents.

But when I try the passcode, it fails.

All the questions and suspicions I've had since Bram's story last night trickle into my brain. Why would Henry change his passcode? Have I been a fool this entire time? Has Henry been lying? He told Adam he has feelings for me.

Was he actually seeing Kennedy in secret?

And how am I supposed to get into his phone? I can't ask Bram for help. Not just because he's infuriating, but because he'd never betray Henry. It was hard enough getting him to tell me the truth about the fire alarm last night. He'd never give me the passcode.

A traitorous thought sneaks in: Bram wouldn't share the passcode, but Adam might.

My mind drifts back to that huge blowup between Henry and Adam last year before Christmas, right outside these rooms. Henry completely lost it in a way I'd never witnessed before. There's bad blood there. The question is whether or not I'm willing to betray both of them by taking advantage of it.

I know the answer the moment I ask myself. Defeated, I head back toward the chair, only my gaze hitches on Henry's desk drawer, which I somehow left half-open.

I pad back over and push on it, but something inside keeps the drawer from shutting all the way. I dig my hand inside to free up whatever's blocking it, and my fingers light on what feels like a paperback novel.

As I tug it free, I hear a *rip*. The sound of paper tearing. My heart thumps, and I carefully twist and maneuver the book until it's free.

I'm holding a copy of *The Strange Case of Dr. Jekyll and Mr. Hyde*. Luckily, the cover seems to be intact. I flip through the pages in search of what tore, finding it marked up the way we were supposed to annotate our outside reading novels last year.

But I thought Henry was reading *Frankenstein*, like Adam. He had asked to borrow my copy.

Maybe he didn't like it and moved on to something else. I continue flipping, and sure enough, there's a page torn near the end. But the way the novel was crumpled up at the back of the desk drawer like an afterthought, I doubt Henry will notice.

When I go to put it back, the door creaks behind me.

I turn, finding Henry in the doorway. He's clutching the empty plastic bag in one white-knuckled fist.

He isn't smiling.

HENRY

ONE WEEK BEFORE KENNEDY RUSSO'S MURDER

"At that time my virtue slumbered; my evil, kept awake by ambition, was alert and swift to seize the occasion; and the thing that was projected was Edward Hyde."

—*The Strange Case of Dr. Jekyll and Mr. Hyde* by Robert Louis Stevenson

Henry had been back at school only two weeks when Kennedy Russo asked if he'd tutor her in math. "You're the smartest kid in this school," she said. "And I'll pay you."

Henry didn't need the money, and he was pretty sure Kennedy knew that. He wondered what game she was playing—if she even needed help in math.

"Maybe we could meet at your house for an hour or so after school? Please." She made a pouty face and batted her eyelashes like a movie vixen. It sort of worked on Henry, who saw no reason to say no. Kennedy Russo had been Henry's first crush, back when they were in grade school and she let him borrow her blue crayon. She'd never traveled in his circle, though, existing only in his periphery. A beautiful yet alien-like, elusive being.

But now she was standing in front of him, asking to come to his house.

Henry thought of Hayden then, his best friend whom he loved more than anything. Their friendship had started to feel different lately, and he wasn't quite sure about this new trajectory. Plus, Hayden had never expressed any of this, so it remained merely a feeling. If anything, Henry suspected Hayden felt a certain way about Bram, which wouldn't be surprising; every girl Henry had ever been interested in only seemed to notice Bram. And Henry sometimes wondered if he himself was actually interested in Hayden that way at all, or if he was simply fearful of Bram taking her away from him.

Either way, Henry wouldn't be doing anything *wrong* by tutoring Kennedy. He was allowed to have other friends. And Kennedy had as much sway around school as her father had around town. If she and Henry became friends—or more than friends—maybe the school would finally accept the brothers again.

"I guess," he said, fiddling with his glasses to give his fingers something to do.

"Okay, great!" She smiled and clasped her hands together. "Will your brother be there?"

"Brother?" Henry felt like an idiot for not thinking of it sooner: Kennedy probably wanted to avoid Adam. After the school board fallout, Dr. Russo had essentially dropped Adam as a patient, and

Henry was sure his brother didn't want anything to do with the doctor's daughter, either. "Maybe we should meet somewhere else," he said.

He watched Kennedy's face fall. Maybe this girl only wanted to see the inside of his house, he thought. It wouldn't be the first time a schoolmate befriended him just so they could brag to everyone else that they got inside the "castle."

Just then he remembered that Adam had a physical therapy appointment after school. "You know what? My house is fine."

"Thanks so much, Henry. You're the best." This surprised him; as of a moment ago, he wasn't aware she even knew his name. She hugged him, which surprised him even more—especially because he liked it, the feel of her arms wrapped around him, her hair brushing the side of his face. But what surprised him the most was how her scent tugged at his memory. It was cloyingly sweet, like brown sugar and blackberries. There was a hint of vanilla that made her smell almost like one of the berry crisp desserts Hayden sometimes made, freshly removed from the oven. Only that wasn't quite it.

She pulled back, and the scent picked and pulled at the strings wound deep in Henry's memory, giving him an unsettling sense of déjà vu. He felt frustrated that he couldn't pinpoint it.

"Just, uh, don't mention it to your brother, okay?" Kennedy said.

Henry nodded, knowing she was right. They had to keep this tutoring session to themselves. Maybe he could take her to his room, or they could work under the gazebo. It was a nice day outside after all.

As Kennedy waved goodbye and headed off to class, Bram made his way down the hall. "What was that about?"

"Nothing." For some reason, Henry didn't want Bram to know about Kennedy. Maybe because he knew it was a betrayal in a way, considering Adam's feelings about the Russos.

"Nothing," Bram repeated, clearly unconvinced.

As he eyed Henry suspiciously, the scent memory finally came to him. Mariana had worn this same perfume. Henry had once smelled that scent on Bram in the car the year before; he remembered teasing Bram about how good he smelled after spending time with her. He got a silly sense of relief now that he'd put it together.

"Be careful with her," Bram said in his annoying older-brother voice. "The apple doesn't fall far from the tree."

"Yeah," Henry said, though irritation needled at him. Of course no girl could pay anyone but *Bram* the time of day.

Henry instructed Kennedy to meet him at the gate. He waited for her and, when she arrived, offered to carry her backpack. "You're such a gentleman," she said, and for the first time in his life, it sounded like a compliment. It wasn't like when his brothers said the same thing to tease him.

She handed the backpack to him, smiling with red-painted lips. "I've never been inside your house before."

Henry's heart sank; maybe she really did only want the castle tour. "I was actually thinking we'd hang out in the backyard." He waited for the look of disappointment.

"That sounds perfect," she said, her arm brushing his as they ambled side by side on the walkway.

They wove through the gardens, pushing aside the massive overgrown branches of the magnolia tree that no one ever bothered to trim. As their feet crunched over the once-pink blooms, now withered brown and scattered over the path, Henry half expected Kennedy to start snapping photos, the way Adam's middle school girlfriend had. But she simply took in her surroundings, periodically looking back over her shoulder at the mansion, almost like she was overwhelmed or nervous.

"Adam isn't here," Henry assured her.

"Oh, I know." She smiled, and he helped her get settled at the gazebo table.

"I'll grab some snacks. What can I get you to drink?"

She smiled at him like he was a cute little puppy dog. "You're just the sweetest thing, aren't you?" Henry wasn't sure how he felt about this. "Water would be great."

"Be right back." Henry strode back to the house to gather refreshments, still going over her words.

But when he returned to the gazebo, Kennedy wasn't there. Her backpack was on the seat, math textbook spread open on the table, its pages flapping in the wind. A red spiral notebook and pencil lay there too, and Henry wondered if she'd gotten bored and decided to wander the gardens.

He didn't want to call out her name in case it drew Bram from his dark cave of a room. Instead, he set out the snacks and water bottles, and sat down in the seat adjacent to hers. Another gentlemanly move; he wouldn't sit directly beside her unless she asked.

When he reached for a chip from the bowl, Henry spotted a tube of lipstick wedged in between the textbook and the notebook. The tube looked familiar, and this time, Henry didn't have to rack his brain for where he'd seen it before.

The day of Mariana's accident, Henry had found this same tube of Raving Red on the oil-slicked ground of the garage where the boys had been working on her car. He'd been in a state of shock when the ambulance and the fire department finally left. He found the tube of lipstick and assumed it had fallen from the car or from Mariana's purse when she came to check on it. She was chronically disorganized, always forgetting something in the boys' car or up at the house. Plus, no other women had been in the shop in months. Still in a daze, Henry picked up the tube and shoved it to the back of the workstation, planning on returning it to Mariana whenever she returned from the hospital.

Only Mariana never returned. That tube of lipstick was probably still sitting in the exact same spot on the workstation.

And now, here was the same brand of lipstick in the same shade with Kennedy's things.

Henry knew it wasn't a huge coincidence for two high school girls to own the same lipstick, or to own the same perfume. But it was strange that Kennedy had this particular tube of lipstick and a particular perfume, and that Mariana had owned both.

Something wasn't adding up. He popped off the tube's lid, revealing the vibrant red waxy stick within. He'd seen Kennedy's lips today, this same vibrant shade of red.

Henry didn't know much about makeup, but he knew Mariana didn't wear a lot and that her lips never looked like Kennedy's.

The conclusion seemed glaringly obvious then: Mariana had never worn this lipstick.

A sense of unease flooded Henry. He got up and searched the gardens, but there was no sign of Kennedy. Thinking she may've gone in search of a bathroom, he started in the direction of the house. He found it odd that they'd never crossed paths, but he'd taken a while in the kitchen, trying to make everything perfect.

Inside, finding the guest bathroom unoccupied, Henry wandered from room to room. He still didn't dare call out her name. If he hadn't seen her belongings outside, he would've assumed she'd ditched him.

When he heard voices coming from upstairs, he followed the sound to Bram's room. Unable to fight off his curiosity, Henry tiptoed closer and pressed his ear up against the door to listen.

"You don't have a girlfriend anymore," Kennedy said. "Why can't we—"

"Because I want nothing to do with you," his brother's low voice cut in. "When are you going to get that through your head?"

"Never, Bram. I love you."

All the blood rushed to Henry's face. Kennedy was in love with Bram?

He felt like a fool. She had never been worried about *Adam* spotting her here with Henry. She'd never wanted to tour the mansion. She'd been hoping to see Bram.

"And I've been telling you for over a year that this is not going to happen," Bram said. "Nothing has changed."

"*Everything* has changed," she argued. "You're single; you're back at school. When I see you, I can't think about anything but us together."

"You need to get out of here. And if you show up at my house again," Bram said, voice cool yet bladed, "I'm calling the cops. Stop messing with Henry to get to me."

"You'll change your mind," she said, sniffling.

"No, I won't."

"Is there someone else?"

"Kennedy, get out of my house. Tell Henry you're feeling sick and go home."

"Please, Bram," she begged.

"Let go of me," he said, firmly. "You're—I don't want to have to—"

The voices were moving closer to the door. Henry hurried down the hall and descended the stairs. He couldn't face Kennedy as she made up some excuse to leave, not with the apparent trouble he went to with the snacks on the table, the drinks. Instead, he fled out the front door and raced to the garage.

Apart from investigators, no one had really been in the shop in a year. Henry had taken to hiding his invention in here, stopping in from time to time to borrow tools. This time, he was looking for something else. That tube of lipstick he'd stashed on top of the workstation.

At first, he didn't see it. Dust had collected. Parts had continued to arrive before the boys had a chance to cancel the orders, and they were now stacked high on the workstation.

But Henry moved everything aside, and there it was, covered in a thin layer of soot: the lipstick tube in the same shade as the one with Kennedy's school things.

He doubted very much that the lipstick had been Mariana's. So then, had it been Kennedy's? Was the tube Henry found with her things a replacement for the one she'd lost?

Bram said Kennedy had been chasing him for over a year. He said he'd rejected the girl's advances, and yet somehow, he smelled like her. That sickly sweet perfume scent. She'd clearly been throwing herself at him, enough that Henry had picked up her scent on him. Despite the fact that Bram had been dating Mariana, Kennedy had been obsessed.

And Henry had found Kennedy's lipstick in this garage the day Mariana was killed.

21

Henry steps into the room, dropping the empty bag at his feet, fist still clenched at his side.

I let the novel fall into the open desk drawer. "I'm sorry, I—"

He crosses the room in a flash. "Why are you going through my things?" he demands, reaching past me to push the drawer shut.

It slams, and I flinch. Not knowing what to say, I back away. For the first time in my life, I'm actually afraid of my best friend.

"Henry?" a deep voice calls from the doorway. Bram wanders inside, and I feel a whoosh of relief. "Sorry, I sent her in here to grab a—oh, there's one." He ambles over, picking up a pen from the holder on the desk. "I can't seem to find any in my room, and we all know Adam can't read or write."

Henry's eyes narrow as he scrutinizes us. "Aren't there pens downstairs?"

"Apparently not," Bram says lightly. "Phil, you ready to write up that grocery list?" He keeps his focus on Henry. "She offered to accompany me to the market. Isn't that sweet of her?"

Henry remains unamused. "She's sweet all right. Is it okay if I speak with her in private, please?"

Bram's eyes flick to mine in an unspoken question.

I nod, letting him know it's okay. Henry seems to have calmed down in his brother's presence. Still, I shiver, thinking of the way his temper flipped like a switch.

Bram takes the pen and ambles out of the room, glancing over his shoulder at us before leaving the door open.

"Are you going to tell me what's actually going on?" Henry asks the moment his brother leaves.

I consider this. All signs point to Henry having a secret relationship with Kennedy. To Henry being the hooded figure with Kennedy moments before she was murdered.

Henry, who looked like he might have done something to me if Bram hadn't intervened.

But I can't forget that he's *my* Henry, the boy who sat next to me on the school bus every day until he was old enough to drive. The boy who stayed up with me on the phone every night after my mom died. The boy who listened to me cry when my dad went through a breakdown and deleted the home videos because he couldn't bear hearing his dead wife's voice on them.

Hasn't he at least earned the chance to explain?

"I know you asked Bram to pull that fire alarm," I admit, leaning against his desk. "I know it was you in that school security footage with Kennedy the day she died." It may've been a bluff, but his face falls, confirming everything. "I think you were the boy Lydia was talking about, the one who was secretly dating Kennedy. Maybe secretly because you knew Adam wouldn't approve. Or maybe there were…other reasons." Red-hot shame creeps up my neck.

"*Dating* her?" Henry shakes his head. "Hayden, no. I told you last week, none of us were dating Kennedy."

"But you knew something, didn't you? About why she was on the property like Lydia said."

"Because she was stalking Bram!" Henry pushes his glasses back up the bridge of his nose. "I couldn't exactly tell anyone—especially not the cops—that my brother wanted to get rid of that girl. That he had a motive for killing her!"

He's right about that. Telling the cops that Bram wanted Kennedy out of his life would've been detrimental. "So what happened?" I ask, not sure I'm ready for the answer. "You were trying to help Bram? You had him set off the fire alarm so you could confront Kennedy in the woods, and then…" I don't finish the thought, that something happened there in the woods, something that left Kennedy lying on the forest floor with blood seeping from a wound in her head.

"I was trying to help Bram, yes," Henry says, taking a seat on his desk chair, "but it was more complicated than whatever you're thinking. It was about more than asking her to leave Bram alone." He proceeds to tell me about a tutoring fiasco involving Kennedy. About how obsessed she sounded in Bram's room. About finding Kennedy's lipstick in the garage the day Mariana died.

It tracks with Bram's version of events—at least up until the lipstick.

"I thought," Henry continues, "that Kennedy might've been there in the garage the day Mariana died. I tried talking to her at school, but she refused. She didn't want to talk or even be seen with me. She threatened to call for help if I so much as got near her. I tried getting her number off Bram's phone, maybe to pose as him in order to get her to meet me. But he must've deleted all traces of her.

"That's when I came up with the plan to set off the emergency alarm. While everyone was forced out of the school to the fields, too distracted to notice the two of us, I thought it would be my only chance. I considered pulling her off to the side yard, hoping that if she did protest, the alarm would drown out the sound of her voice." Red streaks up the sides of his neck. "It didn't come to that, though. I was able to trick her into coming with me to the woods. All I had to do was tell her that Bram was waiting for her. She seemed confused at first. Apparently, she'd asked him to meet her *after* school. On the way there, she pulled out her phone, like she didn't quite believe me. I knew why. I'd been trying so hard to talk to her while Bram had been firm that he never wanted to speak to her again. In the end, though, she agreed to come with me." Henry pats down his disheveled hair, and seeing him in his pajama bottoms, his sea green eyes wide, I don't have to wonder why Kennedy trusted him.

"I only planned on confronting her," Henry says, rubbing at his face. "I wanted to catch her off guard, just to find out if my theory held any weight. That day she came over for math tutoring and I overheard her conversation with Bram, she didn't sound…right. But I had no idea if not being *right* meant she was capable of killing a girl."

He inhales, turning away from me to pace the room. "Well, she was furious when I asked if she'd been in the garage the day Mariana died. She denied it, even after I showed her the lipstick." Henry frowns, crossing his arms over his chest. "She threatened to leave, since Bram clearly wasn't there in the woods. So I acted indifferent, saying the cops could just test it for her DNA. And that's when she panicked and demanded I give her the lipstick." His speech comes faster now, breathier. "I told her I would, in exchange for the truth. I said I was sure Bram would be with her now, as long as she confessed. That after the hell she put him and our family through the past year, she owed it to him." He adjusts his glasses. "It didn't take long for her to cave. She started crying, begging me not to tell anyone that on the day Mariana died, she'd tampered with a wire in Mariana's engine while we were out of the shop and then lured Bram away into the woods."

My breath hitches. Kennedy had murdered Mariana Sanchez. And Henry found out.

"All her begging did was spark this overwhelming need to tell

Bram and Adam," Henry continues. "We finally had answers. Our names would be cleared." He stops pacing to meet my gaze, his eyes flooded with sorrow. With regret. "I started walking away, trying to leave the woods. Kennedy was shouting for me to come back. She said I'd promised her the tube of lipstick, but I didn't stop. Then her voice was lost beneath the fire alarm, just as I'd hoped. I headed through the east side of campus, straight for the parking lot. That's all I know. I have no idea what happened after that."

I wish I knew if he was telling the truth. Up until last week, I didn't think Henry was capable of lying to me or to anyone else. But now I think he's more than capable. Now I think that Henry's high intelligence makes lying easy for him. That he's able to think two steps ahead of everyone else and craft the exact story he needs to tell.

"Part of me thought maybe Kennedy couldn't handle the truth getting out," Henry says solemnly, "so she…you know." His gaze lowers. "But Bram said it couldn't have been a suicide, not considering how she looked in the woods." He shuts his eyes as if the gruesome images are right here in the room, displayed before him.

"It wasn't suicide," I say, remembering with a shiver how Kennedy's head was split open, her blood pooling over the forest floor. "But maybe it was an accident, Henry," I press on, even as he shakes his head. "Bram told me Kennedy got aggressive with him, physical even. Maybe she tried to grab you, to keep you from telling. No one would blame you for defending yourself."

"No," Henry says, stepping toward me with his hands folded together. "I swear to you, all we did was talk. She begged me not to say anything, but she never touched me. And I *never* laid a finger on her. When I left the woods, she was alive."

He's looking at me, pleading with his eyes, awaiting a response. I don't have one.

The doorbell below draws Henry's attention, rescuing me from his searing gaze. The sound is followed by loud knocking.

"Some sort of prank?" Henry asks, moving toward the door.

"You're not expecting anyone?"

"Not unless Mr. Swanson decided to pay us a visit."

Through the wall, I hear Adam's thunderous footsteps. Then his voice booms into the hallway, "Is anyone going to get the door?"

I follow Henry out as Bram emerges, dressed for the day in his usual dark jeans and a black graphic T-shirt. Seeing us, Adam retreats back into his room, slamming the door.

The knocking continues as we make our way down the stairs. Just before we reach the door, a muffled voice from the other side yells, "Police! Open up!"

My heart seizes. Police?

Henry and Bram exchange a fearful look. "Go," Henry tells Bram, batting his brother away from the door before opening it.

Bram doesn't obey, remaining at his side when Detective Wilson says, "Bram Abbott, you're under arrest for the murder of Kennedy Russo. You have the right to remain silent." In the commotion, Henry tries to ask questions, demands to see the warrant.

But Bram remains stoic. He practically turns his own back to Detective Chase, helping the man cuff his wrists.

My eyes start to tear, and I want to yell at him to *do* something. To ask for his lawyer, resist somehow.

But then I realize that he's turned to me. "Hey, Phil," he says tipping his head low to meet my eyes, his use of the nickname pulling us back to when we were kids. To when things were light and easy, everything a joke to him. "It's going to be okay. I'm okay." Even as the cuffs click shut and Detective Chase yanks him backward, Bram offers a small smile. "Be strong."

But I can't be, not when they're dragging him off to jail. "Isn't there something you can do?" I ask Henry as Adam appears behind us now, already shouting at the detectives.

"I don't—" Henry turns to Adam. "Get Mr. Swanson on the phone."

Adam nods, pulling his phone from his pocket as he ducks back inside the house.

But it's too late. The detectives are walking Bram down the cobblestone path to the circular driveway where their cruiser is waiting. Watching him placed inside, calm as ever while the world is shattering all around him, feels like some vital piece of me is floating off down the creek. I want to run after him. Only I know that won't help things.

Unable to catch my breath as the car drives off, I lower onto the porch steps. Behind me, Henry is on the phone with his dad. "Just get back, okay? Bram needs you."

He hangs up and descends the steps, standing on the cobblestone path. "This is bad."

"How can they have enough evidence to arrest him?" I ask, trying not to cry. "Just his image on a security camera doesn't prove anything."

"They already subpoenaed his phone," Henry says. "Our lawyer called this morning."

"What? Bram never said—"

"I'm sure he didn't want to worry you," Henry says, lips twisting as he looks up at me. "But by now, they know that Bram was texting Kennedy and that he was supposed to meet her in the woods. They know he wanted her to leave him alone, that he pulled the fire alarm. They'll simply fill in the rest."

"Even if it's not the truth?"

"They need someone to blame. All signs point to Bram." He nibbles his lower lip. "I should tell them it's me in the video with Kennedy. It's all my fault anyway."

"No, Henry. Then they'll pin it on *you*."

He shrugs. "I deserve it. If I'd gone to the cops about Kennedy rather than confronting her, none of this would've happened."

"I understand why you didn't," I say, trying with everything in me not to cry. "Kennedy was a town darling, and her dad has a lot of influence. You needed proof. But I think we have to tell them about Kennedy and Mariana now. It's our only—"

"It will give Bram an even bigger motive," Henry cuts in, his eyes wide. "We can *never* tell the cops that Kennedy killed Bram's girlfriend."

A wave of nausea hits me. He's right. It could look like Bram was seeking revenge—that he found out the truth behind who stole the love of his life. That it sparked a hatred so intense that he murdered Kennedy in a crime of passion.

I must look as ill as I feel, because Henry moves up the steps to place a hand on my shoulder. "I'll get you some water."

"No, you don't have to...I'm going home." He shouldn't be wasting time worrying about me when his brother has just been hauled off to jail.

"You are?" he asks, and when I look up, there's disappointment in his face.

I nod. "Your parents and lawyer will be here soon. I'm in the way."

"Can I call you later?" he asks, his voice meek, sounding less like the man he's become and more like the boy I used to play pirates with. "I could really use my best friend."

"Of course," I say as he tugs me up by the hand. When he wraps me into a hug, I hug him back, desperately wanting to believe he's the boy who sat and held me while I cried over my mom. "Let me know if there's anything I can do."

"Thanks," he says, forcing a smile for my benefit. It's almost impossible to believe he's the same person whose anger less than an hour ago incited true fear in me. That he's the one who violently erupted toward Adam last year.

But he is, and that's why I'm not sure I believe his story. That's why a single question keeps turning over in my mind: If Henry didn't kill Kennedy, who did?

22

I can tell the moment our car pulls up in front of the school that this is going to be the Monday morning from hell. "Wow," Dad says, staring out at the scene.

The first days after Kennedy's murder, a few reporters from local stations parked outside, trying to get students to comment on the case. Now, there are dozens, many from big-city news stations, all here asking people who don't even know Bram Abbott to talk about him.

Henry and Adam are staying home, but I send off a quick warning text just to make sure. Don't come near school today

Of course, Lydia Costas is speaking to a reporter when my dad drops me off at the curb. "Kennedy was my best friend, so obviously

I knew she was seeing Bram Abbott," she says, "even though she didn't tell anyone else. And now that she's gone, it all makes sense. He always seemed like the quiet serial killer type."

I push myself into the frame, startling Lydia. "Bram Abbott is not a killer," I spit. "The police need to let him go and find the person who actually did this."

"What's your name, hon?" the reporter asks.

"Hayden Phillips, and Bram is my..." I freeze, getting absurdly hung up on Bram's words from the other night. *You and I are not just friends.* "Bram is someone I trust with my life," I say. "And he deserves better than what the cops and everyone at this school are saying about him."

When the reporter thanks me, I turn to find Lydia eyeing me icily, her arms crossed. "You're delusional," she says. "And you'll probably end up being the next dead girl."

An unsettling sensation crawls up my spine. Was that a threat?

I should get out of here. I didn't even want to come today, but the only other option was sitting around at home, worrying about Bram's arrest.

Last night, Henry called me. And even though I'd promised to be there for him, I couldn't answer. I was too upset. He said he's the reason Bram is in jail, and deep down, I can't help but agree. I know he wanted to tell the police it was him on the surveillance video, and *I'm* the one who stopped him. At the same time, I resent him for protecting himself, essentially surrendering his brother in the process. For not being the person I thought he was.

Since I still needed an update on Bram, I called Adam. He said his parents had returned home and that Mr. Swanson was working tirelessly to get Bram out. If he fails, they'll have to wait until his hearing to try getting him out on bail. With their fortune and his parents' travel habits, though, Adam said bail wasn't a guarantee. The judge could easily label Bram a flight risk.

After I got off the phone with Adam, I sobbed into my pillow. Bram had instructed me to be strong, and so far, I've failed miserably. Everything seems hopeless.

I stop at my locker, next to two baby-faced freshmen. "Bram Abbott isn't the first serial killer in his family," one of them whispers to the other. "His ancestors were poor until they killed the family who used to live in the castle. The Abbotts tortured the family first and then buried the bodies in the gardens. Bram has been using the same torture devices they left behind in the dungeon."

That's it. I slam my locker door, startling them both. There's no way I'm going to last the day. Though it serves Bram right for doing absolutely nothing to quell that dungeon rumor.

Hoisting my backpack on again, I head out the front door where, according to Adam, no one cares much about the camera that will catch me ditching.

The camera crews outside, however, are a different story. I make it all of two steps when someone calls my name. I turn around, pulse pounding in my ears.

"Hey! Where are you going?" Sage scurries after me.

"Nowhere." My shoe draws a circle over the sidewalk. "I just can't be here today."

"Yes, you can," Sage says, hooking her arm through mine and attempting to guide me back toward the building. "Today is our student council meeting at lunch, and I'm not going to sit there all by myself and listen to Lydia Costas lead it."

"You're not going to be all by yourself, Sage," I say, holding my ground. "The rest of the student council will be there."

"You know what I mean," she says with an eye roll. "You and I are the OGs. No one else will back me up if I need to start a coup to take over the presidency or at the very least, get the homecoming theme changed. Did you hear she wants to make it an underwater theme? What the hell are we supposed to do? Dress as mermaids?"

I cringe. "That does sound horrific."

"See? That's why you can't leave."

I frown and tug my arm away. I'm not looking for an argument, but half of this mess is Sage's doing. "So you want me to help *you*, when you completely ignored the favor I asked you?" If it weren't for her, that video of setting off the fire alarm would've been for the cops' eyes only. Now everyone in town is convinced that they were right about Bram Abbott, "the Girlfriend Killer," all along.

She sighs. "Look, I'm sorry about Bram. I know you're close with the Abbotts. And even though I don't understand *why* you're friends with them, I'm sorry that you're hurting. I guess I'm trying to find a way to make it up to you."

"By forcing me back in there, where everyone is talking about my friend? Who isn't even here to defend himself?"

"I'll tell them to shut up, okay? I may not agree with you on Bram's innocence, but I am a believer in our justice system. Bram deserves his day in court."

How noble of her. "Unfortunately," I say, crossing my arms, "the court of public opinion doesn't tend to weigh evidence. You've always been so sure it was an Abbott. Why?"

"There's just something off about them," she says, picking at a pink fingernail. "And Bram was dating my cousin. Sometimes, the simplest answer is right in front of you. It's always the boyfriend."

"So much for innocent until proven guilty."

"The video *is* proof," she says.

My chest tightens. "Okay, Sage, I tried. But I want to go."

"I'll come with you," she says, already following me through the parking lot.

"*You're* going to ditch school?" I ask, keeping my pace and calling her bluff. Sage doesn't get Bs, and she certainly doesn't ditch school.

"I can tell you need a friend right now."

I wouldn't call Sage a *friend*, not anymore. But seeing as how the Abbotts probably won't be back in school again, she may be the closest thing I have to one at Silver Creek High. She admitted something to me at the coffee shop on Saturday—that she's held a grudge against me, because after Mariana's death, I chose the Abbotts over her. Maybe she thinks we can be friends again, now that they're not here.

I'm not sure I can forgive her, especially if Bram gets convicted for a crime he never committed. Not that it matters how I feel or what I think, since she's still following me. The forested area behind the athletic fields is still a crime scene, so I take the street in front of the school for a while, entering the residential district. Sage follows. She stays silent, and I'm glad for it, though I get the feeling she's antsy to say something, or maybe just antsy about ditching.

When a car slows beside us, the driver no doubt eyeing the two of us out on the street during school hours, I duck between two houses and head down the path that winds through the woods.

"So I heard you were defending Bram out there with the reporters," Sage says, putting an end to the blessed silence. "Pretty wild."

"I don't believe he killed Kennedy," I answer truthfully. I wish I could lay out all the evidence I've collected, just to get one person on my side. To convince her that it couldn't have been Bram. Except I know that the very information that could vindicate Bram could also give him a clear motive.

And it could also point the cops directly to Henry. Instead, I add, "I know Bram can be withdrawn when you don't know him. But off the football field, he's not violent. He's caring and—"

"Oh my god, Hayden," she says, stopping momentarily to curse when her dress catches on a bramble. "Tell me you're not in love with that lunatic."

I start to correct her about the *in love* part, but my tongue fails me. Because the second her words echo back through my head, I realize they're true. Somehow, in trying to fight off my feelings for Bram, I only fell harder for him.

"You've fallen straight into the Girlfriend Killer's trap," Sage says as we press deeper into the woods. "And here I thought you were obsessed with Henry. You're always making eyes at each other in class. Which is also so, completely wrong. Sure, he might look harmless. Not like Bram, who looks like he'd be happy to slit your throat and drink the blood. But he—"

"That's disgusting, Sage." Though I get what she means about Henry, how I was drawn to something about him that was possibly an act. I think I've been telling myself I loved him because I believed that he was the safe choice. *Harmless.* And that Bram was a risk I couldn't take.

And now, nothing about Henry feels safe. He's cunning and volatile, and I'm not sure he's telling the truth about what happened in the woods with Kennedy. And if Henry is lying about Kennedy, who's to say he didn't invent that whole story about how Mariana died?

Maybe one of the Abbotts really is a serial killer.

As hard as it is to admit it—even to myself—the person who truly makes me feel safe and secure is Bram. The person I'd call if I were in trouble would be Bram. Of course, I realize all of this now that he's locked away.

"I'm just saying we're all a little safer now that that bloodsucker is behind bars," Sage says, brushing another leaf from her dress.

Irritation gnaws at the base of my skull. "Can we please steer the conversation away from the Abbotts?"

"Sorry," Sage mutters as we take the shortcut through the thick ferns toward Creek Bridge. Apart from the birds chirping overhead, we push through the feathery fronds in silence. When the lapping of the creek drifts through the trees, I bat a loose hair out of my eyes and speed my steps until the clearing.

It's been ages since I've been out here, and with the familiar sounds come the bittersweet memories. I think of the summers spent swimming with the boys, splashing around and making bets on how long we could remain submerged. The water, sourced from the mountain springs, is dangerously cold year-round, and we never lasted long.

The wooden bridge stretching from one side of the ravine to the other is old and rickety, its low railing missing beams in places. When I was little, Mom used to make me hold her hand as we crossed it and forbade me from playing on it. Since her passing, it's become a place to sit and remember her, to listen to the birds and the water down below.

I wish I could do that now. I've never needed Mom as much as this moment. Dad is there for me, but it's not the same. Instead, I have Sage, who is not exactly an objective or even sympathetic listening ear.

"Shoot," she says, having touched the rail. Now she has to extract a splinter from her finger.

My phone dings from the outside pouch of my backpack, and I dig it out to find a text from Henry.

Please believe in me.

My chest feels heavy. This distance between us is something I never could've predicted in a million years. I had such a different vision of our future.

I read the text again, noting his choice of phrasing. He's not asking me to simply believe his words but in *him*. My friend. The words speak to more than my brain; they appeal to everything I've experienced. To countless moments by his side.

And I get a sickening sense of guilt, because I never should've doubted him. Over the years, I can't think of one time that he's intentionally ignored my texts like I've been doing to him. He's never let me down in a time of need.

The night Dad deleted our home videos, I called Henry, sobbing. He dropped everything to come sit with me here on the bridge. He brought a blanket, and the two of us lay down right on these boards to watch the stars glimmer overhead where the canopy of trees parted. He asked me to tell a story about Mom, and then he listened, the way Dad simply couldn't. Not back then. One story led to another, and before we knew it, hours had passed. Mom's favorite song, or at least the song she always sang to me, "Daydream Believer," was one her mother had sang to her when she was a child. When I told Henry, he started to hum it as we lay there, staring at the sky.

Sage glances over to see the phone in my hand. "Who are you texting?"

"Nobody," I say, putting my phone away.

"Henry's a sicko, Hayden. I tried to tell you." Over in the trees, an animal rustles—something large, possibly a deer. I start to turn, but Sage's next sentence slices through the air like a knife. "How demented do you have to be to take a girl to the woods and hit her over the head with a rock until she dies?"

"What?" I ask.

An uncanny sensation is zinging up the back of my neck. How does she know the way Kennedy was killed? I saw the body, and not even I know the details, apart from what Lydia let slip. "Why did you say *Henry*?"

Sage's eyes widen. "I did? Oh, whatever. The triplets are all the same to me. I meant *Bram*. Like I said, though, I don't trust anyone in that whole family."

"Who told you how Kennedy was killed?"

Sage turns to face the creek, as if admiring its beauty. But she's playing with the collar of her dress, and the skin at her clavicle and all over her neck is blotchy red. "I think it's common knowledge. My mom is a friend of the Russos, so they probably told her, and she told me."

"Right," I say, but I don't buy it.

Did Sage see Henry in the woods? Did she see how Kennedy was killed?

Or is there more to it than that?

I try to remember what Henry told me, but my adrenaline is kicking in hard. My heart is pumping louder than the water below, and I can barely string a thought together. He confronted Kennedy about Mariana's death. She'd confessed to tampering with Mariana's car.

Kennedy killed Mariana, Sage's cousin.

And Sage may have overheard the confession.

What if Henry was telling the truth? What if he left Kennedy behind in the woods, and Sage, overwhelmed and alone with her cousin's killer, couldn't control her rage?

Or maybe saying *Henry* when she meant *Bram* was a simple slip of the tongue. Even so, I start to back away from her, pulling my phone out again to text Henry. "Did you see Henry in the woods, Sage?"

She shakes her head. "No. I told you, I meant Bram."

"Sage, I know that Kennedy confessed to killing Mariana. I know she killed your cousin, so it wouldn't be—"

"Stop it," she cuts in, her voice high-pitched. It's clear she isn't hearing this information for the first time. She knows about how Mariana really died. When she glances over from the creek and our eyes meet, I know everything.

But before I can blink, she's rushing at me with her hands outstretched.

ADAM

Adam gripped the phone tightly as he made his way through the woods. His jaw clenched as he reread the text from Henry: I'm going to tell the cops I'm the guy in the video.

He never should've left the house to go for a walk.

No, you're not, Adam had replied. I'm on my way home. Don't move and don't talk to anyone.

For all of Henry's brains, the boy was an idiot. Did he think the cops would just send Bram home if someone else confessed to being the unidentifiable hooded figure from the video?

Even worse, Henry seemed more worried about what Hayden thought of him than of the consequences of his actions. Last night he was a mess because Hayden was ignoring his calls and texts.

He'd started to worry that she might go to the cops, that she didn't believe his story.

Adam wasn't even sure *he* believed Henry's story, but he couldn't let his brother go to the cops. He talked him down from his panicked ramblings. But Henry was still so on edge when Adam finally went to bed. Adam doubted the boy got a minute of sleep, which meant he wasn't thinking clearly.

That was why Adam had to be the one to do the thinking. It wasn't exactly his forte, but with Henry a stress case and Bram behind bars, Adam was the only option. He'd come to the woods to clear his head and think about what had to be done.

He kept walking, following the path that led to the creek. Hearing movement, Adam froze like a deer in a hunter's sights.

Two girls ambled out of the trees and into the clearing. Right away, Adam recognized Hayden and Sage. He took a step back into the trees. Hearing Bram's name, Adam's attention perked up, but the girls continued traveling on ahead, and the sounds of the nearby creek began to muffle their conversation.

Concealed by the trees, Adam followed them.

"Nobody," he heard Hayden say.

"Henry's a sicko, Hayden." Adam flinched at the vitriol behind Sage's words, rustling a branch and nearly giving away his cover. He froze, watching Hayden start to turn in his direction, and silently pleaded with her to stop. "How demented do you have to be to take a girl to the woods and hit her over the head with a rock until she dies?"

It took Adam a moment to put together what Sage was saying. Then his heart plummeted. Hayden must have told her something. After all these years of friendship and being the only schoolmate not to turn on the triplets after Mariana's death, she had finally jumped ship. She was siding with Sage Wheeler and all the others.

Of course Henry would have confided in Hayden. He loved and trusted her, and because he couldn't keep his guilt-ridden conscience to himself—he'd made this monumental mistake of telling her about his plan to confront Kennedy.

Now, Hayden was telling everyone that it had been Henry in the woods with Kennedy, not Bram.

It wouldn't be long before the cops went from arresting one wrongly accused suspect to another. In fact, the girls could be talking about going to the cops that very moment.

Adam's fears had been blaring in his head so loudly, he'd missed the point when the girls' conversation had taken a turn, becoming more heated.

Hayden was pleading now. "Sage, I know that Kennedy confessed to killing Mariana. I know she killed your cousin, so it wouldn't be—"

Adam's blood began to boil. She had no right to tell Sage, Silver Creek's biggest gossip and snitch, what they'd learned about Kennedy. That would be the final nail in Bram's coffin. He wanted to go over there and tell Sage it was a lie.

But before he could decide what to do—before he even knew what was happening—Sage was barreling toward Hayden.

Then Hayden was toppling over the low railing of the bridge. Adam heard her scream; he watched her body fall. Heard the *smack* as she hit the water.

Adam sprinted into the open, still struggling to comprehend what he'd seen. The quickest way to Hayden was a dive off the bridge, but the creek was laden with huge rocks beneath the surface. Everyone knew it was too dangerous to jump or dive. Adam's mind brought up the horrible town tale of Ronny Ackles, the only person who'd ever tried to make this jump. He hadn't survived.

If by some miracle Hayden had managed to survive, Adam needed to remain in one piece to help her. He raced through the brush and dried grass to the ravine, but the incline was steep. Short of throwing himself down, descending the ravine would take far longer than he could afford. As it was, when he looked out over the rushing water, there was no sign of Hayden.

He'd have to risk diving.

Adam charged toward the bridge, where he spotted Sage staring at him in horror. "Call for help!" he shouted at her as his footsteps thundered over the wooden planks.

Once he reached the place Hayden had gone over, Adam kicked off his shoes. He climbed up onto the bottom rung, splinters piercing the soft flesh of his feet. He searched for a sign of life, and for a split second, saw Hayden's hair bobble toward the surface. Stepping onto the top rail with one foot, still bent over and grasping the wood with one hand, Adam scanned the creek for rocks.

The water was dark and frothy. It was impossible to be certain, but he thought he saw a clear area below. Adam let go of the rail with his hand and, in one fell swoop, pushed up onto it with his remaining foot.

Then he leapt off.

ADAM

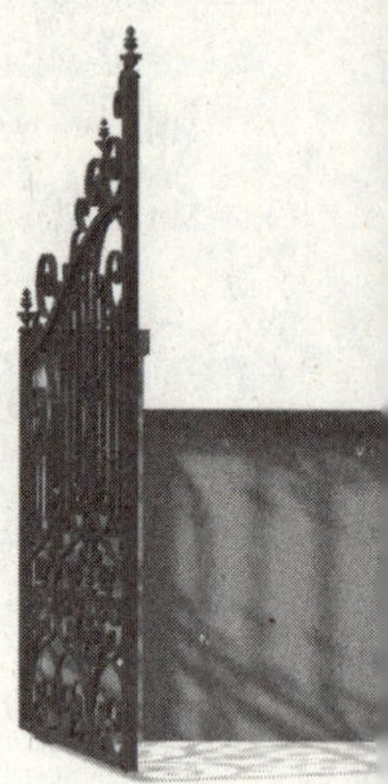

The instant Adam struck the water, panic consumed him. It encased him the way the icy water did—filling his nostrils, his throat, his chest. He began to sink, and when he tried to fight the pull, his foot struck a rock.

But he was surfacing. His head breached the choppy water. At first he couldn't take a breath, the cold was so fierce. But his body was intact, the pain caused by the frigid water.

Frantically, he began to search the creek. He ducked back down, but the lapping and bubbling tide kept visibility low. Instead, he swam, feeling around the whole time, thinking that Hayden must've continued to float downstream. There were many things that Adam couldn't do while his hand was in rehab. But he could swim just fine.

He kept moving with forward strokes until an image of Hayden's lifeless body flashed in his mind. Then the panic rose again, and his limbs flailed. "Sage!" he screamed without sparing a glance up at the bridge. He hoped and prayed that she was on the phone with neighbors and an ambulance. That help was on its way.

Out of breath, Adam waded into the shallows to get footing. He used his positioning to scan the water, but there was still no sign of Hayden.

A sudden sense of dread pummeled Adam, so fast and intense his vision blackened.

The waterfall.

If Hayden had drifted through this next section of deep water, she would either get snagged in the shallow rocks beyond it, or the current would carry her through to a fifty-foot drop.

Adam started to run, forcing his legs through the water like paddles, forcing his burning lungs to work. When the shallows gave way to deeper water, he took a leaping dive and swam with everything in him.

Adam's strokes were long, his feet kicking to the point of numbness. As his arm cut through the water on the next stroke, his bad hand hit rock. Pain radiated through the already-paper-thin skin.

And the water was getting deeper. Just as Adam's vision became fuzzy around the edges, he saw it: Hayden's head rising to the surface.

Only she was face down.

Adam couldn't stop, even though his hand throbbed and the burning in his lungs brought him back to the days after the car explosion. He swam until he reached her, turning her over and looking into her lifeless face.

Adam dragged her to the nearest bank, pulling her onto the thin stretch of sand at the base of the ravine. "Hayden," Adam said, trying to shake her awake. There was blood in her hair, and her skin was scraped and cut from when she'd been thrashed against the rocks. He couldn't tell if the gash in her scalp was serious.

He glanced up at the bridge, but the sunlight was blinding. "Did you call?" he yelled out to Sage.

There was no answer. Adam retrieved his own phone from his pocket, but of course it was waterlogged. He couldn't even turn it on.

With his eyes better adjusted, Adam squinted up at the bridge again. He spotted Sage with her phone, only she wasn't calling anyone. Instead, she appeared to be filming.

Adam's frigid blood went warm. Sage was filming him and the unmoving body on the shore. Hayden's body.

"What the hell are you doing?" Adam shouted up at her.

"I've got it all on film!" she called over the rushing creek. "You pushing Hayden face down in the water. Drowning her to keep her quiet about your brothers' crimes."

Adam couldn't process Sage's words. Hayden still hadn't taken a breath in far too long. "Please, Hayden," Adam begged. "Wake up." He pictured Henry's and Bram's faces when they discovered that their closest friend was gone, and a piercing agony tore through his chest. Adam's extremities shook with fatigue, but he racked his brain for what he'd learned about CPR in health class.

He pressed his palms to Hayden's chest, leaning his full weight as he gave compressions to the beat of "Stayin' Alive." Only he couldn't remember how many to give and the worries over whether he was pressing hard enough or too hard clogged his mind.

Having lost count, Adam pinched Hayden's nose and tilted her head back. Forcing a breath into his raw lungs, he leaned down to put his mouth to hers. He tried giving air, but her chest failed to rise.

When Adam moved to pump on her chest again, tears streamed down his cheeks. He'd lost her. He hadn't reached her in time, and now she couldn't be revived.

In Adam's fire-damaged peripheral vision, he spotted Sage carefully descending the ravine. Had she finally decided to help? He continued compressions, water and tears dripping down onto Hayden's lifeless face. The horror and anguish mingled. Like ingredients in a potion, they conjured up a memory so vivid, it felt as if it were taking place right now.

Mariana sat in the driver's seat of her car, making eye contact with Adam through the windshield. A little nod—she'd done it. She'd broken up with Bram. Adam felt hope and guilt hit him in equal doses. The car continued several yards down the driveway when suddenly, Adam smelled smoke.

The car was halted now. But the engine was in flames, smoke billowing up into the air.

Mariana was still inside.

Adam never thought about what to do. He charged straight up to the burning car, shouting at Mariana to get out. She blinked, clearly in shock, then tried to move, only her seat belt stuck, the retractor having locked with the force of her braking. She started yanking on it, fighting to release it.

As the flames leapt from the engine, Adam called to her to ease the belt out. But in her panic, she only tugged harder, more frantically. The fire grew, creating an oven of the entire car. The smoke thickened, and she was coughing and choking.

Adam pulled the door open and reached over Mariana in an attempt to free her, holding his breath. His eyes stung from the smoke, so bad he could barely see as he fought with it. Mariana was losing consciousness, fading as the smoke spread and the flames lapped.

Then came the *bang*, sending Adam flying through the air. Everything went black..

The vision melted away, along with the freshly awakened sense of suffering and loss, leaving with it only a stark realization: Adam had tried to save Mariana, just like his brothers and Hayden claimed.

Sage's words from up on the bridge finally echoed back into his ears. She was going to make this look like murder. Adam had tried to save Hayden's life, but Sage was going to twist it, painting Adam as a monster. Just like she and the rest of the town had done with Mariana's death.

When he tilted Hayden's head again, leaning down to place his mouth on hers, he'd already given up hope. His friend's face was deathly pale, lips blue. He gave her a slow breath anyway, doing what little he'd been trained to do until the ambulance arrived.

But of course, no ambulance was coming. Even if Sage had actually called, the hospital was an hour away. In desperation, he tried shouting to her again, but there was no response. It wasn't until he heard the splash that he realized Sage was in the water.

At first, Adam thought she'd gone completely mad. But when she ducked her head beneath the surface, it all made sickening sense. She had only filmed Adam holding Hayden face down in the water. She'd stopped the camera before the rest of it: Adam turning Hayden over, carrying her to shore. Attempting CPR. Of course she'd stopped filming. Now, Sage was trying to make it look like *she* was the one who'd jumped in to try and rescue Hayden. Like *she* was the one who'd dragged Hayden's body to shore.

With Hayden gone, no one would be able to refute Sage's version of events. No one but Adam, whose word was as worthless as his CPR skills.

Adam barely cared about Sage's plan. Once again, he'd failed a girl. Another girl who meant so much to him. Going through the motions, he pushed a hopeless breath between Hayden's blue lips.

And she coughed.

Adam flinched, wondering if he was the one who'd gone mad. But he watched as her chest moved, and water bubbled up through her lips.

He snapped to, sliding his hand under her back, folding her upper half forward as she expelled a river full of water, then took her first gurgling breath. He patted her back, called her name, and listened to the blessed sound of her wheezing breaths.

Adam held her, supporting her flaccid body, checking her for a phone and finding nothing. As he did, he spotted Sage emerging from the water, clothes soaked and hair dripping.

She scanned the bank for a moment, and Adam's attention diverted back to Hayden, who coughed in his arms. He listened and found that she was still breathing. "Are you okay?" he rasped, his own breathing shallow.

Hayden worked up a nod, opening her eyes for the first time, blinking away the water. And then her eyes widened in terror. Adam followed her gaze to the bank, where Sage now charged at them, a large rock in her hands. She raised it high, aiming at Hayden's skull.

Adam whipped his body around to shield his friend, taking the blow in the shoulder. He grunted, agony rocketing through his arm.

His sight blurred by the pain, he glanced back to where Sage was stumbling, her clothes squelching. The rock had slipped from her grasp. She clutched her hand for a moment, like it might be injured, then quickly bent to retrieve the rock.

Adam had only seconds to lay Hayden down in the sand and struggle to his feet. But his weary body swayed, and Sage was already skirting past him. She wound up her arm, hand gripping the rock, and let out a guttural roar.

Adam clenched his jaw and lunged forward, knocking the girl's feet out from under her. Sage screamed, the rock falling as they both toppled into the sand.

Adam lifted his head, blinking away the dizziness. He was weak, but he had to get Hayden away from here. Mustering all the grit he could—the kind he needed at the end of the second practice of the day during hell week, when nausea struck and his muscles felt like they'd melted off his bones—Adam stooped to lift Hayden.

Beside them in the sand, Sage groaned and tried to get up. She looked disoriented, and Adam could only hope it would last. He lifted Hayden in his arms and forced his tired legs to move in the direction of the road. He craned his neck enough to check behind him, where Sage was still gathering her bearings.

Adam hurried on, his bare feet stinging the more they warmed up. His injured shoulder cried out. *Don't come after us*, he silently pleaded with Sage. He would do whatever it took to keep Hayden safe, but he hoped it wouldn't come to that.

When the sound of the creek died out, he left the path, clomping straight through the trees. His phone still useless, he forced a deep breath into his lungs and screamed, "Help! Someone, call 911!"

But the area was vacant. When he made it through the trees and onto the road, Adam screamed again. He panted, eyes panning in both directions. Hayden was alive in his arms, but he couldn't hear the sound of her breath over his own laborious huffing. Her skin was cold, and her eyes had fallen shut again. She needed medical care.

It was a mile to town, and Adam knew he didn't have that sort of trek in him. He started downhill toward it anyway, calling for help with what little breath remained in his lungs. The adrenaline that had fueled him was dwindling, and his legs began to give way. Thorns, twigs, and rocks had ripped his feet to shreds, and every step on the rough pavement was torturous. But he had to stick to the road, to keep out in the open until someone found him. "I'm sorry," he whispered to Hayden as his legs shook and faltered.

She was turning blue again. There must've been some water still trapped in her lungs. He was losing her. He remembered the lone farmhouse off the beaten path. Lydia Costas's house, though he'd never given it a thought before. He had no idea what her parents did for a living, but he hoped one of them would be home.

He trundled along up the narrow dirt road, Hayden's wet body slick in his hands. The farmhouse was in view, but there was no car out front. Adam's hopes fell.

Then he thought of breaking in. Maybe the Costas family had a landline. He'd call for help and deal with the consequences later.

When he reached the corner of the property, Adam set Hayden down beneath the shade of a sycamore. He noticed the dirt below him, painted red by his bloodied feet. "I'm going to get you help," he told Hayden, even though he doubted she could hear him. Then he hurried up the driveway.

At the sound of a car approaching the property, Adam's hopes lifted again. But when it turned into the driveway, he peered through the windshield, finding Lydia's terrified eyes on him. Adam knew how he looked, wet and bloodied, like some sort of swamp monster. He folded his hands in front of his chest and mouthed, "Please."

Lydia stopped the car and squinted at him through the windshield.

Having her attention, Adam gestured over to the sycamore. "Please!" he shouted now. "It's Hayden!"

Lydia glanced over in the direction he'd pointed, stretching her neck for a glimpse. She quickly trained her eyes back on Adam, who knew that out of view, somewhere on the dash, her hands were moving to her phone.

The passenger's side window rolled down the faintest crack.

"Please!" Adam shouted. "Call 911! Have them send an ambulance!"

Lydia hesitated, licking her lips, and when her hand darted forward, Adam felt despair come over him like a black cloud. She was going to drive off. She wanted to be as far away from Adam as possible.

But Lydia brought the phone to her ear, and the car engine shut off.

Adam collapsed to his knees.

EPILOGUE

HAYDEN

ONE WEEK LATER

I'm lying on the couch, all comfy in front of the TV, when there's a knock at the door. I start to call for Dad but remember that I'm on my own today. It's the first time he's left me alone since Sage Wheeler tried to kill me.

I get up to find Henry in the doorway. My heart goes through a gamut of feelings—first delight, then disappointment that he's alone. I know it was too much to hope for. "Come on in," I say, heading back to the couch.

"Actually," he says, reaching for my arm, "would your dad kill me if I took you on a field trip?"

"Yes," I say. "But it's a risk I'm willing to take." I'm desperate to get out of here, to see something other than a television screen.

He laughs. "Glad my life is so valuable to you. But it's just a trip to my house, so don't get too excited."

"Your house is a museum with its own movie theater and botanical gardens. It's like taking multiple school field trips all in one day." Remembering my current disheveled, pajama-clad state, I frown. I've showered at least, and Henry has seen me at my worst; still, I'm self-conscious. "I'm a disaster."

"You're never a disaster," he says without a hint of sarcasm.

"But I—"

"Go," he says. "I'll"—he glances around the living room, then gestures to the dishes on the coffee table—"clean up a bit."

"Thanks."

A few minutes later, I'm dressed in jeans and a T-shirt, my hair thrown up into a ponytail. I dabbed on some blush and tinted lip balm too, since I look like a walking corpse. Henry hovers closely, guiding me to the truck like I might keel over—even though I'm feeling much stronger today. Then we're making the short drive up the hill in Henry's truck.

I fight the urge to ask about the case, to ask about Bram. If there'd been any news, he would've told me by now. But every day that goes by without hearing from him carves a bigger hole in my chest.

Once Lydia called the ambulance, Adam started to worry that it would take too long. I was frigid and breathing poorly, going in and out of consciousness. He convinced Lydia to drive us until we met the medics on the road.

Before I was rolled into the ambulance, I had a rare and fleeting lucid moment. All I could think about was how I knew the identity of Kennedy's killer, and if I didn't survive, it would be Adam's word against Sage's.

Lydia, who'd only returned home to grab her notes for the lunchtime student council meeting, was standing by my stretcher, looking lost. So I grabbed her wrist and used my remaining oxygen supply to whisper, "It was Sage. Tell the cops she killed Kennedy and tried to kill me."

I didn't get the chance to see her reaction before the medics pushed me inside the ambulance. I wasn't sure if she believed me and would follow through, or if she rolled her eyes and drove back to the farm.

Adam rode with me in the ambulance, holding my hand the whole way. I later learned that when we arrived at Central Springs Hospital, he insisted on making sure Dr. Russo wasn't at the hospital that day. I was given oxygen, treated for hypothermia, and checked for myriad infections and ailments that can occur after near-drowning. Once they got my breathing under control, I was closely monitored in the hospital for three days.

Dad stayed there with me, and Henry came to see me every day, both when I was too sick for visitors and afterward. Even Lydia came to visit, right around the time I started staying awake for longer periods. She let me know that she'd gone to the police but wasn't certain they'd taken her seriously.

I kept staring at the door to my hospital room, wishing for it to open, praying to see a familiar broody face.

Two of my earliest visitors were Detectives Chase and Wilson. I answered their questions, told them how I'd figured out Sage Wheeler killed Kennedy right before she pushed me into the creek. As I was relaying the events, I had the nauseating realization that my theory wasn't rock solid. I had no evidence, only Sage's slip of the tongue and my belief that she tried to kill me to keep me from telling. I recounted how Adam saved me and tried my best to convince the detectives that Kennedy—not Adam—had killed Mariana Sanchez.

The entire hospital stay, and even the first couple of nights after I returned home, my sleep was restless. I kept worrying there was a possibility Sage could get away with all of it. What if she told the detectives I'd fallen? That I was delusional? Would they take her word over mine and Adam's? I hoped they might find the rock that had killed Kennedy, so they could test the DNA against Sage's. But the detectives weren't saying anything.

And then last night, Dad got the call from the lead investigator. On the day Kennedy was murdered, the detectives had discovered an acrylic nail at the crime scene in the woods—painted a brick orange shade, perfect for fall—which explained why the detectives had checked my hands during that first interview. It turns out they hadn't suspected the Abbotts right from the start. Only they couldn't ignore the camera footage or the eyewitnesses, so they eventually focused on the brothers, figuring the nail could have come from any of the dozens of students who took shortcuts through the woods and wasn't forensic evidence.

But after I'd told them about Sage, they tested the DNA on the acrylic nail and compared it to hers. Last night, they got the results back. It was a match.

Ever since Dad relayed this information, I've been picturing Sage's manicured fingers wrapped around the rock. The orange nail bending and ripping with the force of the rock coming down on Kennedy's skull. The nail popping off, layers of Sage's real nail along with it.

The mystery of Bram's missing hoodie was solved too. Neil Chen came forward with it. Apparently, Neil spotted it on the benches during the fire alarm and, unhappy after the way Bram embarrassed him in the cafeteria, snatched it. He'd planned to deface it and hang it on Bram's locker, but when Bram was thrust into the spotlight for the murder, Neil thought it was best to lay low and hide the sweatshirt in his own closet.

The little twerp's guilt must've finally caught up with him as Bram sat in jail for the murder, since Bram couldn't possibly be the hooded figure caught on camera with Kennedy.

Now, Henry stops the truck and gets down to open the gate. When he climbs back into the cab, he squints at me. "You okay?"

"Yeah," I say. "Just nervous, you know..."

Henry faces forward and starts the truck. "About Bram."

"Aren't you?" I shift my weight, then fiddle with my seat belt.

"Bram can handle himself," Henry says almost flippantly, like his brother isn't locked away in a cell. "And with Sage's arrest last night, it's only a matter of time."

That is true. The Abbotts' lawyer is working around the clock to get Bram out. But the cops have Sage now, so what are they waiting for? What if she already managed to worm her way out of this?

After parking in the circular driveway, Henry helps me down.

"I'm not an invalid, you know," I say when he keeps my arm on the walk up the stone steps.

"Oh, I know. I'm doing this for my own safety, since your dad will murder me if I don't bring you home in one piece."

"Fair enough. So where exactly are we headed?"

"The theater," he says, and I get a sinking sensation in my chest.

"We're going to watch a movie?" I ask, barely able to keep the disappointment out of my voice. I thought maybe we'd spend the day in the gardens, talking and breathing in the fresh air that I've missed for the past week.

"Not exactly," he says, motioning me along.

When we reach the foyer, Adam is there, wearing workout clothes, a gym bag in hand. "Hey," he says, a brighter smile on his face than I've seen in a long time. "You're up."

"I am." I can see he's getting shy, probably afraid I'll cry over the fact that he saved my life, like I did when I finally woke up in the hospital. But I won't scare him off this time. "How was physical therapy?"

"Really good, actually."

Henry feigns shock, throwing a hand over his mouth and exchanging a wide-eyed look with me. "Did he just use the word *good*?"

I punch him in the arm and turn back to Adam. "Making progress, then?"

He nods. "I started with a new physical therapist a couple weeks back, and this guy treats our sessions like the sky's the limit. He says he's not ruling out playing football next year." Adam frowns. "Granted, I'd be a walk-on, but—"

"But," I interrupt, "you'll be playing football. And any college would be lucky to have you."

He grins, nodding to himself, a little bit of that cockiness of old shining through. "Well, I'm off to shower. You nerds stay safe."

"As long as I'm not around your pool or your pond or your parents' jacuzzi tub, I think I'm good," I say, unable to fight off my own smile at seeing him so happy.

Henry and I continue to the home theater. Inside, he shuts the door behind us and turns off the lights. When he takes both of my hands in his, my heart cracks a little. A few weeks ago, Henry pulling me into a dark room for our first kiss was something that played on repeat in my daydreams. Now…I can't put this off any longer.

"Henry," I say, flipping the lights back on, "there's something I need to tell you." My eyes are tearing up, and not because of the bright lights. I don't want to hurt him.

Henry lets out a soft laugh. "Hayden, I know," he says, letting go of my hands and playing with his glasses. "And I think…I think I feel the same way."

"What—no." My cheeks burn at how horrendously I've botched this. I'm about to lose my closest friend forever. "No, it's not—"

"I love you," he interrupts, startlingly serious now. I want to throw my hand over his mouth to keep him from talking. "But," he continues, "I love being your friend. I think I might've confused that with being in love *with* you. And I think that...for us, *just* friends is pretty great." He glances thoughtfully upward. "Perfect even."

I stand, stunned for a moment before letting out a breath of relief. "Yeah," I say, smiling back at him. "Me too."

"Now, are you going to let me show you the surprise or not?"

"You never said anything about a surprise," I say as he moves to the space behind the seats.

"It's just a project I've been working on. An invention of sorts." He retrieves a small white box with what looks like a lens on the top and takes it to the corner of the room. After plugging it into the electrical outlet, he says in a showman's voice, "The lights, if you please."

I flick them off, casting us in darkness again. There's a faint *click*, and then light bursts forth from the little box on the floor. Overhead, bright yellow stars paint the theater ceiling before fading into glimmery silhouettes of trees. A crescent moon peeks out from behind the leaves of a sycamore.

My heart hitches. It's our view of the sky from the creek, replicated to the letter. The scene is hand drawn, each feathery leaf and twinkling star carefully sketched. But before I can get out a word, music starts up. A familiar piano tune.

"Shall we?" Henry asks, taking my hand and leading me to a reclining theater seat.

He takes the seat next to mine, and the moment I start to lean back, something unexpected happens. Instead of Davy Jones's tenor, I hear my mother's voice, soft and airy, singing the lyrics.

My throat tightens, and my eyes sting. "How did you do this?" I choke out.

"That night when you called me about your dad and how he deleted those home movies, I sort of hacked into your family's cloud. It took me ages, but I finally managed to recover some of them. I saved them for you on a USB, including this part with your mom singing." He shrugs. "Then I decided to make something that would keep her with you forever."

"It's amazing," I say, basking in the sound.

"I built the motor myself." He turns a dial until the scene shifts from yellow to glittery green. "There's a setting with creek sounds too," he adds in an apologetic tone. "Obviously, I created it before you nearly died in that water. Probably too soon for that."

"Probably," I say, a smile on my lips as I watch the stars cycle through all the colors of the rainbow, listening to "Daydream Believer" resonating through that little box. Hearing my mother's voice for the first time in three years, my closest friend at my side.

A knock at the door interrupts the moment. Probably Adam, finished showering.

"You should get that," Henry says, turning off the music but leaving the glow of the stars to illuminate the room.

I side-eye him. "You picked a really inopportune time to lose your chivalrous habits. Don't you want to save me the trouble? Not to mention, it is *your* house."

"I think it'll be worth the trouble," he says.

I pretend to be annoyed as I get up. Then I pad to the door and pull it open to find Bram standing there.

"Hey," he says, rubbing his hand over the back of his neck, a shy smile on his lips.

A flood of emotions hits me so hard and fast, I'm dizzy. "Hey," I say, the word coming out choked. My feelings graze right past relief, landing on irritation. I glance back to dart a look at Henry.

"Oh, didn't I say?" He grins coyly. "There was a second part to the surprise."

I turn back to Bram. "When did this happen?"

"Early this morning."

Behind me, Henry clears his throat. "I'm, uh, going to see if I can get the sound quality a little better on this. I'll be in the garage." He unplugs the star projector, tucks it beneath an arm, and tries to slip past us.

"Wait," I say. "Can you come over tonight for dinner? My dad's going to attempt to make my mom's famous lasagna, and I don't want to be the only guinea pig."

He smiles. "Yeah, sounds good," he says. "Or, you know, completely terrible."

I laugh, bumping his arm as he skirts by. And then he's out the door, and I'm alone with Bram.

My pulse thrums as he peers down at me, eyes flooded with concern. His skin is pale as always, a stark contrast against the black T-shirt. "I'm so relieved that you're okay," he says. "When I heard you—"

"Why the hell didn't you call me the second you got out?" I interrupt. Up close, I can see that his hair is still damp from a shower. I inhale the herbal scent of his shampoo, the cedar and smoke of his cologne. "It's all I've been thinking about. *You're* all I..." I hesitate, not sure how to stop the words from pouring out.

"I'm all you *what*?" he asks, a soft smile on his lips.

But I don't need words to tell him. I step closer, throwing my arms around his neck, digging my fingers through his hair. I tug him to me, pressing my lips to his.

He flinches, stunned at first. And then he's kissing me back, urgently, his hands on the small of my back.

When we part, breathless, Bram blinks. His dark eyelashes flutter like he's coming out of a daze. "Can't say I was expecting that." He pretends to look serious as he squints at me. "Should you be doing *that* in your condition? What with oxygen deprivation and all?"

"Sorry," I say, my face heating.

"Phil," he says, head titling as he smirks, "don't apologize for something we both know you're going to do again very soon."

I start to protest, but he pushes open the door, reaching back for my hand. I want to refuse it, but my need to be close to him wins over and I take it, letting him lead me down the hall.

"What should we do today?" he asks as though it's any other day. "You're still recovering, so maybe you should just—oh!" He turns to give me a devious smile. "Have you been on a tour of our dungeon?"

I roll my eyes. "Let's go out to the garden."

Bram sighs dramatically. "Fine." He pulls me closer, lips grazing the top of my head. "I guess we could both use a little vitamin D after our stints indoors."

"I know how much you love the sun," I tease as we step outside.

"It's true that vitamin D and I have had our differences," he says, pretending to be scorched by the slanting rays. We amble along on the pathway, our fingers interlocking. He glances over at me, and his gray-blue eyes catch mine. "But you, my dear, look awfully pretty in the sunshine."

Read on for a sneak peek of

WE WERE WARNED,

another thrilling read from Chelsea Ichaso!

PROLOGUE

The figure knelt over the body at the edge of the ruins. Nearby, a streetlamp crackled before succumbing to the night. Gray clouds tumbled closer. As the ocean waves crashed, the wind whipped against the figure's black hood and rattled the chain-link fence.

The figure glanced back to peer beyond the mist. A rock wall lined the front of what was left of Fairport Village, separating the clifftop property from the beach below. Among the other rocks, a long granite one stood out, smooth and flat as a tabletop, specks of mica gleaming beneath the moonlight. It formed a plank over the sandy beach below: the Founder's Slab. Back in the 1800s, a horrible plague struck the first settlers, and it's been said that in their desperation, the sick carved their prayers into that sacred rock.

Only those prayers went unanswered, as if the land had other ideas. The figure could almost hear its call, a wicked drumbeat, demanding more blood. The figure turned back to the body.

This girl—this *child*—sprawled lifeless on the gravel was far from the first to die on this land.

This child wouldn't be the last.

And so, tucking the note within the girl's sweatshirt pocket, the figure scanned the ruins once more, then vanished into the night.

October 4

Dear Diary,

I saw her again today. In the girls' bathroom. I had just washed my hands when I heard a noise. A swish. I spun around as the tail of her long black shawl fluttered across the back wall. Just a flicker before disappearing into the bathroom stall.

The stall door rattled, and my heart stopped. For a moment, I watched that door with my feet frozen in place, hands dripping water on the floor. I didn't dare take a breath. I wanted to sprint for the exit and never look back, but some reckless part of me had to face it. Had to find out for sure. Legs quivering, I forced two quick strides and flung open the door.

She was gone, of course. Vanished, like the ghost she is.

But I know what I saw.

She's following me.

1

The moment the corroded fence comes into view, the sky betrays us, clouds shifting to cover the crescent moon. I click on my flashlight, even though Fairport Village isn't something you need to see to know it's creepy.

You can feel it.

Not just the smooth sand from the beach below transforming into rubble and grass up on this cliff. It's something in the air. Something darker than a pitch-black night that seeps into your skin whenever you get this close to the ruins. Something that makes the little hairs on your arms stand up, that whispers with a tiny buzzing voice, *Go back*.

I'm tempted to obey the voice. When Henry De Rossi's wide brown eyes meet mine, I can tell he feels the same way.

But I'm going in if it's the last thing I do. And let's be honest, if the legend is true, it very well could be.

Everyone else has already made it inside, which means we're missing valuable footage. "Go on, or I'll murder you myself," I say, because I've never been good at encouraging words, and I need this paycheck.

Henry adjusts his glasses. His dark-brown hair flutters in the breeze as he raises his video camera to his eye and clicks it on. Then he waves me along, and we approach the rusted chain-link fence, broken hinges reinforced with steel chains wrapped around the posts. The weathered *No Trespassing* sign has been there since before I was born. I hike his equipment bag up higher on my shoulder and ignore the words, along with the enormous crooked *Condemned* sign, its letters flashing white in the silvery moonlight. I pry the two flaps of chain link open. Henry takes a deep breath, staring down the gap while I try to avoid cutting myself on this broken, rusted metal.

Finally, he exhales, the sound lost beneath the whistling wind and the crashing waves, and ducks through. His sweatshirt snags on a sharp steel end, but I jostle it loose, and he slips free.

He turns the camera off and lowers it, meeting my gaze through the chain link. I pass the equipment bag through to him. "Well, good luck to you, sir," I say, saluting him. "I just remembered there's a thing I've got to do." I spin around on my heels.

"Oh, come on, Eden!" Henry bites out. "Thought you weren't afraid of some stupid curse."

"I'm not," I say like a defiant toddler. "It's the tetanus that worries me." I gesture to the fence. "And, you know, the prospect of falling through a rotted floorboard."

He rolls his eyes in the filmy moonlight and tugs the fence open. "You want to get paid or not?"

Letting out a huff, I duck through the opening. "Two hundred bucks seems like a lot until you crack open your skull." I grab his equipment bag and heft it over my shoulder. Henry and I aren't exactly friends, but we had a film production elective together last year. He heads the audiovisual team at school, and now he's in the advanced film class. As part of his application to some fancy film school, he's chosen to make a short documentary on the Fairport Village legend. Capturing the senior overnighter will be a huge part of it. I opted not to stick with the film classes, but apparently Henry liked my short feature titled *Fairport High Teachers Who Are Secretly Aliens* enough to offer me a paid assistant job tonight.

Either that, or everyone else was too scared of the curse to take the job.

Voices trickle out of a nearby bungalow, and Henry doesn't miss a beat, his camera rolling, its light illuminating the broken cobblestone path.

"Which bungalow is that?" I ask, struggling to keep up with his long strides, the equipment bag slapping at my side.

"Shouldn't I be asking *you*?" he says without slowing.

"Oh, right." I dig into my pocket, pulling out the little map Henry told me to study in preparation for our documentary. In its heyday, the six cottages of this bustling clifftop resort were painted various shades of pastel—delicate pinks, greens, and blues—so they lay like seashells under a glimmering sun. The Blackmores gave each one a charming name, like Sunnyside Cottage and the Village Jewel. Unfortunately after the resort closed down, the effects of salt water and wind took their toll. The new paint began to oxidize and peel. The walls rotted and buckled. A storm tore apart roofs and the once-pristine Fairport Village sign. Looters, either ignorant of the curse or unfazed by it, shattered windows and removed anything of value from every residence.

In the daylight, you can still make out the faded hues from the beach. But here in the dark, they all look identical, except for the varying degrees of devastation. I squint down at the map, still scurrying along after Henry. "It's the Darling Daisy," I say, reading off my own scribbles as I add, "known to the Fairport youth as Aunt Gertrude due to the facade's uncanny resemblance to an old lady's face."

I glance up, and a chill snakes through me. There's no electricity in the place. Of course, there hasn't been in twenty-five years. So when light gleams through the cracked window eyes and spills through the open mouth of a door, it's like seeing the dead raised.

ACKNOWLEDGMENTS

Beware the Abbott Boys is a nod to my love of gothic monster novels, namely *Frankenstein*, *Dracula*, and *The Strange Case of Dr. Jekyll and Mr. Hyde*, so it would not exist without the brilliance of Mary Shelley, Bram Stoker, and Robert Louis Stevenson. In addition to these beloved and inspiring authors, I have many people to thank for helping me work my creepy little idea into a twisty thriller that readers can hold in their hands.

To my fantastic editor, Wendy McClure—thanks so much for your wisdom and enthusiasm with this story. I've been beyond fortunate to work with you on yet another book.

To my fabulous agent, Uwe Stender—for your belief in my writing, encouragement, and unwavering support along the way.

A huge thanks to the team at Sourcebooks: Thea Voutiritsas, Karen Masnica, Lia Ferrone, Hannah Son, Jenny Lopez, Michelle Lecumberry, Jessica Rozler, and Aimee Alker. Thank you so much to Corina Lupp for designing the perfectly chilling cover!

I am forever grateful to my dear friends and critique partners, Julie Abe and Laura Kadner. Thank you for your invaluable input on this story. You two have earned a lifetime supply of cupcakes.

To my parents, George and Rebecca Kienzle—for listening and cheerleading through all of the publishing highs and lows. To my Ichaso, Kienzle, and Lewis families, your support means the world.

To my husband, Matias—for always being my first reader and the person who talks me through every single new idea or plot struggle. I couldn't do this without you.

Kaylie, Jude, and Camryn—thank you for being my sounding boards on all the things.

To the book bloggers and influencers—thank you for supporting my books. Every post and photo means so much to me.

And of course, thank you, dear reader! You're the reason I get to keep writing, and I'm endlessly grateful that you picked up this book.

Finally, all gratitude and praise to my Lord and Savior.

ABOUT THE AUTHOR

© KIM PECKHAM PHOTO

Chelsea Ichaso writes twisty thrillers for young adults and is also the author of the adult thriller, *So I Lied*. Her novels have been Junior Library Guild selections, TAYSHAS reading list selections, and have been published in multiple languages. Chelsea currently resides in Southern California with her husband and children. When she's not writing, she can be found cheering from the sidelines at her kids' soccer games or attempting to strum a tune on the guitar. You can visit her on Instagram @chelseaichaso.